Albuquerque NM
August 14 2005

To Jo Anna Belle
With Best Wishes
on your Bat Mitzvah

A SCANDAL IN YVONSK

AND OTHER STORIES

AVRUM ORGANICK

JoAnna Ruppa
from
Cliff & Sandra Richardson

RED LAKE PRESS
NAVAJO, NEW MEXICO 87328

Red Lake Press
PO Box 951
Navajo, New Mexico 87328
e-mail: avrumorg@aol.com

Printed in the U.S.A.

10 9 8 7 6 5 4 3 2 1

ISBN: 09671068-6-9

Cover illustration: "The Old Synagogue," woodcut (1928) by Solomon Judovin

PREFACE AND ACKNOWLEDGMENTS

Like a painting by Seurat, where disconnected bits of color produce a picture, the disconnected bits of narrative in this short story collection produce, in their own way, a life picture of the writer. I have chosen to arrange these stories in the roughly chronological order of the events that are described though not necessarily in the order that they were written. I have made some effort to distance myself from myself by the perhaps feeble device of simply changing names and places in some instances or in changing from the first person to the third person. What has resulted is the confusion some readers may experience in distinguishing between the writer's own name and his *doppelgang,* Jack Berkowitz. In other stories I have broken down any pretense of narrative objectivity by simply calling some of the pieces what they are, namely, memoirs. With all of these problems I hope the reader will sense the excitement of being carried across a sweep of time and history, experiencing contact with so many engaging characters, and enjoying the sight and color of many different landscapes.

Eleven of the stories in this collection have appeared previously in print while thirteen appear here for the first time. I am indebted to the late Jack Schwartzman, editor and publisher of *Fragments* for publishing the title story, *A Scandal in Yvonsk. Twins* appeared in *The Santa Fe Literary Review* published by Colleen Mariah Rae; she has continued to encourage me in my work over the years and in all respects she has been my mentor. *Twins* was reprinted and appeared as one of the four short stories in *Blessings: A Novel and Four Short Stories* by this writer and published by Red Lake Press. *Bugler, Bicycle Dreams, The Hamilton Railway Special,* and *Squirrel's Ears* appeared in different issues of *Serape Anthology*, edited by Kevin McIlvoy of New Mexico State University in Las Cruces, New Mexico. My thanks are due to Professor McIlvoy for his support. *Squirrel's Ears* appeared as well in *Blessings,* and a portion of that story appears in the children's book, *Canyon Boy,* illustrated by Navajo artist, Irving Toddy, and published by Red Lake Press. *Fort Defiance Revisited,* and *Cecile Comes West* appeared as two of the short stories with *Blessings,* while *A Slice Venison* is a chapter taken from that novel. Finally, *Lo, I Have Wrought in Common Clay,* appeared in *The Elchanite,* the senior high school yearbook of the Talmudical Academy High School (of the Yeshiva College) over sixty years ago.

Many of the previously unpublished stories represent work done in undergraduate and graduate creative writing seminars in the Department of English at the University of New Mexico in Albuquerque. Professors Tom Mayer, David Dunaway, Laurie Alberts, Lewis Owens, and Sharon Warner as well as fellow students in those classes provided criticism and advice. Each of my adult children, Desbah, Aliza, Shoshana, and Benjamin have encouraged me in this work. My wife, Ida, arranged for recording of the stories by her father in *Squirrel's Ears,* and Alvin Kenny recounted for me the tale of the witches that appears in *Twins.* Dorothy Kavka of Evanston Publishing, Inc. has done the typesetting, design and production of the book.

CONTENTS

A SCANDAL IN YVONSK

I knew it wasn't right and it's still not easy for me talk about it. After all, I was the son of a *melamed* (a teacher). But I did steal two kopeks from the *pushkeh* (the coin-collection box) in the *beth hamedrash* (the house of learning and prayer). It was a small amount, and I really did plan to replace the coins. How could I have known then that my little crime, in the sweep of events that followed, would make the difference between my being alive and dead?

But first, let me take you back to the year 1905, when I was sixteen, when it all started. The earth seemed to be shaking with the thunderous events that were taking place beyond Yvonsk, beyond our little *shtetl* (rural village) in *Radomeh Gubernyeh* (the province of Radom). We lived about sixty *versts* south of Warsaw in what was then Russian Poland, but the news was coming from Saint Petersburg in Russia itself. There was a railroad strike going on. Can you imagine such a thing happening in the land of the Czar? It seemed as if this would lead to the end of oppression, and that there soon would be freedom for all, for both Jews and Gentiles. A *Duma* (a parliament) was called; a democratic representative government would be a reality at last.

I was hungry for more news. The only way I could get it was from an underground newspaper printed illegally in Warsaw. A subscription cost twenty-five *kopeks,* and I was short. I was usually able to earn a little money for myself by helping my mother at her stall on market days. But that Fall the rains and early snows turned the roads to mud. Trade at the market dwindled to nothing, and so did my hopes for making enough for my subscription. I felt cut off from the world, and I could stand it no longer.

With the dizzying thought that a subscription to the newspaper could be in my grasp, and with the certainty that the world would open before me, I stole into the darkened *beth hamedrash.* There the hammered copper coin-collection box was in its usual place near the door. I used a flat blade, and making as little noise as possible, I pulled two *kopeks* from the *pushkeh.* The two coins would never be missed. And besides, I would surely be able to replace the missing coins within the next few weeks before the Passover when spring would come.

With my heart beating wildly, I headed for the passageway toward the side door — when I brushed against a figure in the darkness. It was Itzik Mayer, the *shamesh* (the sexton). Neither of us said a word. I was certain the Itzik Mayer had recognized me. But had he heard the rattling of the coins that were purloined from the *pushkeh?* If he had heard the rattling, would he know it any of the coins was missing? There was a chance nothing would come of my having brushed against Itzik Mayer in the darkness.

But I was wrong. Word of the theft was brought quickly to my mother and to her brother, Aharon Laib Teitelbaum. The words *"A Shondeh!"* and "*A Charpeh!*" (A Shame! A Disgrace!) thundered forth from the lips of the mighty Teitelbaum. "A shame like this has never been brought upon the name of our family!"

"*Shaa! Shtill!*" hissed my mother. "Word of this scandal must never get beyond this room!" My mother made her decision swiftly, even though it meant pain, sending me away, never to see me again. Pain was to be preferred to shame.

"There must *not* be scandal in Yvonsk. Moishe must go. He is to go to *Amerika!"*

In the Fall of 1906, I landed in Halifax, Nova Scotia. The revolution of 1905 in Russia had been crushed. The first parliamentary *Duma* in Moscow, that glimmering hope of democracy, was called in to being, and, almost as quickly, dissolved. The Czar had struck down democracy with his iron fist.

*****

In the dining room of my home in Washington Heights, one evening in 1950, Chaim Perlstein, my cousin on the Teitelbaum side of the family, gave this report:

On September 12th, 1942, the Jews of Yvonsk, young and old, were summoned at gun point and gathered in the marketplace. From there, the Nazi SS marched the people to the railroad station where they were loaded into cattle cars. My brother, Benjamin, his wife, his grown sons and daughters with their spouses and their children, and my sisters, Sara Malka and Esther Dvora, with their husbands, children and grandchildren, did their best to stay together. They'd been told they would be settled on farms in the east. But rumors of the new camp, Treblinka, that had been constructed outside of Warsaw, had reached their ears and they feared the very worst.

When the train pulled north from Yvonsk, Chaim forced his way through the chute normally used to shovel manure from the cattle onto the tracks, and managed to find a handhold beneath the car. For more than an hour, with the railroad ties whizzing by only inches from his head, he managed to hold on. When he sensed the train slowing down, Chaim dropped between the rails and when the last of the cars passed over him, he rose and escaped into the woods.

Now, with chilling accuracy, with the giving of the exact date of the deportation, and with the recitation of the names of my brother and my sisters, last seen together in the cattle car, I saw the end with crushing clarity. For forty-four years I'd borne the weight of my guilt over the stealing of the two *kopeks* from the *pushkeh.* Now I realized that the part I played in creating what *might* have been a scandal in Yvonsk no longer had meaning — because on September 12, 1942, Yvonsk disappeared from the face of the earth.

BUGLER

At 11 A.M. on November 11, 1938, during the hours of Hebrew study, I stood at attention with my classmates to observe a moment of silence, twenty years after the signing of the Armistice that ended World War I. The impressions of that brutal war were still fresh in our collective memory. We had not yet recovered from that war, the war that had been called "The War to End Wars" and "The War to Make the World Safe for Democracy." Yet the shadow of a new world war was already upon us. It was the shadow of Hitler's war. Just two days before, on the night of November 9-10, Hitler declared war on the Jews. Under his direction, Nazi mobs attacked and destroyed Jewish homes, synagogues and business all over Germany, killing Jews and imprisoning thousands on *Kristallnacht,* the night of shattered glass.

My father had sent me and my brothers to one of the first of the all-day Jewish schools to ground us thoroughly in the traditions of our people. How else could we be prepared with the moral strength to face the onslaught of hate that was building against us? Anti-Semitism, similar to what my father and all Jewish immigrants had experienced in Europe, was increasing in virulence here in the United States. Native-born Americans Gerald L.K. Smith, William Dudley Pelly, and Father Couglin were as openly vicious in their verbal attacks on Jews as was Hitler himself. Fritz Kuhn, a naturalized American citizen of German birth, had breathed new fires of hate in the German-American Bund. The activities of the Bund were documented in the newspaper accounts of the time.

The *Yeshiva Etz Chaim* (Academy of the Tree of Life) or the Hebrew Institute of Boro Park, a school for some 200 boys, provided five half-days of instruction in Hebrew and religious studies in the mornings. This was the first yeshiva to introduce Hebrew as the sole language of instruction in the Jewish subjects. Five half-days of regular public school subjects were taught in the afternoons. The twenty hours devoted to Jewish studies each week in that program represented five to ten times the number of hours other Jewish students obtained in Jewish afternoon or Sunday schools.

By the age of eleven I had already learned the basics of the Hebrew language. I had studied all of the *Chumash,* the five books of Moses, and had read some of the simpler *N'Viyim,* the books of the prophets. I was comfortable with my knowledge of Hebrew. The Old Testament stories were full of passion and drama. How could I not be touched by the dilemma of Abraham when he was told by his wife, Sarah, that he must banish his concubine, Hagar, and with her, his own son, Ishmael, perhaps to perish in the desert? How could I not be moved when Abraham was commanded by God to sacrifice his own son, Isaac, the one born of Sarah? I was a good student and second only to Mayer Fish, my rival, the asthenic son of a dentist. Mayer was always at the top of our class in both Hebrew and English studies.

But now it was time for us to begin the study of the *Gemorrah* or the *Talmud.* Rabbi Binimovich was the one to initiate us into the *Talmud.* To me, Rabbi Binimovitch was Tradition itself. He was tall and broad-shouldered, and towering in his traditional, calf-length, black caftan. He was old, perhaps as old as seventy, yet his great beard was not yet totally white. It was said that he had been an officer, a Jewish chaplain in the army of the Czar in Russia. He was a figure of power and dignity, an ancient wise man. In his declining years he was to carry that delicate flame, the heart of the Jewish tradition, the *Talmud.* He would now pass it on to the six or seven boys who sat before him.

At the rabbi's class each of us had a copy of the *Gemorrah* before him. A center panel carried the text. The text would start with a short section of the *Mishneh,* an earlier text written in Hebrew. This was followed by sections of the *Gemorrah* itself whose language was not Hebrew but Aramaic. I had little difficulty in understanding the Hebrew of the *Mishneh* but understanding the Aramaic, the language of the Babylonian rabbis, was another matter. Futhermore, and making it more difficult for me, there were no subscripts as guides to pronunciation. It was here that I began my great struggle to enter into the core of Jewish tradition, to achieve full membership in the community of Jewish scholars, to join the two-thousand-year continuum of Jewish learning.

Rabbi Binimovitch, according to custom, presented to us the simplest of the *Gemorrahs* in hopes of instilling in us the confidence we would need to go on to more difficult tractates in the future. The rabbi began slowly enough, but it was clear to us that he was carried away by his own enthusiasm. Before long we noticed, and we soon began to imitate, (and some of us to ridicule), the mannerisms of this new Russian rabbi who had been transported somehow into our world in Brooklyn.

Rabbi Binimovitch had a curious manner of rocking back and forth as he read aloud. Soon he would lapse into a sort of sing-song, a new and strange melody to the ears of the boys of Boro Park. As the rabbi's finger flew across the column line by line his eyes would flash and saliva would fly out of his mouth. Droplets of spittle that were not caught in his greying mustache and beard sailed across the space between his desk and ours, and the droplets landed in a shower on the open books before us or in our faces.

But now the rabbi, having run through several lines asked me to read and to explain the passage he had just read. My heart leaped into my throat. Without the subscripts to guide my pronunciation, I stumbled repeatedly. I was mortified at my stupidity. I was angry at myself for having made fun of the great man before me, even if I had done so only secretly. And I understood *nothing* of what I was asked to read. The few words I was able to force from my lips became more difficult and a lump grew larger in my throat. Finally the words stopped completely. I remember how my lower lip trembled uncontrollably, and how the tears that welled up in my eyes splashed on the page of the open book before me.

The rabbi looked up from his page and fixed his gaze on me and the fierce intensity of his eyes was replaced by a look of the greatest compassion.

"Avromeleh," he said softly, using the Russian-Yiddish affectionate diminutive of my name, "*Ha'Shem,* (the Holy One whose name is simply 'The Name') looks down from heaven. To Him every tear shed in the learning of the Torah is as precious as a pearl and He gathers each one up and He holds onto it forever."

With this my tears flowed more freely as the sweetness of Rabbi Binimovitch eased my pain. I tried again and again over the succeeding weeks and months to master the intricacies of the language of the *Talmud* and the involved logic over points of law, but the difficulties of the task were simply beyond me. It would never be possible for me to overtake my rival, Mayer Fish, or to enter into the fraternity of scholars of Israel.

But something else had entered my life: it was music. I heard the offstage trumpet call from Beethoven's *Leonore Overture Number Three*, and so I chose the trumpet. My lessons began when I was eleven, at the beginning of the 1937-1938 school year. It didn't take me long to produce some musical sounds with that instrument. After a few weeks I was able to play the mournful, solo trumpet theme of Sibelius' *Finlandia* with great feeling, and the music teacher pointed me out to others as his prize pupil.

After my studies of the trumpet began, I made a discovery. On the ground floor of the apartment house I passed every day on my way to school, a window was open. A musician was hidden in some inner room. Through the open window and close to my ear, I heard the sound of a trumpet. But the pure, crystal sounds of the trumpet told me that this was an accomplished professional who was playing. My heart soared as I listed to the faultless way he carried out his exercises. I lingered listening to his brilliant tone, to his perfect phrasing, to his double and his triple tonguing. This was joy. This was coming close to God.

When I realized that I'd failed to achieve success as a *Talmud* scholar, I turned instead in hopes that one day I would be able to play the trumpet with the faultless technique of the unseen player. I practiced and I did become better. My lessons were interrupted, however, with the coming of the summer when I was to leave Brooklyn for three weeks of summer camp at Camp Lehman in Westchester. What I did not know as the summer approached was that it was my trumpet playing that would earn me three extra weeks away from the city. And there, at Camp Lehman in the summer of 1938, I would meet the young men and boys who would be swept into the impending storm of war.

On the twenty-second of July, 1938, our chartered bus drew up to the curb at the 92nd Street Y.M.H.A. on Lexington Avenue. We would be heading north and I was glad of it. 92nd Street was just a few blocks away from 86th Street and the Yorkville neighborhood of Manhattan, home of Nazi sympathizers and of the German-American Bund. The Brownshirts held there rallies there, at the *Turnhalle* on 85th Street and Lexington Avenue. The Bundists had displayed the Swastika flag before thousands of supporters at Camp Nordland in New Jersey in May of that year. At their Fourth of July celebration at Camp Siegfried on Long Island they had preached their vicious, anti-Semitic sermons and had raised their arms, Swastikas showing, in the Nazi salute. The Nazi threat and terror were close by. All of us Jews knew it.

We had all seen the first German Jewish refugees in Brooklyn. The boys wore shorts (we wore knickers), and they wore grey socks to just below the knees. They carried their books in leather cases under their arms while we carried our books in briefcases that we held by their handles. In the years that followed there would be thousands of Jewish refugees in Washington Heights in upper Manhattan, an area to which we also moved from Brooklyn. You could spot the women by the clothes they wore. They all looked the same. They all dressed in two-piece grey suits. They wore grey, broad-brimmed fedora hats and their high-heeled shoes were of alligator skin. You could tell them by their accents and by their liquid "L's." In the synagogues they pronounced the Hebrew blessings "*Baruch Ataoow Adonai*" instead of our Polish-Jewish "*Baruch Ataw Adonoi.*"

Now we were lined up on the sidewalk, boys mainly from Manhattan's lower East Side, some from the Bronx, and I from Brooklyn. The camp counselors, young men in their early twenties, serious about their responsibilities, did their best to restrain us as we shouted or jumped or wandered off. At last, at the signal, we lifted our duffle-bags on to our shoulders, mounted the high step, and disappeared into the bowels of the bus. The great machine then growled off, picking its way through the grim streets of Harlem, heading north to the green of Westchester, to the estate of Judge Irving Lehman. The judge, older brother New York's Governor Herbert Lehman, had set aside part of his estate for the camp. We marveled as the great size of the judge's house (most of us city boys had never seen a house like that) and then we reached the camp at the rear of the estate by a winding dirt road. Camp Lehman lay before us, a breezy, tree-bordered retreat from the heat of New York City.

This is a *real* camp, I thought. My heart swelled with anticipation as I looked about at the scene. A flag flew from a flagpole behind the central campus and baseball field. Eight very large pyramidal tents were arrayed on the south side of the field, and each tent was mounted on a raised wooden platform. The khaki-colored sides of the tents were trim and tight and without a wrinkle, and the tent flaps were rolled up. In the cool interiors we could see the neat, iron cots, each cot with its own wooden, Army-colored foot-locker.

We were hungry now and we were marched to the mess hall for our first meal. We were greeted there by Mr. Kastenbaum, the camp director, who introduced us to the cook and his helper. We, members of the 'second trip' of the summer, were introduced to our counselors, and they, in turn, told us of our assignments to each of the tents, according to our ages.

"This is a working camp," Mr. Kastenbaum explained. "Each tent must take its turn for a day at its different duties," and we learned that day the meaning of the term "K.P."

"Who here can blow the bugle?" was the question put to us at assembly at flag-lowering by Aaron Lazerson, the assistant camp director. Aaron Lazerson was the sort of no-nonsense man, a man of authority, whose questions demanded answers. He had steel-blue eyes and an unsmiling expression on a face that showed the scars of acne. He was the rule of law. When no one else raised his hand I raised mine.

"I can play the trumpet," I said.

"Then you can play the bugle." He produced a brass bugle and handed it to me. "You will play 'Taps' tonight."

The transition from the B-flat valved trumpet to the bugle was not as difficult as I feared. The different notes of the bugle, I found, could be produced entirely by changing how hard I changed the tightness of my lips, or the *embouchure,* when I applied my lips to the mouthpiece. I was familiar with the melody of he "Taps." Yes, I could do it.

In the evening hours I practiced. I played softly as my lips became accustomed to the new brass mouthpiece. I knew I could produce the plaintive and dramatic melody of"Taps" with feeling.

The other campers, with some difficulty because of their excitement on their first day of camp, were settled down on their cots in the tents at last. I was more tense as I waited to be called to play. At last I was led out of my tent in the gathering darkness to the foot of the flagpole in the center of the campus. I took a deep breath, raised the instrument to my lips and I played:

"Day is done
Gone the sun
From the earth, from the hills, from the sky
All is well
God is nigh
Good night!"

Over the next several days I was coached by the counselors who knew the bugle calls. I learned the melody of the Mess call, Assembly call, Flag Raising, and Flag Lowering

"Reveille" was a difficult call. It required a rapid series of rising, then falling notes, and it was particularly hard for me to do this crisply with the bugle cold and without the chance to practice in the quiet of the morning. Even when I warmed the mouthpiece and I when I worked out the tonguing with the mouthpiece alone (detached from the bugle) it didn't help. What was supposed to ring out as a crisp and rousing wake-up call in the early morning often came out as series of blustering, unmusical, missed notes without tone or form:

Ya gotta get up
Ya gotta get up
Ya gotta get up in the morning
Ya gotta get up
Ya gotta get today!
Tat tat/tat tat/tat *tah* da
Tat tat/tat tat/tat *tah* da
Tat tat/tat tat/tat *tah* da
Tat tat/tat tat/tat *tah*!

"That one sounded like one of your usual cold farts," was the comment of Benjy Goldman, one of my tent-mates. I'd just returned after blowing "Reveille" one cold morning and I decided to ignore him. Benjy was a tough kid from the Lower East Side, and I knew he was a little envious of my beginning chumminess with the counselors. He was a short but muscular blondish boy, and he'd learned to fight on the streets. He'd boasted that when attacked by gangs of Italian boys and called "Jew Boy," and "Kike" he would call back at them: “Greaseballs” and “Wops.” Then he would fight it out with them and he said he usually came out the winner. I admitted to myself that I admired him for that toughness. But this Benjy was one *I* didn’t want to tangle with.

It was true I was spending more time with the counselors. I was becoming more a member of the staff than a camper. The few quiet moments after the last drawn out notes of the “Taps” were my favorite times. I would be invited to linger at the base of the flagpole and even walk back to the steps of the social hall instead of going back to my tent. There, with the counselors relaxing after the day’s activities, I would join them in their discussions. Even the tough face of Aaron Lazerson would ease at those moments, especially if the “Taps” were blown particularly well, and he would offer me a pinch of *Shmectabak.* The snuff from a can of “Copenhagen” was foul-smelling, it was true, but after I pushed it into my nostrils, as Aaron instructed me to do, it produced a new, deep sensation and a delicious, powerful sneeze. I felt I was initiated into the inner sanctum, and I gained Aaron’s unqualified approval.

Now I was on a first-name basis with all the other counselors. Jeff I remember particularly well. He was short, with curly, reddish blond hair and heavy blond eyebrows. He had what seemed a constant smile that was the result of his large over bite. He had a quiet ambition: to fly. He’d been taking lessons at Floyd Bennet Field near Far Rockaway.

A Jewish boy flying an airplane! I thought. What a far cry from the usual yeshiva-boy image of a Jew. Jeff would be the one who would tell me of the fate of other Jewish flyers and of Aaron Lazaerson in the war that was to come.

Marvin Blumberg was a second year medical student at New York University. He was short and dark-complected, and he conducted his office and his little, one-bed infirmary with reassuring, professional coolness. In the years that followed I kept in touch with Marvin since he and I were both from Brooklyn. It was four years later that he invited me to spend an evening with him at the hospital where he was then a pediatric resident. “Have you heard of the new miracle drug?” No, I hadn’t. “Watch this,” and he showed me a vial of yellow powder which he diluted with sterile water from a syringe. “This is penicillin, and I am going to give it to a little girl with endocarditis (infection on the heart valves) and she will then have a chance to live."

My popularity with the counselors continued to grow and I was cast as the young "David"in the camp play.

"You looked just like a fairy" was Benjy's taunt after the performance. "You must really *be* a fairy. You and Stanley probably sneak in bed together."

This new attack brought me down hard. I'd been elated after being on the stage with my sword and slingshot in hand, headband on my forehead, Israel's hero. My face stung with indignation, feeling as much for Stanley Penso as for myself. Stanley, one of the other boys in our tent, was, it is true, as feminine-looking as a girl. He had the smoothest, unblemished skin, the most luminous brown eyes and the slenderest arms and legs. He would curl up on his cot during rest hour reading a book like a girl with his legs tucked underneath him. And his voice, at twelve, was also that of a girl. Yet nobody, up to that moment had made fun of Stanley. He'd been able to maintain his quiet dignity up until that time and Benjy had violated that.

I was raging inside, and a little blind. I stepped forward and pushed the shorter Benjy out of the way. This bully, I thought, is nothing but a shrimp anyway. The response came quickly with a sharp left hook and a stinging pain to my face that sent me sprawling to the floor.

"Don't try that again," Benjy muttered breaking it off, and the fight was over. I didn't feel humiliated by the defeat. Even though it had been stupid of me to try, at least I'd pushed the little man.

I was the bugler at Camp Lehman. I was kept on as the bugler when the second "trip" of the summer left and a new group of campers rolled in on the bus. The summer ripened for me. There were no more bullies. I was part of the staff. The "Reveilles" got better. The flag-raising and the flag lowering bugle calls stirred the emotions and the last sounding of the "Taps" became a memory. The tents were struck, the windows of the mess hall and the social hall were shuttered and the latrines were closed. The last bus rolled out past Judge Lehman's house on August 31st, 1938. A year and a day later

Hitler's armies rolled across the border into Poland. The war had begun.

*****

Jeff drove his convertible through the quiet streets of Mohegan Colony in Westchester where my parents had a summer home. He was able to drive as slowly as three miles an hour. He wanted to savor the quiet. He needed it as an antidote for the throbbing in his ears, the throbbing that always stayed with him from the four radial engines of the B-17's he'd come to fly. He'd gone through the war as a pilot in the "Flying Fortresses" as they'd been called, and now, in 1947 he was still flying, flying B-17-loads of rifles and machine guns from Czechoslovakia to the *Haganah* in Palestine. The Zionists were preparing to fight, if necessary, for the Jewish State and for the War of Independence which was to come.

Jeff had followed the fate of many of those who'd been at Camp Lehman with us and he told these two stories:

Aaron Lazerson had become a navigator in a B-17 and was killed in the massed, daylight raids over the ball-bearing plant at Schweinfurt in Germany in August, 1943.

Stanley Penso was drafted when he turned eighteen late in 1944 and he was sent as a replacement to an infantry unit with the advancing army in Germany. Jeff could not know the irony of the story he was about to tell, not remembering as I did, the girl-like child curled up on the top of the cot reading a book during rest hour. Nor could Jeff understand why I suddenly became very quiet. On April 1st, 1945, just a few weeks before the end of the war in Europe, Stanley was killed, a German bullet striking him in the eye, shattering his skull and splashing his brains inside his helmet.

BICYCLE DREAMS

There's this great feeling of blinding joy that stays with me and that I must write about. It's about speed, and balance, and blossom-perfumed sea air rushing into my face, and the power of the light of the summer solstice all rolled into one. It's the remembrance of a dream that came true.

Imagine where the dream began: the sidewalk of a tree-lined street in Brooklyn, Fifty-Second Street, that ran south toward Fourteenth Avenue. I'd roller-skated down that sidewalk many times. I knew something of the feeling of speed, of balance, and of air rushing into my face. I'd felt the power of the muscles of hip, thigh, and leg, pushing forward, to the side, and back, right side, then left side. But skating was noisy: crash! Steel wheels hitting cement. Front double-steel wheels, rear double-steel wheels. Right skate crash, roll, left skate crash, roll. Click-click: steel wheels hitting the cracks, front wheels, rear wheels right. Click-click: front wheels, rear wheels left.

What I longed for was to speed down that sidewalk on a bicycle with big, rubber-tired wheels that would roll swiftly and quietly. With a bicycle you wouldn't hear the crash of steel on concrete nor the clicks going over the cracks. But I didn't have a bicycle. My brothers didn't have bicycles. It was the Great Depression. My father was out of a job; my mother had just gone back to work as a sewing machine operator to pay for food and rent. I didn't dare ask for a bicycle. Even my girlfriend, Marilyn Bernstein, whose father had a furniture store on Thirteenth Avenue, didn't have a bicycle. The skates had been sacrifice enough.

Then I had the dream. I dreamed I was riding a bicycle down that sidewalk. It was swift and quiet. The air rushed into my face. When I got to the corner at Fourteenth Avenue I leaned to the left and I didn't fall. I rounded the corner, headed east on the sidewalk on Fourteenth Avenue and I didn't fall. When I woke up it was as if it had really happened.

When school was out the last week of June, I stayed with my Aunt Bessie in Far Rockaway. My cousin, Edith, was only a few years older than I and she had a bicycle, a girl's bicycle. It was one you could get on easily, and if you felt you might fall, it was easy to get off. And she took me out on the street with her bicycle one morning saying, "I know you can do it."

I remember the smell of the sea that morning and the sound of the surf at the beach, though you couldn't see the ocean because of tall hedges that grew to ten or twelve feet and that were blossoming at that time of the year.

"You just sit on the seat and hold onto the handlebars. Then you find the pedals and off you go." Edith held the handlebars as I mounted the seat and then I found the pedals. I pushed down with my right foot and I went forward. Then I pushed down with my left foot and I kept on going forward. From that moment I knew I would not fall. Right foot down, left foot down and I shot ahead, the wind coming into my face. I could feel the power in my hips and thighs and legs, and I knew I would not fall. The turn at the end of the street was easy, and I leaned a little into the turn without fear, just as in my dream. And the air in my nostrils was perfumed with the smell of the blossoming hedges, and the smell of the sea, and the summer solstice sun bore down on me and filled me with joy so great that God was there, and I knew it.

It was more than a dozen years later that I spied the slender Raleigh English Lightweight with the hand brakes and the three-speed Sturmey-Archer gears in the window of a bicycle shop on Boylston Street in Copley Square. It seemed fitting that the English bicycles, a pair, a man's bike and woman's bike, each with slender front and rear fenders, the same color, deep gray-green like the classic MG roadster, would be displayed in Boston, genteel Boston. The message of the pair of English bicycles in the window was that you and your girl might soon be riding together on those perfect English bicycles (your girl would be perfect, and lovely, and, perhaps English too) on some tree-lined lane in England, or New England.

I still hadn't owned a bicycle of my own, but at that time the three-speed bicycle had replaced the heavier, baloon-tired Columbias and Schwinns. It was possible to rent one of those lightweight beauties for a day or an afternoon almost anywhere. In my college days in New York there was a bicycle rental place near Columbus Circle and you could ride for an afternoon in Central Park. And on Cape

Cod, at Eastham, you could rent one at the gas station on the main road. I did that one time on a weekend, off alone from the hospital in Boston where I was interning, and I bicycled off to the beach at Chatham, to the taste of salt air, where I sketched the skeleton of a wreck half-buried in the sand.

It was in Texas that I bought my first bicycle, a black three-speed with an odometer and a generator-powered rear light. It was not a Raleigh, but it was English to be sure, and it bore the crest of its manufacture, like the Raleigh, in Nottingham. It was on this bicycle that I began my summer adventures on long-distance rides on the back roads of America.

Imagine a road that winds through the Hill Country north of San Antonio, north to New Braunfels, through German farms, each with its shiny, "A-O Smith," blue-painted glass-lined silos glistening in the sun. Imagine the smell of freshly-turned earth, of honeysuckle, and of pig-shit as you pedal silently by. Imagine the long, hot ride through live-oak forests near San Marcos, then down the long hill to Austin.

Imagine a summertime ride through flat, green Wisconsin country, westward from Milwaukee across fields where the air is laden with perfume of alfalfa from the drying ovens, and of sassafras; where you cross the Rock River on the wrought iron bridge at Jefferson, and then, after more miles across flat green land, descend into the cool bowl of Madison at night. Imagine also rolling down farm-filled "coolies" of Hamlin Garland's Western Wisconsin, down to the broad Mississippi.

When the ten-speed bicycle replaced the three-speed, I was able to buy a Raleigh at last. It was a top-of-line Raleigh "Competition," only twenty-four pounds in weight, with that slender, hard leather Brooks saddle, and with Campagnola headset, crank, and gears. It was then that I trained on the road around the lake in Washington Park in clear-aired Denver for the Century Run. The hundred-mile course runs north along the South Platte, then east out on the prairie and away from the Front Range, and comes near the old trading fort of Saint Vrain where, one hundred-fifty years before, barges laden with beaver pelts began their journey to Nebraska, to the Platte, to the Missouri and down the Missouri to the Mississippi to St. Louis.

Imagine cranking your way up the canyon roads of the Front Range west of Denver: Boulder Canyon to lofty Nederlands, Bear Canyon to Evergreen, and the South Platte Canyon where the narrow-gauge trains no longer run and where the water ouzel has reclaimed the tumbling water.

And now each April, at the "Tour of the Rio Grande Valley," with the gay throng at the chilly morning start, then soon enough alone as the others pass me by, I drift down past the earliest green of the cottonwoods, down the valley of the Rio Grande, down past the dam at Isleta, past the old adobe church at Bosque Farms on a street that bears my name, "Don Abran," past Los Lunas and Tome to Belen.

"You shouldn't be riding those long distances any more," my wife says. "You might get hit, slow as you are now. Or you might have a heart attack."

But the dream of riding the bicycle down the sidewalk on Fifty-second Street to Fourteenth Avenue stays with me. So does the blinding joy of my first ride on that summer solstice day. The dream has taken me beyond Brooklyn, beyond Manhattan, beyond Cape Cod, beyond the Hill Country of Texas, beyond the greens of Wisconsin, beyond the Front Range canyons of Colorado, and now to Aprils on the Rio Grande.

LO, I HAVE WROUGHT IN COMMON CLAY

It was March. The white romance of winter had passed, leaving only stale crusts of gray snow patching the hillside. A cutting wind slashed my cheek; yet cold as it was, there was a sweet taste of Spring in it.

I was pushing through a strip of greenery, a park lining the river. It was late afternoon; an orange sun was just sinking behind the cliffs across the water. Directly ahead, a Colossus, a great bridge throwing a noble roadway across the river to the opposite shore. I stood insect-like at the base of one of the giant towers. I gazed at the modern maze of intricate steel bracework soaring dauntlessly upward. I thought of the men whose brains had planned it, the engineers at their slide rules, the mathematicians at their tables, the draftsmen at their charts. I thought of the men whose brawn had built it, the men at the cranes, the hoists and the pulleys, the men at the riveting machines and the welding torches, the joiners, the fitters, and the steeplejacks, the men who had wielded the sledge hammers and heard the singing metal resound in their ears. I gazed at their work, their harmonies and counterpoints blended into a symphony of steel.

I passed under the roof of the roadway and out again into the fading sunlight. Once more I turned my eyes upward to the sky-scraping tower. Suddenly, as I stood marveling at the combined result of many men's efforts, an intense creative desire surged through me. It seemed to charge my hands with some strange new pulsating power which throbbed at my fingertips in search of an outlet. I clenched my fists savagely, stared at my idle fingers and cursed them. I thrust my useless hands into my pockets and trudged dejectedly along.

The dirt path which I had been following now led me upon a little rocky knoll where brittle crusts of snow wedged themselves among the bare brushes. I came upon a little clearing in the shrub where the snow had thawed out. I stooped down to dig my yearning fingers into the moist brown earth. In my craving desire to create, to build, to imitate in my own humble way those men who had built the gigantic bridge which towered above me, I molded a tiny brick of the mud in my hands. I viewed my creation triumphantly. I pressed out a second brick between my fingers and then went on to form another, and still another. My fingers soon became deft at it; a sizeable pile accumulated.

I had created! My hands had shaped the formless. Now I could build. I stood up, stretched, and scanned my surroundings. A broad, flat face of granite rose from under the mud and slush to project over the winding path below. Carefully I brought my unbaked mud bricks to this high, dry site. I lay out about fifteen of them in a circle. Upon this first row I built up a slightly smaller ring of ten bricks which leaned a bit toward the center. As I lay the next row, I could see the shape of a dome taking place. Flushed by my promising start, I pressed on quickly and assuredly. More bricks were formed, new rings were laid out. I was working, I was building, I was happy.

The sun, whose last rays purpled the clouds, had sunk. It was twilight. On a flat rock jutting over a pathway in a park along a silver river squatted a tiny model shelter. In the semi-darkness I could see the vague shape of some prehistoric mud hut. The haughty bridge tower, crowned by her twinkling lights, noble in her evening silhouette, looked down at the low clay at her feet. Yet it was that clay, the feeling of it underneath my fingernails, the fresh smell of it on my hands, that had satisfied my desire to build. Some expressed that desire in steel. I, as my primitive ancestor, had expressed it in clay. Yet whether we build titanic bridges of steel or tiny dwellings of crude clay, we the builders, sense the joy of creating and earn the repose of the worker whose house is built and whose job is done.

A brisk wind blew in on the darkness. I tasted its sweetness and went home happy.

ODOR OF GARLIC

"K'im dumani sheh yesh kahn ayzeh rayach shel shoom." (It seems to me there is a certain odor of garlic here.) With these words Rabbi Doctor Zigmund Vilts, with a sniff and a dour face, would begin each day of instruction at the Talmud class, level *gimmel* (three) at the Hebrew Teachers Institute. He enunciated the words in crisp, perfectly correct, idiomatic Hebrew and in the Sephardic Hebrew pronunciation. Of course we knew it wasn't garlic he smelled. It was just the usual stuffy classroom smell of varnished desks and seats, and of chalk dust and ink in a room where the steam radiators had been left on and where the windows had been shut tight all night..

We all thought Rabbi Doctor Vilts was a singularly humorless fellow. Actually he was just a real mean sonovabitch. We thought his lack of discernment in not recognizing the true nature of the odor that greeted his nostrils each morning just represented another instance of his being totally out of touch. Out of touch with our feelings, that is. He never smiled. He showed us no mercy when we stumbled over difficult passages in the Talmud tractate, *Babba Kammah,* the first of a series of three volumes on codes of civil law. Actually, I'd never got to first base as a student of the Talmud. The first difficulty was that the language of the Talmud (actually the Babylonian Talmud) was Aramaic, not Hebrew which I knew fairly well. The second difficulty was that I could not actually follow the complexities of logic of the legal arguments as expected of me. Yet the Talmud was the cornerstone of Jewish learning. If you were to get anywhere you had to be able to study the Talmud. I knew I just wasn't up to it.

I admit that I and the others in our class had a certain grudging respect for Rabbi Vilts. He was not only a rabbi but a rabbi *Doctor.* He had a Ph.D in something, we never learned what. Dark complected, clean shaven but with his blue beard still showing, he wore thick glasses. He had a short, straight nose, and, as I've said, he never smiled. He was born in Europe, we were told, probably in Lithuania, where the real Jewish intellectuals are said to come from, and that he lived and studied in Palestine before coming to America.

We never learned anything about his personal life, whether he was married or had children.

Unlike the rabbis in the Yeshiva (the rabbinic seminary that was part of the same building complex as the Hebrew Teachers Institute) who taught the Talmud in Yiddish, Rabbi Vilts taught it to us in Hebrew. Hebrew was not his mother tongue (as it was not ours) but he spoke it with a crispness that amazed us. And furthermore, as I have said, he spoke Hebrew with the Sephardic pronunciation. When I would try to speak in the Sephardic fashion it required special concentration. I had to be careful to "translate" from the Ashkenazic Hebrew that I'd learned in the lower grades of the Hebrew school I attended in Boro Park in Brooklyn. I had to change the terminal "S" sound of the letter "Toph" and to pronounce it as "T." But if the terminal "S" sound was of the letter "Sin," it was to be left as "S." Then I had to remember that the vowel sound, "Kamets' ("aw") had to be changed to the flat "Patach" ("ahh"). But *he* had no difficulty making that transition to the perfect Sephardic. We did not like the Rabbi Doctor Vilts.

If I was falling behind in my Hebrew studies, I was having much greater success in my secular studies with classes in the afternoons. I had won a New York State Regents scholarship on the basis of competitive Regents examinations given at the end of each semester. I remember how proud I was to see my name in fine print in *The New York Times* among the list of winners from all the high schools in New York City. I would soon be leaving the Hebrew Teachers Institute. My application had already been sent in to Columbia University.

Then there was heady success in extra-curricular activities. I was editor of the class newspaper, a mimeographed weekly set out in columns with justified right margins to make it look like a real newspaper. I remember what pains I took using the typewriter to make the extra spaces between the words to make a neat-looking column. The campaign I championed as editor was an effort to get trees planted in front of the school building which had no grass or space or greenery. I missed the trees that lined the streets in Brooklyn that had been our home before we moved to Washington Heights.

The end of my senior year was approaching and the pace of extra-curricular activities increased. First there was the senior class play, a series of skits and lampoons. Sol Reichel was the cleverest, round-bellied buffoon and chief performer. Izzy Finkelstien and I wrote the comedy lines and the lyrics to the songs. Then there was the job I had as assistant editor of the school year-book. Carmi Charney, the editor, wrote a serious and scholarly essay on the book of Jeremiah. A story I wrote was more personal and introspective. I described a walk along Riverside Drive at the end of winter. Where a patch of mud had appeared among the crusts of snow, I kneeled down, fashioned tiny bricks and built a mud hut. I described my exaltation, the joy that all men must feel when they create something useful, an exaltation similar to that of the Creator himself, and I titled the piece, "Lo, I Have Wrought in Common Clay!"

And then I had a girl. We'd met the summer before at camp. She was not a sweetheart and I was not in love with her. Charlotte Pearlberg had a boyfriend who was already a freshman at Columbia University so she had no need of me, but she was content to have me squire her around, and she was somebody to be seen with. Charlotte was an outgoing, bright, and pretty girl with a Russian face. Her father was a pharmacist in the Kingsbridge section of the Bronx near Riverdale, which I considered to be kind of a romantic place. Little Mr. Pearlberg with his turned-up nose, mustache and his thick accent seemed like a *real* Russian.

My classmates, particularly the Yeshiva boys who were more religious than I and who were shy with girls, envied me. Charlotte, with her great personality would have conversations with these boys on serious subjects. Then she would laugh, flash her merry eyes, toss her head, show them her profile, the one with the turned-up little Russian nose. Then she would show them her full Tartar face, then turn and walk away showing them her little ass, and they would swoon.

So my life had two parts, the heady, successful part, and the level *gimmel* Talmud class with Rabbi Doctor Vilts. I fell further behind in the studies of *Babba Kammah* with each passing week. I could see now that, unlike my triumph in high school, where I learned at about this time that I would be class valedictorian, I would never be able to pass the final examination in Talmud, scheduled just a few days away. My anxiety, distress, and guilt at the failure that lay ahead grew day by day. It would be the first time in my life that I would fail in anything.

It was now the first week of June. The steam radiators had been turned off for some time and the windows of the classrooms were allowed to remain open during the night.

K'im dumani sheh yesh kahn ayzeh rayach shel shoom," intoned Rabbi Vilts in his usual manner at the beginning of class one such fresh June morning.

Odor of garlic! I thought. I was filled with a passion toward my tormentor unlike any I had ever experienced before.

Early the next morning I slipped into the Talmud *gimmel* classroom with a large clove of garlic in my pocket. Earlier I'd peeled off the outer, dried garlic leaves and I was ready to go. I came up to the teacher's desk, the large one that faced the students' desks, the one that belonged to Rabbi Vilts. I pulled out the shining and moist, plum sized garlic and I smashed it as hard as I could on to the surface of that desk. The juice splashed out onto its pitted surface and it oozed between my fingers. I ran the garlic back and forth until I covered every square inch of it. I continued to rub it until the garlic disintegrated under the constant pressure of my hand, leaving bits of garlic pulp trapped in the little pits in the wood surface.

When I finished this, I ran to the bathroom and I scrubbed my hands with a brush and soap I'd brought, scrubbing and rinsing over and over again, but I couldn't get rid of the smell.

If he ever decides to find out who did this, and if he ever checks us over to see who has the odor of garlic on his hands, I'll never get away with this, I thought. On the other hand, if I don't show up in class today, he'll surely know I was the guilty one.

So with my heart pounding, I went back into the classroom and took my regular seat which, fortunately, was not too close to the rabbi's desk. The other students, as they came in a little later, smelled the garlic vapor which filled the room, spilled out into the hall, out the windows, and down into the street. They winked knowingly at one another, not asking who'd done the deed, but delighted that *some*body had.

Rabbi Doctor Vilts came into the room and approached his desk. He raised his head and sniffed the air. There was no change in the expression on his face. Then he put his book down, opened his mouth, and started the day's lesson in perfect Sephardic Hebrew.

For the very first time he said *nothing* about the odor of garlic. *Nothing!*

The next week I just didn't show up for the final exam in Talmud *gimmel.* It didn't matter. I would not be coming back.

Later that summer I found that I was not accepted at Columbia University. I went to City College instead.

THE SECRET — A MEMOIR

I.

In the summer of 1942, the year I graduated from high school and the year I turned sixteen, I had my first job. I was delivery boy for a fruit and vegetable store on upper Broadway in Manhattan. The orders were big and heavy, thirty or forty pounds, packed in split wood bushel baskets, and I transported the baskets to customers in a pushcart that had steel wheels.

I can still feel the jolt of the loaded pushcart as it bounced down off the sidewalk, over the curb and into the street on my way to make my deliveries. I would push the cart in the street until I came to the apartment house where I was to find the first customer, sometimes three or four blocks away. Then I would have to lift the cart up on to the sidewalk and park it there while I carried the bushel basket down the steps into the basement and to the dumbwaiter. There I would press the button to signal the lady upstairs her delivery was on its way. If I looked up the dumbwaiter shaft I would usually get a load of dust in my eye. Then I would raise the heavy order by pulling on the rope until it was delivered. When I would return to the store I would collect my ten cents per order.

The physical work was hard, yes, but what galled me most was that I was paid so little for it. The previous winter or two I used to deliver chickens from the kosher butcher. The chicken orders weighed no more than five or six pounds and I was able to carry them by hand. For these I got fifteen cents each order. But that was only part-time work, on Fridays or before the Jewish holidays; this was my first full-time job and I wanted to prove to myself that I could do it. I stayed with it for two weeks.

"Get a mop and clean the bathroom. You know, the little toilet in the back of the store," the store owner ordered. It was a filthy little bathroom the owner hadn't seen fit to clean himself for months. I struggled with a bucket and a mop in the tiny, cramped, poorly-lit bathroom and I mopped the floor. Then I just walked away.

Although I took some satisfaction in just quitting, at the same time I felt I'd failed at something. But more humiliation was to come later that summer.

In the Spring of that year I'd set my hopes on entering Columbia College, and Columbia would offer the best chance of going on from there to medical school. When I received my first response from the Office of Admissions containing the application blank, the return address that was printed on the envelope, "Columbia University in the City of New York," produced a magical effect. It made me believe I was already in. All it needed was to complete the application and an autobiographical sketch, and I did so with confidence. But then there was the personal interview. That went badly from the beginning. I could see that the interviewer, a Mr. Ireland, knew I was not going to be "Joe College," a football player or a member of the Varsity Crew at that Ivy League school. The only school letter I'd earned at the Talmudical Academy High School, was for debating. Then there was the written examination, to be held on a Saturday morning. I hadn't anticipated that I would have to violate the Sabbath.

"Would it be possible to take the examination at another time?" I asked. Yes, an examination would be given again on a weekday but later in the summer, but by that time most of the places in the incoming class would have been taken, I was told. I made my decision then and there. I would not violate the Sabbath. I would take my chances on the slimmer prospect of admission with the later examination. When, weeks later, and the letter came, I found my application for admission to Columbia was not accepted. I applied for admission to City College and I was accepted in a few days.

There was still work I could do that summer. I took a job as junior counselor at a summer camp. The work was certainly easy enough and I found the nine- and ten-year old boys responded to my even-handed treatment of them. But my disappointment at being rejected from Columbia weighed heavily on me, as did the physical effect of the previous very hard delivery job. I soon began to feel curious waves of fatigue that I'd never experienced before. I took to resting more and I was encouraged when I began to feel better. As the last weeks of summer passed, the country air, the good food, and the easy companionship of the boys I was in charge of led to improvement. The episodes of fatigue became less frequent. I was encouraged and I looked forward to starting the new school year at City College.

I was delighted to find that the campus of City College, the Main Uptown Center, was indeed a campus very close to what I imagined a campus should be. There was a quadrangle with a central flagpole and there were trees and benches and walkways across the open space. The buildings were of gray stone of a uniform and pleasing "University Gothic" architectural style. The Main Building boasted a lofty, square tower, and inside, a Great Hall from the rafters of which hung flags bearing the emblems of the ancient universities of Britain: Oxford and Cambridge, and those of Europe: Paris, Bologna, and of the Charles University in Prague.

City College was a place I could be proud of. I would remain at City College. When the time came I would seek admission to medical school in spite of what everyone knew at the time, that a quota system for Jews was in place in most medical schools in the United States; that the chances of a Jewish boy from New York getting into medical school from City College were virtually non-existent. I would make it from City College or not at all.

I took delight in exploring the campus. The main library, a somewhat newer building but with a Gothic facade compatible with the others, lay just outside of the north gate at 139th Street and Convent Avenue. The main reading room with its tall ceiling, its north-facing windows, its rows of long tables with their green shaded brass lamps, the hushed students scattered here and there in the huge hall poring over their books, presented a picture any college or university could be proud of.

I made another discovery, the old library located on the ground floor of the Main Building just beneath the tower. In contrast to the expanse of space of the main library, the old library was compressed into a small but cozy space filled floor to ceiling with cast-iron stacks that were reachable by means of narrow, cast-iron spiral stairs. The shelves were filled with old books bound in leather bindings. Three or four small wooden tables on the floor between the towering stacks received their light from Gothic casement windows that looked southward onto the green swath of the lawn.

Before starting classes I had to complete a physical examination. In my case, because I noted a family history of tuberculosis, I was sent to Dr. Solomon Lubin, a tuberculosis specialist, for a chest X-ray. The X-ray taken in his office showed an abnormality in the left upper lobe, a "lesion," Dr. Lubin said.

"What is a 'lesion'?" I asked. Dr. Lubin was Russian and he had a sweet Russian accent, like that of my Russian Aunt Henya, Uncle Laibish's wife. He was short, about five-feet two, and he had a little turned-up nose and a graying mustache.

"A lesion is a 'spot,' a little area of beginning trouble," he said. But he said it in his Russian accent, in a comforting and reassuring way as he addressed me by my first name.

"Avrum, you may start college, but you must be careful and take only a limited number of courses. If you avoid extra-curricular activities, avoid over-exertion and take a rest every afternoon, you will be all right. We will watch you closely."

I turned in the khaki uniform I'd drawn for the R.O.T.C. course I signed up for. I felt sad to do this because I'd looked forward being a full participant not only in campus life but also in the national effort. And I signed up for only three courses.

But by this time I felt well and I was ready to start my college life even though on a limited basis.

There was one activity, however, that I did not give up, my regular Saturday mornings leading the Junior religious services at the Washington Heights Congregation on 159th Street near Amsterdam Avenue where our family was a member. This was not a *college* activity, so I thought it would be O.K. Besides, I felt an obligation to help our rabbi, Rabbi Weinberg, because I'd just graduated the Talmudical Academy High School the Spring before.

I found my first college courses easy because I avoided taking those that required laboratory. But as the Fall term progressed, I began to experience again those waves of fatigue that I'd first felt in the summer. At certain times of the day, usually about eleven o'clock in the morning, the fatigue, often accompanied by nausea, took total possession of me. Though I tried to sit up and to stay awake in class, I would fall asleep, my head on my arm, bent forward in my seat. After a short sleep in this position I would be relieved of my fatigue and nausea but I would feel completely spent. I would be moist with perspiration. But I would be able to stay awake for the rest of the class and for the rest of the afternoon. When I came home I would rest some more. Then I would feel well enough stay awake and to study while lying in bed until late the evening. But the next day I would be swept again by the same wave of extreme weakness and sleepiness. And this pattern continued as the weeks went by. It was clear to me that I was now in trouble.

At the end of the semester I went back to Dr. Lubin's office for another X-ray. Now, where the "spot" had been seen in the left upper lobe, there was now a cavity, about the size of large cherry, with a wall of uniform thickness surrounding it. The diagnosis was now clear: *active, cavitary, pulmonary tuberculosis.* Dr. Lubin was now in charge. He would not send me to a tuberculosis sanitarium but he would manage my case allowing me to stay at home. In addition to having me rest in bed, he would use a form of treatment that would put my *lung* at rest as well. The treatment was called *artificial pneumothorax,* a process by which the lung would be made to collapse by introducing air into the pleural space. The walls of the cavity would then come together and this would promote healing. Dr. Lubin admitted me to the hospital for this procedure which required the skill of an experienced specialist such as he was. During the process I experienced a new, curious discomfort that I had never felt before. The discomfort lasted only a short period of time but I was to feel it many times over the next several years. It was the sensation one feels as a needle penetrates the pleura. When new x-rays were taken I was told that the pneumothorax was only partially successful.

"Avrum," Dr. Lubin explained in his kindly way in his Russian accent that was so musical it took the terror out of waht he was saying, "the lower portion of the lung has collapsed nicely, but the upper portion of the lung, the part that contains the cavity, remained expanded. The reason for this is that the lung beneath the pleural membrane that covers the lung has been inflamed, and that because of the inflammation, that membrane has become adherent to the membrane that lines the chest cavity, and the two membranes have become 'stuck' together. But there is chance I can 'tease' the two membranes apart when I give you repeated injections of air. Meanwhile you will have to remain at home in bed."

I was satisfied with this explanation and I agreed with the plan of treatment that Dr. Lubin laid out. I withdrew from college and started my bed rest. Within days I began to feel better. The spells of enervating fatigue were gone. I had a corner room of my own (my two brothers, Elliott and Harold, were away at college) with three large windows on the sixth floor of the apartment where we lived. The south window brought in the light of the low-lying sun and of its comforting warmth nearly all day long on most days that winter. Two west-facing windows provided a splendid view of the ice-packed Hudson River, of the Palisades on the New Jersey shore, and to the north, of the span and the towers of the George Washington Bridge. In the evening I would take delight in the colored sunsets over the wooded Palisades, and as night fell, in the specks of light that outlined the curves of the great suspension bridge.

One night, as I gazed across the dark river and at the still darker mass of the Palisades, I made a discovery. I saw a tiny light moving along a course halfway between the crest of the cliff and the water's edge. The light had to be the headlight of a moving automobile, and therefore, of necessity, there had to be a road. The car, driving slowly and steadily along the road at night, filled me with wonder and imagining. The road must be narrow with a sharp drop-off of hundreds of feet to the river below on one side, and with a rocky cliff towering hundreds of feet above on the other side.

There must be trees in that wild place, I thought, and bare at this time of the year. What could the driver of the car be doing on such a road on such a winter's night? I wondered. Perhaps it's a criminal escaping from the police on that dark and seldom-traveled road; or perhaps it's a lover with his girl, she sitting close to him and silent at his side. The actual distance between me on my bed in the apartment on upper Manhattan and the road on the other side of the Hudson River could not have been more than three miles, but the night and the mystery worked their magic. The road could have been in a far-off place hundreds of miles away, in a wilderness somewhere, in a land not hemmed-in by brick apartment houses like those on Washington Heights, a land free from an illness that promised to keep me bound to a bed for six months or a year.

When daylight would come my spirits would revive. I sought many ways to reach the world outside of my room. The little Emerson radio with its two dials and with its cracked Bakelite case provided a way. The "Make-Believe Ballroom" program on New York's station WNEW brought a morning's worth of pleasing, popular tunes of the previous decade, 1930's. Bing Crosby's tender, soothing, mirthful, whimsical interpretations of the old songs would bring on a smile. "A Fine Romance" was one of my favorites because of the wonderful irony of the lyrics:

A fine romance with no kisses
A fine romance, my friend, this is,
Why you're as hard to land as the "Isle de France,"
I haven't got a chance,
This is a fine romance!

And I loved the tender lightheartedness of the song,

I met a million-dollar baby
At the five-and-ten cents store!

After a morning of light diversion such as this I would turn off the radio and I would read in the early afternoon. I found a volume of great American plays and I was thus introduced to the pleasure of reading contemporary drama. From this reading I got first hand knowledge of some of the famous Broadway plays of the 1930's that I'd heard about. Elmer Rice's "Street Scene" was close to my own experience growing up as I did at about the same time in New York City. Eugene O'Neill's "Mourning Becomes Electra" showed me how a playwright could introduce psychological probing using two sets of dialogue, one set to be used in conversation and one set as asides. From there my reading led me to Greek drama and to "Oedipus Rex" with its spine-chilling conclusion of the hero gouging out his own eyes.

Someone had given me a "Modern Library Giant" edition of the librettos of W.S. Gilbert. I'd been familiar with Gilbert and Sullivan's operettas, "The Mikado" and the "Pirates of Penzance," but I took particular delight in making discoveries of my own, the less-well known "Gondoliers" and "Iolanthe." My heart would laugh and I would feel a tingle up the side of my face as I followed the printed page while the tenor sang (in the opera's recording on the radio), describing his delight in a maid who cried,

Kiss me, kiss me, kiss me, kiss me
Though I die of shame-a!

And of his response,

Please you, that's the kind of girl
Sets my heart aflame-a!

I found more serious reading in a college text-book of philosophy. Notions of truth were being ever expanded as new discoveries were made in the physical world and in the universe.

When I set the book down I considered the vastness of space, the distant stars and galaxies, and, in comparison, the smallness of our own planet and of the lack of significance of my own situation.

I listened to serious classical music (in addition to Gilbert and Sullivan) in the afternoon and evening over what was then the first classical music station, New York's WQXR. I would listen late into the night until the dream-like theme of the final sign-off (from Glazunoff's 'Scenes de Ballet.') I never tired of the announcer reading the voice-over of the closing verse from Longfellow's poem 'Day and Night':

And the night shall be filled with music,
And the cares that infest the day,
Shall fold their tents like the Arabs,
And, as silently, steal away.

I looked forward to the weekly trip on the bus down to Dr. Lubin's office for a "refill" of air to maintain the pneumothorax. I found in those trips out into the world a refreshing counterbalance to the isolation and to the introspection of my days in bed at home. One of the routes of the Fifth Avenue Bus Company in upper Manhattan came down Fort Washington Avenue. The bus stop was on the corner directly in front of the apartment house in which we lived. The Fifth Avenue bus was special. The fare was a dime, compared to a nickel for other bus lines and for the subway. There was no fare-box at the front of the bus. You just went in and took a seat. Each bus had a two-man crew, the driver and the conductor and it was the conductor who collected the fare. After you found your seat the conductor would find you and, usually with a smile, would present you with a shiny little metal collection box for the dime. And usually he would say "Thank you!"

The route taken by the Fifth Avenue Bus was also particularly pleasant. At 158th Street Fort Washington Avenue swung to the left and joined Broadway, that wide thoroughfare with a tree-lined median. At 155th Street the route turned west to Riverside Drive and the great open space above Hudson River. Further south the route crossed a high-level viaduct over 125th Street to Morningside Heights and the lofty, graceful Riverside Church, and then Grant's Tomb. At 110th Street the bus turned east, along the northern margin of Central Park to Fifth Avenue and then turned south along the eastern margin of the park. There were trees and lawns on the park side to gaze upon, and Mount Sinai Hospital and the imposing apartment houses and mansions on the east side of the avenue. Once past the Metropolitan Museum of Art with its broad steps and its colonnaded facade, I would step off the bus at 86th Street to catch the cross-town bus through the transverse across the park to Central Park West and to Dr. Lubin's office. I never tired of those adventures.

Dr. Lubin would begin by taking me into the dark, black-painted X-ray and fluoroscopy room. He would stand me behind the fluoroscopy screen and switch on the machine which allowed him to see my collapsed lung and how much air was left in the pleural space. From time to time Dr. Lubin would allow me to bend forward and to look into the dimly-lit, green-tinted screen to see inside myself. What I found more fascinating than the collapsed lung was my heart, beating with a series of successive, rapid, complex movements.

How fragile we must be, I thought on first seeing those contractions of the heart. How helpless we are to control those marvelous contortions, how helpless we are, in fact to control our own destiny.

Dr. Lubin would then take me to the procedure room where he would have me lie on my right side on the examining table. I would feel the cold of the alcohol on my skin as he prepared the site for puncture. Then I would feel the sting of the needle as the Novocaine, the local anaesthetic, was injected into the skin and then into the muscles between my ribs. After a few minutes the sting was gone.

"Now, Avrum, you will feel a little pressure," the doctor would say as he prepared the longer needle that would penetrate the skin, the muscle, and finally the pleura. When the needle punctured the sensitive pleural membrane I felt that curious, momentary, dull ache that shot through my whole body, the same sensation that I'd felt earlier when Dr. Lubin induced the pneumothorax in the hospital. Over the weeks and years that followed I became accustomed to that feeling though I never liked it.

The air to collapse the lung further was delivered through a simple pneumothorax apparatus, an arrangement of two graduated two-liter bottles. When the upper bottle, filled with pink-dyed sterile water, was permitted to drain into the empty lower bottle, the air displaced from the lower bottle flowed through a length of rubber tubing attached to the needle and into my chest.

Dr. Lubin controlled the quantity and the rate of air to be delivered by opening or closing a series of stop-cocks or valves within the system. After he delivered some seven- or eight-hundred cubic centimeters of air he withdrew the needle. He would then take me back to the fluoroscopy room where he could see how much more the lung had collapsed with the injection of that additional amount of air.

After several weeks and after five or six of these air-injections (a certain amount of air would always be absorbed between treatments) Dr. Lubin brought me to his consultation room.

"Avrum, I am sorry to say that after all these injections of air I have not been able to tease the adherent layers of the pleura apart. It will be necessary to readmit you to the hospital in order to cut the adhesions. Those adhesions are pulling on the upper portion of the lung, not allowing that portion of the lung to collapse."

"How will that be done?" I remember asking, trying not to show my disappointment.

Dr. Lubin went on to explain the procedure.

"The cutting of the adhesions will be done by a thoracic surgeon under local anaesthesia. The surgeon will introduce a lighted instrument into the pleural cavity. Through a cannula introduced into the thorax in another location, a cautery instrument will be introduced that will cut the adhesions by means of an electric current."

"O.K.," I said. I had complete confidence in Dr. Lubin who I now regarded as my wise old Russian friend.

I remember the scene in the operating room: the penetrating light above, the surgeon and Dr. Lubin in mask, surgical cap and gown holding up their gloved hands in preparation for the procedure. The same steps were used as in the office to sterilize and to anaesthetize the skin. When the Jacobeus thoracoscope, the name of the visualizing instrument, and the cannula for the cautery were introduced, I felt the same deep discomfort I was now familiar with. I remember the conversation between the surgeon and Dr. Lubin.

"One must be careful not to cut too close to the lung," the surgeon said. "That might cause a major tear in the pleura covering the lung and infected material might spill into the pleural cavity."

I'd not been told that the procedure carried any particular risk or that a complication might occur. I felt powerless lying on the table, my life and my future entirely in the hands of the two men who conversed about it so casually.

The procedure went well. The feared mishap did not occur and I was returned to my room. Now I could go home with the promise that the pneumothorax would be effective and that I could go on with my cure.

Word got around that I was a patient in bed at home. I received a few visitors. I received one visit that touched me deeply because that visitor hardly knew me. He was the *shammas* (sexton) of the Washington Heights Congregation and he was fulfilling the *mitzvah* (good deed) of *bikur cholim* (visiting of the sick.) He was an Orthodox German Jew, one of many refugees who began to come to our synagogue and to our community. He spoke with the quiet, accented speech with the "liquid L's" that we, the older *Ashkenazim* (Jews of Polish-Russian-Eastern European background but now Americans) recognized immediately. He was a shy man with glasses and a little black goatee, not comfortable in doing what it was his obligation to do for the community. But I was grateful, nevertheless, that he came.

Much more light-hearted and joyful to me was the visit from my old Talmudical Academy High School classmate, Jack Scharf. Jack was the younger of two sons of grocery store owner on Girard Avenue in the Bronx. The older brother, who Jack described to me as brilliant, morose, and restless but who felt trapped, accepted his role, which was to remain in the store and eventually to take over the business. Jack, because of his brother's sacrifice, was the one who was free to strike out on his own. Although he'd not talked to me about his ambition when we were students together at the Hebrew high school, Jack chose engineering. That sounded to me like an adventurous leap forward. Now Jack, with his great height (he was over six feet tall), his Tartar face, with ruddy cheeks and slanted eyes that nearly came together in a grin, and his bounding optimism, came to cheer me up.

"When you regain your health you must go forward and you must accomplish something in life."

"I don't feel sick anymore," I assured him, "And I know I'll be able to go back to school. But I'll have to look around for something other than medicine. To get into medical school for a New York Jew from City College is hard enough to begin with. But with the added handicap of tuberculosis, I know it will be impossible."

Jack's advice came as a refreshing breeze. "When you get back to college, take the vocational aptitude tests and then see the counselor, a Dr. Dan Brophy. He's a good man and he helped me choose the right direction. I'm sure he'll give you the guidance you need."

The winter was passing. I continued my bed rest at home. The weekly trips to Dr. Lubin's office from Washington Heights to Central Park West became increasingly enjoyable. The slopes along Riverside Drive became alive with the blaze of flowering Forsythia before any green appeared. The air became milder and it was sweet to breathe deeply. When the leaves were young on the trees I was allowed the additional privilege of leaving the house even on days not scheduled for my treatment. Riverside Drive was only one block west of Fort Washington Avenue. From the front door of our apartment house it was any easy walk to the curving pathways of Riverside Park and to views of the Hudson River, now free of ice, and to the panorama of the sun slanting on the steel towers and the suspended roadway of the George Washington Bridge. I was still serious about my rest cure and I would often take it on my back on a sun-warmed wooden park bench looking upward at the clear sky through the branches of a tree and through its newly-sprung leaves.

The "cure" was working well and I was allowed even more privileges. When the summer came my parents took me to the country, to Mohegan Colony in northern Westchester near Peekskill. A cottage on a cool, tree-shaded lane and a lake nearby proved an escape from the increasing heat of the top-floor apartment in Manhattan. Here I was allowed to resume a near-normal level of activity. Weekly "refills" of my pneumothorax continued and there were day-long excursions to maintain the treatment. First, there was an early-morning, seven-mile bus ride through pleasant, green, rolling country down to the river-level train station at Peekskill. Here I would board a city-bound commuter train of the New York Central, or, on some occasions, and this would be a special thrill, a ride on The Pacemaker, the major, all-coach luxury transcontinental train from Chicago on its way to New York City. A ride on a train, specially one drawn by a great steam engine, was an adventure. For me it was an affirmation that I was a participant in the active life of the time; it was a confirmation that I was continuing to get better.

The trains were drawn by steam engines along the eastern shore of the Hudson River as far as Harmon, about thirty miles from the city. Here electric engines took over. From here there was a smooth pull to the confluence of the Hudson with the Harlem River just above the northern tip of Manhattan. Here the tracks swept along the western shore of the Bronx under the spans of bridges that crossed the Harlem, the steel arch of the Washington Bridge at 181st Street, and the stone arches of High Bridge. The train would then slow to cross a low-level bridge to Manhattan, stop at 125th Street, then plunge into the tunnel beneath upper Park Avenue to its final stop at Grand Central Station. When I would step off the train, I would be greeted by the smell of ozone and of engine oil, and I would feel the excitement of the hurried passengers on their way to work in the city. I would then leave the terminal, take a few breaths of the still-cool summer morning air, take the Lexington Avenue bus to 86th

Street, and then take the 86th Street Crosstown bus to Dr. Lubin's office.

The return trip to Peekskill in the late afternoon completed the day's excursion. I soon became familiar with the names of the station stops along the Hudson River route: Yonkers, Hastings-on-Hudson, Dobb's Ferry, Tarrytown, Ossining (under the gray, stone walls and under the forbidding towers of the famous prison, "Sing-sing,") and then Croton-on-Hudson. It was peaceful to gaze across the widest portion of the Hudson, the Tappan See, and to watch the trees and grasses along the right-of-way set off into wild and waving motions with the passing of the train.

I was soon enjoying a near-normal life. I was permitted the privilege of evenings out for what quiet entertainment I could find. Mohegan Colony, where my parents had found a summer cabin, had been established many years before by a group of Anarchists and free-thinkers, and later by Socialists, Communists, and Zionists. The children of these intellectuals, were not politically active as were their parents, but they were mentally alert, and keen in their interest and accomplishment in many fields including music. What a joy I found when I was invited to an evening of chamber music played in a small living room! I'll never forget one such summer evening, in the soft light of a living room in a house just at the end of the lane, where two earnest young girls of fourteen and sixteen, with piano accompaniment, played Bach's double violin concertos in E-minor and in A-major.

By the end of the summer I was up and about all day without fatigue or distress. I felt ready, at last, to pick up the threads of the life I'd left off.

II.

When we moved back to Manhattan at the end of the summer, Dr. Lubin agreed I could return to school provided I would take only a limited number of credits. After my first semester at City College I followed the advice of my friend, Jack Scharf, and I sought out the student counseling service. There I took the Minnesota Vocational Preference test series. When the tests were done I was called to meet Dr. Daniel Brophy, a man who would play a major role in my future and who would set me on a course so exciting that I felt impelled to keep the whole matter a secret for the next four years.

Dan Brophy was a man in his early fifties with a large frame, a barrel chest, and an apoplectic complexion. He was a cigarette-smoker and he had a fine tremor that he could not suppress. One might have taken him for a truck-driver, a longshoreman, or a street-car conductor. Instead of a booming voice or a blustery manner, however, he spoke in a barely audible, almost monotonous tone, and his face displayed little emotion. At City College his appointment was in the Speech Department, and at the same time he functioned as a guidance counselor. The "Doctor" of his title was for the degree of M.D. He was a graduate of Cornell University Medical College, but, for reasons he never disclosed to me, he chose not to practice medicine but rather to teach and to advise students.

"You've done very well in several areas," he began when he sat down with me to discuss my test scores. "What field were you thinking of going into?"

I explained that though I'd considered medicine as my first choice, I was forced to consider alternatives because of my recent illness. It was necessary, I added, to avoid the risk of a "breakdown" of tuberculosis. I knew that the stress of long hours in medicine increased that risk. I did not say to this apparently friendly Irishman that what troubled me more was the basic difficulty a Jewish youth from New York experiences getting into medical school from City College.

"Your tests show strength," Dr. Brophy went on in his analysis, "In the following areas: 1) interest in people, 2) facility with language and expression, and 3) science. These are the attributes of persons who do well in medicine. The grades you achieved in your college courses last year and in your first semester this year have been excellent. If you continue to do as well over the next several years you should have no difficulty getting into medical school. Keep in touch with me. When the time comes I will help you."

I was stunned. I was delighted. It was as if a light had turned on for me after the gloom of the diagnosis of tuberculosis. Dan Brophy's words, "I will help you," rang in my ears. I found it strange that this man, who I had met only moments before and on the basis of only a few college grades and some scores on a test, would come forth with such a promise. It was simply *wonder* that this great, good fortune should come to me. I would not betray this trust; I would not dissipate the strength of the promise now by telling others who would be certain to seek similar favors. So I kept the secret.

With the promise that I would be helped, I plunged forward into my studies. I wanted to get the good grades necessary to maintain Dr. Brophy's respect. I knew how to study and I enjoyed learning. From my previous experience I had a sense what was expected when it came to taking examinations in every course. I was free from the constant anxieties that were the lot of other pre-medical students. When they asked me what my major was, I said only that I was a "biology" major.

I came to Dr. Brophy only once each year when I'd accumulated another measure of the necessary good grades. I wanted to be sure this association with my mentor would not grow thin.

At last it was the Fall of my senior year. I'd already completed my applications to several medical schools when I presented myself to Dr. Brophy. It was time for the promise to be fulfilled. I'd completed my part of the bargain. With the exception of a single "C" in mathematics, the vast majority of my grades were "A's."

Dr. Brophy sat behind his desk (with me waiting quietly) and he picked up the telephone. He said he would be calling Dr. Joseph C. Hinsey, Dean of the Cornell University Medical College.

"Joe," he said, "I have a lad here who would like to come to our medical school and I would like you to meet him."

My heart raced. This was really it. It was really happening. I thought it a bit strange that I, a Talmudical Academy High School graduate, should be called a "lad," but it was in keeping with the Irish in Daniel Brophy.

Within a few days Dr. Brophy and I were sitting in Dr. Hinsey's office on the ground floor of the Cornell-New York Hospital Medical Center.

"This is the lad I told you about," Dr. Brophy said. "He's done very well at City College and I think you'll agree he'll do well when he's admitted to next fall's entering class."

There could not have been a stronger endorsement. Dr. Brophy had not only made good his promise to "go to bat" for me but he'd followed through. Dr. Hinsey turned his earnest gaze on me and he addressed me by my first name.

"Avrum, I'm pleased to meet you. I'll see to it that you have interviews with members of our admissions committee."

Dr. Hinsey was a remarkable man and I came to know him better over the next several years. A professor of anatomy with a distinguished reputation in studies of the brain, he possessed enormous personal magnetism as well. He was famous for his ability to remember people. Years later, when I visited the medical school, I would observe Dr. Hinsey greeting people in the hallways and calling them correctly by their first names.

"Avrum," he asked me one time (and this was long after his retirement) "How are you? Where have you had your internship? What are your plans?"

The first of the admissions committee members I went in to see was Dr. William Herrick, a young professor of bacteriology. The meeting went very well. We had many topics of mutual interest and I felt very comfortable with this soft-spoken man. Then the subject of my health came up. By the time I was speaking with Dr. Herrick, I was in my fifth year of pneumothorax therapy. I had still not passed, what was considered at that time, the last critical milestone in the "arrest" of tuberculosis.

"Do you think you will be able to maintain your good health without the "crutch" of the artificially maintained pneumothorax?" Dr. Herrick asked. Dr. Herrick ended the interview with statements that were both encouraging and discouraging.

"You are obviously qualified to enter medical school and I would have no hesitation in supporting you were it not for the fact that, by going to medical school , you run the risk of seriously jeopardizing your health. It would do no good," he concluded, "To get in to medical school and soon thereafter go to your grave."

My optimism was still riding high with Dr. Brophy's support and Dr. Hinsey's cordiality. I did not for a moment believe Dr. Herrick's dire prediction. Nevertheless I was realistic enough to see that the only obstacle to my admission was the perception that tuberculosis was a disqualifying condition. I knew it was possible that I would not be accepted, but at least I would not be rejected because I was a Jew.

The tall, gray-white, art-deco, neo-Gothic buildings of the Cornell-New York Hospital towered above me as I left that interview with Dr. Herrick.

"So long, great buildings and great institution," I soliloquized (over dramatically, I thought, even as I said it). "I've seen you today and I'm glad I've come this far, but it's likely I'll never see you again."

The conclusion of this memoir, of the secret so well kept and of the promise so faithfully carried out, is soon to be revealed. But as I passed those buildings over the next ten years, I remembered the apostrophe that in my heart, even at the time I first uttered it, I did not really believe.

The question of my admission to the Cornell medical school was submitted to Dr. Carl Muschenheim. Dr. Muschenheim was Clinical Professor of Medicine, a practicing physician specializing in tuberculosis, and, at that time, a participant in exciting research on the usefulness of the new drug, streptomycin. Furthermore, Dr. Muschenheim had had tuberculosis himself as a young man, and had "taken the cure" at the famous Trudeau Sanatorium in upper New York State. I was instructed to bring all my chest X-rays with me for review and I would be examined by Dr. Muschenheim in his office. My own doctor, Dr. Lubin, was happy to comply with the request that my case be reviewed by another expert in the field.

It was a dimly-lit office with a dimly-lit examining room with a dark fluoroscope and X-ray suite adjoining. Dr. Muschenheim placed the X-ray films on the view-box. He had no difficulty identifying the lesion, now not much larger than the size of a pea, in the collapsed left upper lobe "under" the pneumothorax. A physical examination then followed which consisted principally of Dr. Muschenheim listening to my chest with a stethoscope. Then he told me that I could get dressed, and I did so, and I returned to the consultation room where I found him seated at his desk and I sat down opposite him. For the longest time, it seemed, he said nothing. He hummed to himself in a soft, unmusical way. At last I spoke.

I was somewhat surprised at my forthrightness, but I found I had to end the suspense.

"Well, Dr. Muschenheim, what do you think? Do you think I could be accepted to medical school and that I could survive without a breakdown?"

Dr. Muschenheim's reply was brief and I never forgot it.

"I don't see why not!"

I knew at that moment that his decision would be honored. I would be accepted. Confirmation came in the mail a few days later. The years of uncertainty were over. What had made the uncertainty bearable was that Dr. Brophy had made a promise, and that I had kept the secret.

III.

Some six or seven years after Dan Brophy had made good his promise and some eleven years after we first met, I saw him again. I was dressed in the starched white uniform of a New York Hospital house officer, and in my final year of residency in internal medicine. Dr. Brophy was now a patient in a four-bed room in the hospital teaching unit. He had serious heart disease with a dangerously enlarged heat and with the irregular rhythm of atrial fibrillation.

I greeted my old mentor warmly and said what I thought would be some encouraging words. But he seemed unemotional, maintaining the same almost expressionless face. He seemed not to want to talk to me. I was saddened by his coolness. I came to him the next day in hopes I would find in him some of the warmth he had shown me before. But the stubborn old Irishman maintained his distance. I visited him less and less until finally he left the hospital without offering me the chance to meet him again. I learned that he died a few weeks later.

It was only after the passage of years that I came to understand why he'd been so cool to me. He knew that death was upon him and he did not wish to re-establish a bond that he knew he could not sustain.

OFF-LIMITS

Jack Berkowitz turned seventeen the first summer he spent at Mohegan colony and there he found a fifteen-year old girl living next door. It was Nina Podrenko.

Jack still considered himself an fairly observant Jew, and Nina, whose father was a Gentile Russian, placed her off-limits even though Nina's mother, was Jewish. Nina was, in a way, typical of the off-spring of many of the Anarchist couples who had founded Mohegan colony in the 1920s. The land had originally been purchased by Baron de Hirsch as an agricultural colony a generation before as one of the many schemes to settle European Jews on the land in America.

For the first time in his life Jack could see Jews and Gentiles in these now aging Anarchist couples now living together. Jack tried not to register shock, however, when, from the kitchen below where his parents rented an upstairs apartment, Sonya Levy, married to Tony Dobrochuk (another pairing of a rebellious Jewish woman and a Gentile Russian), came the aroma of frying bacon. Jack had never smelled bacon before, but he learned before long what it was. And yes, to Jack, it was indeed a shock to his Jewish sensibilities.

So Nina Podrenko was off-limits from the start. Besides, Jack was in love with another girl, a Jewish girl from the Bronx named Jodi Mogilievsky. But even with Jodi, both of whose parents were Jewish, Jack was having difficulty. Jodi's parents were secular, and indifferent to the Orthodox observances that Jack felt important. Jack was determined that somewhere along the line, when he could win her heart, he would teach her Hebrew and how to keep a Kosher home. Jodi was a prize that Jack truly yearned for. She was, at fifteen, beautiful beyond belief, with gray-blue eyes, dark hair, a perfect straight nose, and clear, white skin. When Jack got his first good-night kiss from this fairy queen, he nearly swooned, having felt for the first time in his life the combination of physical passion with exalted love. But Jodi, though fey, romantic, accomplished and cultured, a student at upper Manhattan's High School of Music and Art, was not completely within his grasp. The winter before, when Jack was in the hospital, Jodi had sent him a letter that contained a silver bracelet. The inscription on the bracelet said in Russian, "Ya Tibya Lublu." Jack was swept away with joy when Jodi explained its meaning, " I Love You." But them she added in the letter, "I don't really mean it."

That summer with Jack in Mohegan Colony and Jodi in the Bronx, Jack spent painful hours walking to the little post office on Crompond Road hoping to receive a letter from Jodi in response to his, but no letter ever came.

So, though Nina Podrenko was "off-limits" for any serious entanglement, she was there, right next door. Jack spent many hours with Nina. She was an eager listener and Jack was willing to answer her many questions on a variety of subjects. Nina saw Jack as sophisticated coming from the great city of New York while she came from this little country place. Nina asked him about music and Jack described how his older brother Howard had forced him as young boy to sit down and listen to classical music on New York's first classical music station, WQXR. That's where Jack got his start. He told her of his own classical music library on the old, 78 rpm records offered (as a promotional) by the then, new New New York Post. The collection included orchestral works, the symphonies, Beethoven's Fifth, Mozart's 40th, Schubert's Unfinished, Tschaikowsky's Fifth, and the tone poem, Rimsky-Korsakoff's Scheherezade. And he told her of Gilbert and Sullivan's operettas, and that he had seen the D'Oyle Carte Opera's performance of "The Mikado" at the Brooklyn Academy of Music. So Jack felt it was pleasant to be with Little Nina.

"Little Nina" she was, slender, no more than five feet-two, with a turned-up little Russian nose and a pretty-enough face with glasses.

And there was a variety of other girls at Mohegan Colony that summer. Jack always liked girls. He had no sisters, only two brothers. And the names of the girls, delicious of themselves, gave a history of the social make-up of Mohegan Colony. Nina, of course, with her Russian surname, told of the anarchist background of her parents, early settlers of the Colony. Iris Millet's father had been a French anarchist who found his way there. Then came the girls whose first names reflected the politics of settlers in the colony who came later. There were Peninah and Avivah, daughters of Zionist parents who were partial to the Hebrew language. Then there was Faige (and her brother, Velvel) whose parents were Yiddishist Socialists. The twin pretty girls, Sonya and Irena, whose parents, the Slavsky's, were simply Russian language lovers. Later colony settlers had no politics or Leftist leanings, simply business men who saw the chance of a large country house with a tennis court. Bunnie Kaye was the blond daughter of one of those businessmen. She had a smashing serve that Jack admired and wondered at, besides Bunnie herself.

Besides the names and the pretty faces, there was talent. Peninah, in her mid-twenties was a pianist, and Avivah, her sister, at seventeen, was a cellist. One summer evening Peninah invited Jack to a private chamber music concert. Jack, whose musical taste up until that time consisted only of orchestral music, was taken by the beauty and the clarity of Bach's double violin concertos he heard that evening. With Peninah at the piano, two girls that Jack had not met before, Lenore, sixteen, and Judy, fourteen, played the violins. With what perfection, what energy those girls played, bodies and arms swaying, heads tossing! The visual experience, and the close-up of hearing live music played before him enlarged his musical experience and gave him a new taste for music played by stringed instruments. He no longer needed to hear a full orchestra.

Nina was next on the program. She was newer at the violin and she stood up straight and nervous but she played with feeling the lovely Schubert Sonatina for violin in A.

The memory of Jodi Mogilievsky faded that summer and Jack never saw her again. Nina, the girl with glasses, the serious and earnest fifteen-year old, was right next door.

Jack was returning on the train one evening from a trip in the City. Nina's parents, Bill and Rose, and Nina with them, picked him up at the railroad station in Peekskill to take him home. The late summer night was hot and dark, but there was a breeze through the open window of the large, black Dodge sedan Bill Podrenko was driving. His wife, Rose, was with him in the front seat. Nina sat to Jack's left in the rear seat. Nina was quiet as usual as the car climbed up out of the valley into the cooler air of the hills.

"Can I put my head in your lap?" Nina asked. Jack was surprised by the suddenness of this request, but he was even more astonished when, lying with her face looking up at his, she took his right hand and placed it on her breast. It was a small breast but soft and it fit nicely in his hand. Jack had never felt a girl's breast before. It was more delicious than he'd ever imagined. His heart was racing now, and he had to hold back his breath that also was coming fast. She kept his hand there and he did not dare to, nor did he want to, take it away.

How brave she is to do this, he thought, with her parents less than two feet away int the front seat. It must be that she loves me! He smelled an acid, oniony odor from her perspiration and it excited him. They did not speak, but she pressed her head against his lap and held his hand on her breast until the car turned into the driveway.

The days went by. Jack did not find or make any opportunity for them to be together. They never spoke to one another of what had happened in the car. There was never any embrace or a kiss. Nina had given what signals she could for Jack to respond to, but for Jack, Nina Podrenko was off-limits.

PRINCESS

Abraham Foxman, born in 1940, was a Polish infant whose parents were taken off to the Ghetto. They left their baby in the care of a nanny, Bronislaw Kurpi, a Catholic who, at the risk of her own life, took the child into her home. She changed his name, falsified documents, and, with the collusion of a Polish priest, had the baby baptized as if he were her own child. As a result, he survived.

The same thing happened all over occupied Europe, and today, according to Foxman's estimate, there may be more than ten thousand sons and daughters of Jews who were saved by "rescue baptisms." These survivors have come to be called "The Hidden Jews."

–from an article. "The Silence,"
by James Carroll in *The New Yorker,* April 7, 1997.

Elsa, born in 1936, was a Jewish child who survived the holocaust as one of the "Hidden Jews." I knew her in 1946 after her great-uncle, Max Schoenfeld, a friend of my parents, brought her from Poland to America. She was ten years old and I was twenty. I was in love with her.

It was easy to love this child for her wistful blond beauty, for her freckled nose and cheeks, and for her blue eyes.

"You are my princess and I will marry you," I told her. She accepted this calmly, with such poise and equanimity. It was just so. That's the way it would be.

"You know it looks a little silly," my mother would say, "You, a young man, walking to the Schoenfeld's every day to pay court to a ten year-old girl." And every day I would walk to that part of Mohegan Colony where the Schoenfeld's lived to see Elsa. The Schoenfeld's didn't see it strange that I would visit their niece. She was princess to them as well.

Elsa possessed that curious mixture of innocense and worldliness. Perhaps she sensed what I saw in her, what she had experienced but never talked about, a symbol. She was a symbol of Jewish survival, living proof of escape from death, a princess rescued from imprisonment in a castle when the evil monster had lost his power over her.

In her blondness I saw the beauty of Poland, my father's birthplace. Like Isaac whose wife, Rebecca, was brought to him from the land of Abraham's birth, and like Jacob, who loved Rachel of his father's people in the land to the north, Elsa would properly become my wife.

Elsa would greet me when I came to visit her with innocent grace. I presented her with a gift, a pen-and-ink drawing I had made of the tree-lined lane where the Schoenfeld's lived, and I'd placed the sketch in a mat and frame.

The visits lasted most of the summer. Elsa, though real in life, was actually more a spirit, diaphanous, an allegory, an archetype. If I touched her substantial hand in greeting or in taking leave, her skin was cool, almost rough, without electricity or the beginning of sex. At no level, neither at the conscious, or even at the deepest subconscious, was there any of the heat or the chemistry of the sex I had known with others.

The magical summer ended. I returned to the city, to medical school with its power to absorb me so completely in its grasp. The pastoral idyll with Elsa passed completely from my mind. Taking her place were real human beings with whom I reacted with deep emotion. At a conscious level, I experienced the joy of certainty that medicine was the right choice for me.

"Have you written to Elsa?" my mother would ask me. "You spent all that time with her before."

"No, I haven't."

It was not laziness. It was inconstancy. What meaning could there be of a silly promise made to a pretty child, a child more unreal than real. And there was no pain. Elsa did not write to me or try to reach me either.

After medical school I started my internship in another city; more joy, more certainty that medicine was my life, and more fires and passion, and more intimacy.

Five years passed. It was another summer with one evening free to visit my parents in the summer place outside the city.

"Why don't you go to see Elsa? She's baby-sitting at the Kaufman's just down the road. I'm sure she'll be glad to see you."

Baby-sitting! I thought. The ordinariness, the banality of it! Not a proper duty for a princess. I found her in a cottage in a poorer lane nearby, not the airy place of the Schoenfeld's.

I hardly recognized her. She was sixteen, the age for baby-sitting. She had lost her blondness, her freckles. She was heavier, more substantial, though not fat. Her breasts were high and full in front of her. Her spirituality, her airiness, her mystery had vanished!

There was no reaching out, neither I for her nor she for me. There were no reminiscences of that summer in the past. I had communicated to her none of my life, my joy in medicine, nor she of her life to me. Neither of us mentioned either in seriousness or in jest my old promise, and her seeming acquiescence at that time, that she would be my wife.

And that was that. My visit lasted no more than half and hour and I left. I never saw Elsa again. Nor did I think of her until three years later when I received her letter, the first she had ever written. (My mother had given her my new address.) By that time I was two-thirds of a continent away, in Arizona, working in a tuberculosis sanatorium on an Indian reservation. Our worlds by that time were even further apart. My passion was for the landscape of pink, sandstone cliffs, of piñon, cedar and sage, and for a slender, dark-eyed Navajo girl who would be my wife.

"I am in college now," she wrote, "and I am married." I remember nothing else of her letter but I remember my reaction, my momentary pangs of regret. How swiftly and how irrevocably the distance now between us. I was living in an exotically new world with a new lover. Why did it matter to me? But it did touch me that she wrote to me, that was reaching out to me as she never had before. She had moved along swiftly, it seemed to me, in the three years since she'd been a high school baby-sitter. And married! Somehow I sensed by her her tone that the marriage was a complication of her life rather than a joy. She'd not described her young husband (I presumed he must have been young). She did not say anything about love.

I may have written her a letter in response, but I'm not certain I actually did. Inconstancy again. I did think about her. I saw her in my mind again as the Polish Jewish child who'd been rescued, the lovely, blond, fairy-child of that long-ago summer.

My parents flew out from New York to visit me in Arizona. I have photographs and memories of that visit, of our drive to Tucson in a convertible with the top down under the crystal blue dome of the sky, of desert and of saguaro cactus, so different from the canopy of the green of New York summers. And they brought me news of the Schoenfelds of Mohegan Colony. Elsa was dead. A suicide at twenty.

I was struck again, as I'd been when I'd received her letter the year before, only so much more so. That letter was of her unhappiness, her despair. Why else would she have written, why else would she have reached out to me? First inconstancy, now guilt. Why had I not been available to her? Why had I not perceived her needs? In my foolish romancing about her, Elsa, the fairy creature, I had never asked her to tell me her real story. She might have been old enough at the age of four or five in 1940 to have known she was Jewish. There might then have been the memory of terror, fear of discovery, knowledge that her parents had been stripped away from her, later knowledge that her parents had been killed. Did she have memory of brothers, sisters, cousins, uncles, aunts, grandparents, who were also killed? If her memory as a Jewish child had faded, was there not pain as she was pulled away from her new Catholic Polish parents now at the age of ten? What meaning could there have been for her coming to America, to a new set of parents, to meeting a young man, a *luftmensch,* who would spend a summer with her declaring that she was his princess, that he would marry her one day and then abandon her?

Such were my thoughts in the pure Arizona air. Later I would learn some of the psychiatric terms that might have been applied: "survivors guilt," " post-traumatic stress syndrome." The complexities of depression and suicide among the young cannot be made simple by giving them a label. The guilt and self-examination of parents and of any who have known a suicide weigh most heavily and that guilt lingers on among the living.

Nearly fifty years have now passed. The Navajo girl who became my wife became Jewish by Orthodox conversion in a *mikvah.*

Our four children were educated in Jewish schools, and one of them, our son is now on a *kibbutz* in Israel. If I failed to play a meaningful part in the life of Elsa, a "Hidden Jew,' nevertheless, *Am Yisroel chai,* The People, Israel, live on. The memory of the freckled, Polish Jewish child, Elsa, lives also — and I have told my story and hers.

INNOCENCE

I was luckier, in a away, than most beginning medical students because I had chosen a career within medicine even before I started medical school. That field was pharmacology, the study of drugs and their action. I chose pharmacology because it satisfied my scientific curiosity and because, as a field of research, it would allow me to avoid some of the rigors of private practice. I was just then completing my own course of treatment for tuberculosis; it was important for me to avoid having a "breakdown."

Walter Richter, the young professor of pharmacology, was delighted to welcome an eager student such as myself into his laboratory. It was a compliment to him to have a protege, a young person who was enthusiastic and willing to commit himself to pharmacology in his very first year in medicine. By the summer break between the first and the second years I was working full-time in Dr. Richter's laboratory. Dr. Richter had even found a small salary for me out of his research grant money. I was further pleased that he used a piece of my work in one of his publications. It was a tracing on a smoked drum of the contractions of the muscle of frog's leg. In the experiment those contractions were slowed dramatically when sodium fluoroacetate, a powerful metabolic inhibitor, was added to the bath containing the frog's leg muscle.

It was a great start for me. I felt that I was on the right track, that my life was turning out exactly as I had pictured it.

But the laboratory, I soon found, was a lonely place. Late one summer evening, long after Dr. Richter and the other laboratory staff had left I completed one more smoked drum tracing of frog leg muscle contraction. I dipped the tracing in shellac to preserve it and I hung it up to dry. I was hungry and tired and I wandered over to the hospital cafeteria, open for the nurses' ten o'clock supper. I was drawn to the lights, to the pleasant sound of people's conversation. And there I met Millie Thomason.

The hospital cafeteria, during regular hours, had a smaller dining room set aside for doctors and resident physicians on the staff. The larger section was for the nurses. But at night this social barrier would break down. With fewer persons on duty during the evening shift and with everyone more eager for companionship in those late hours, it was acceptable for everyone to eat together, and so I was introduced to Millie.

Millie Thomason was tall, dark-eyed and dark-haired, and she carried her somewhat straight figure with quiet reserve. She had a placid disposition and she spoke in a low voice. It was her calm and lovely face with its tinge of sadness that attracted me. I was buoyed up by the feeling of confidence I gained in my work and I would make her smile. I was bold yet I approached her with kindness. I was twenty-two. I knew she must have been older, perhaps twenty-four or twenty-five. There was some fascination in this for me. She was an older woman, a mystery woman. She said little about herself at first, only that she had graduated from a school of nursing in California and that she had been a staff nurse at a university hospital there for about a year. I had never been out of New York. I found her exotic; she had come from far-away, romantic California.

We met at the late supper several times. At last, my heart pounding, I invited her to come for a walk with me after her shift was over, and Millie, the sad, calm, and lovely woman accepted. We walked quietly in the cool night along curving pathways leading toward the Hudson River. The necklace of lights across the mighty George Washington Bridge cast its sparkling reflections on the dark expanse of water. For long periods we watched as tugboats, with three lights on their single mast indicating a string of barges in tow, glide silently in the distance, far out on the water. I touched her hand and she returned my grasp. It took little to make me happy.

I showed her more of New York. Fred Bevans, an eccentric classmate of mine then and probably still more eccentric now, found an apartment in an old-law tenement in the East Village. I was proud to bring Millie to meet my classmates at one of Fred's riotous parties. When the noise and confusion of the gathering reached its peak we stole up to the darkness of the tenement roof. In the summer night we sat quietly together above the merriment of the apartment below and far above the night noises from the street. With our backs against the parapet, we gazed at the lights of the towers of midtown Manhattan to the north and our lips touched with cool and gentle kisses.

Slowly, Millie told me a little more about herself. She showed me a photograph of herself, a bit younger and a bit happier, standing taller than her parents in the driveway of a very modest house with a one-car garage. Her hair had been longer then, piled in a pompadour in the style of several years earlier. I guessed from Millie's sadness now some untold great loss, that of a lover or, perhaps, even of a husband. Perhaps she came to New York to forget, or to find someone who could make her forget, I thought. And she is so fragile. I never intruded upon her and I never asked. She would tell me if she wanted to; that was up to her.

If Millie came from a modest home in California, her circumstances in New York were modest as well. She shared an apartment with Flo, another nurse, on East 84th Street, just off Third Avenue in Yorkville. The apartment, on the second floor of an old tenement, faced the street. After an evening out in Manhattan at a restaurant or at a party, I would bring Millie home on the Third Avenue "El." I thought a ride on the "El" was a little adventure, and I hoped that Millie, who was a tourist, a newcomer and an outsider visiting New York, would consider a ride on the "El" an adventure too. How much fun it was that the seats on the old, rattling cars were just long, wicker benches that ran the length of the car and on either side of it. From where we sat we could have a good time just looking at all the other people, the old, tired people riding the train at night, the "characters," the ordinary citizens of New York. Millie, at my side, would be content to put her arm in mine and to rest her head on my shoulder. When we would get off at her station, and step off at the platform we would watch the train rumble off to the north. Then we would take the stairs down to the quiet, darkened street. I would take her to her door thinking it was sad that a quest for a better life had brought her to no more than this.

Yorkville's main thoroughfare, East Eighty-Sixth Street, lay only two blocks away. This center of Manhattan's German neighborhood caused me some uneasiness. I remembered photographs of the street as the site of pre-war, massed rallies of brown-shirted, pro-Nazi, Jew-hating members of the German-American Bund. East 86th Street, after the defeat of the Nazis in World War II, retained some of its pre-war character. Many little German restaurants and cafes still lined the broad and brightly lit thoroughfare that ran from Central

Park to the East River. Since there might be entertainment so close by, I brought Millie to 86th street and to one such café where from the front door came the happier music from an earlier era. On a little raised platform three musicians stood, two played violins and a third a bass viol. One seated musician played the zither. How charming it seemed, little waltzes and landler, music from Austria and the Tyrol. I was struck, however by the appearance of one of the violinists, a short man with dark hair who reminded me of the actor, Peter Lorre. Could this man be, like the actor, Jewish? If so, how could he have survived the hatred and fear of the Nazi era on 86th Street? My old anxiety and fear of the place returned but I said nothing and we left. Had I known then, as I know now, that a sensitive and nurturing woman would have responded to my emotion, how a confession of mine would have changed our relationship, how she would have enfolded me in her protecting arms... But I would not tell her what I felt. I was the strong one. I was the one who was protecting her.

A little later in that summer Millie told me that she was about to leave, to return to California. We would have a simple farewell dinner in her apartment. I would bring a symbol of the summertime, a cool, sweet dish of strawberries and sour cream, a dish that was my mother's favorite, a token of love. We lit candles as the daylight faded. We looked out on to the street from the kitchen window. Flo, Millie's roommate, appeared.

"Join us," we said. Flo was part of Millie's life. She belonged with us at the time of tender parting. But Flo, a little older than Millie, a little plainer, a little coarser, looked nervous. She, too, was expecting a visitor. Flo fidgeted, had little to say. The doorbell rang and a Mr. Coughee appeared, a short man with flushed face, sweating in his suit coat and tie. After the briefest of introductions and no further conversation, Flo rose, took Mr. Coughee by the hand, led him into an inner room and closed the door behind her. Millie and I stared at the table in front of us, her face sad and lit by the flickering of the candles. Our hands touched but we said nothing. Soon, from that inner room, came soft sounds of fabrics rustling, soft sounds of clothing dropping to the floor, then human sounds, muffled, then rocking sounds, bed-squeaking sounds. Fucking! They were fucking in there!

Without a word Millie rose, led me out of the apartment door and we sat down on the landing of the stairs. This was our farewell. We wept and we kissed and embraced in the stairwell. We held each other, our faces wet with tears. After a while the apartment door opened, Mr. Coughee came out, passed us on the stairs and disappeared out into the street. It was quiet now. The tension and the pain were gone. Then, with the salt of our tears on my lips, I rose without turning around, walked down the stairs, and out the front door. I was still weeping when I found a waiting streetcar and rode home.

A KOSHER BUTCHER IN SCARSDALE

Max Rausch and I had been classmates in medical school and his wife, Bev, was always the principal "mover" in keeping our families together. When I returned to New York for further residency training, I brought my young Navajo wife, Ida, with me. Ida was just twenty-one, and a stunning, exotic, and proud beauty. Yet, with the exception of Bev, Ida had felt unsure of herself in the circle of ambitious young wives of the other residents at the hospital. Ida sensed their coolness to her and their competitiveness. I am sure it was jealousy on their part. But Bev took her in with a kindness and an openness that made Ida feel very much at home.

Over the years Bev worked heard to keep the friendship between our two families even after Ida and I had settled in the West while Max set up his practice in Westfield, New Jersey. Bev kept her connection with us through her energetic correspondence. It was upon her insistence that we met again at our twenty-fifth medical school reunion. As our families grew (we each had four children now) Bev arranged for us to be together at family celebrations such as a Bar-Mitzvah in Corrales, New Mexico and a wedding at the Temple in Westfield.

Bev also served as a "bulletin board" for any significant events that occurred in the larger family of our medical school class, such as divorces and deaths. In fact she had been a keeper of records of all sorts for many years, and among these records was the photograph album.

Bev pulled out the photograph album on a pleasant Spring evening after Ida and I had come out to Westfield after a visit in New York City. With us was the oldest of our three daughters, Yanabah Yonah, a gracious beauty with two names, Navajo and Hebrew.

"You know," she said to Yanabah Yonah, "When your dad was young he was kind of 'cute.'" (I saw it coming: I'd heard her tell Ida that story before.) "Three of us Jewish nurses had our eyes on your father back then. If we hadn't succeeded in getting our own husbands from among the small group of Jewish medical student in the class at that time we would have gone after him."

When she said this, she opened the old album of black and white snapshots and she pointed to a photograph of a young man and a young woman. The two were sitting on a grassy knoll, propped up on their elbows and they were looking at the photographer. I had difficulty recognizing that it was me in that picture. I had only the vaguest recollection of the occasion, perhaps some sort of class picnic that had taken place — a third of a century ago. The photographer was probably Bev Rausch herself, and she was, even then, preparing herself for her future role as class historian.

We all bent forward to look more closely at the photograph. I was slender then, about one hundred fifty pounds for my five-foot eleven inches of height. The glasses I wore then had plastic frames. My hair, trimmed at the sides, left enough at the stop to show that it was thick and wavy. I was surprised that the expression on my face was that of such calmness and equanimity. The girl at my side had a small but pleasant face and she was dressed in a a peasant blouse and a three-quarter length skirt. It was Margaret Ann Richardson.

Now my head began to swim. I felt I was tumbling into flood-tide of memories and emotions. My face must have revealed some of this to Ida, but she chose at that time not to notice or to make a scene that might embarrass me before my friends.

Margaret and I were lovers. Although the snapshot was a casual one it captured the essence of the relationship between us. We were comfortable with one another. We felt the presence of one another without the need to touch or to look at the other.

Margaret Ann had presented a curious combination of the sophisticated and the ingenuous. I suppose it was the ingenousness that had captivated me. She had come from a comfortable, upper middle class family. Her father had been in the publishing business. Originally from Nebraska, he had become highly successful in his field and had been brought to the East where he settled his family in Scarsdale, north of the city in Westchester County, and where he provided a summer home in the Berkshires. Margaret Ann had gone to Smith and from there to medical school. In spite of these advantages of background and of accomplishment Margaret Ann was nervous and shy. She was the least prepossessing of the eight women in our medical school class. I responded to this shyness. I was optimistic and outgoing; she was reticent. By the end of the first year of medical school we had found one another. The differences in our background and in our personalities must have added to the attraction we felt for one another. Friendship led to a growing appreciation of one another, to exploration of one another, and to love.

Margaret would declare her love in the simplest of terms and these declarations, though they lacked "style," had the most telling effect. When I arrived late at a class party, I found her waiting for me and we danced.

"I thought you would never come," she said. We'd been just friends until then. Now she'd turned her sixteen-inch guns on me. She fired those guns with devastating accuracy.

In the friendly atmosphere of the medical school class our love was acknowledged and accepted. In many respects, too, the world was developing into a more accepting place.

Some enchanted evening,
You will meet a stranger,
You will meet a stranger
Across a crowded room,

sang Ezio Pinza in the great love song from "South Pacific." The melody and the power of the words filled the air.

Once you have found her, never let her go.
Once you have found her, never let her go,
Never let her go!

was the message.

Perhaps, I thought, perhaps it might be possible.

I was a graduate of the Flatbush Yeshiva in Brooklyn, of the Talmudical Academy High School of the Yeshiva College, and of the City College of New York, and I had entered upon a dangerous course.

"Jack, you must not do this," warned my father. Morris Berkowitz had fled Tzarist Russian Poland at the age of sixteen. He'd sent his three sons to Hebrew day schools to instruct us in the language, culture, religion , and history of the Jewish people. My mother,

Cecile, stood by her husband. She met Margaret Richardson one time outside of the hospital. She would have wanted such a shy, quiet woman, so much like herself, for her son.

"She has reddish hair and a small, turned-down nose. She almost *looks* Jewish,' she reported after their meeting. But she, too, said, "Son, you must not do this."

After a while, there was anguish, too, for Margaret. She had entered into the love affair more innocently than I had. I had known from the start that I "must not do this," but Margaret was simply in love.

"Why can't we just run away to some desert island and have a lot of little Berkowitzes?" She declared herself in the same ingenuous way and I knew how much she loved me and I loved her.

Margaret Richardson had character and she would fight. There was a tradition of rebellion in her family. Her brother, Rob, had dropped out of college and had become a jazz clarinetist. Margaret was proud of her brother and found an occasion at a Dixieland concert to introduce me to him.

Now Margaret would have me up to Scarsdale to meet her parents. So on a cool Spring evening I borrowed my family's old La Salle and set out from Washington Heights where my parents lived. When I drove north up the Bronx River Parkway, I entered Bronxville, a world of cool, green trees and lawns and of English Tudor homes half-hidden in well-tended shrubbery. Further north into Westchester I began to experience a growing uneasiness. I was entering a place of loveliness but a place I had known from my earliest childhood to be "Restricted." "Restricted" was the "polite" term which meant "No Jews or Negroes allowed."

In Scarsdale that evening the tree-lined streets curved graciously this way and that, the 1920's style street lamps on short, cast-iron posts threw their soft light into the greenery. Here the homes were mainly two-story frame houses of an earlier era with open porches running the full length of the front of the house, the porch roofs supported by white-painted, rounded wooden pillars.

I remembered the old joke that served as the epitome of a place where there were no Jews. "What is the definition of the Yiddish word, *farblunget*?" the story-teller asks. (At its simplest, *farblunget* means *lost.* But it means more than just *lost.* It means *completely, utterly, totally, hopelessly lost.)* "What is the definition of *farblunget?*" the jokester asks once again. He gives his own answer: "A kosher butcher in Scarsdale!"

I felt the uncertainty, the old fear of rejection, fall away in the warmth of Margaret's welcome. She led me across the broad front porch into the gracious home where she'd grown up. She led me upstairs to show me her bedroom, small, light, airy, with wallpapered walls and white curtains and with the smell of lilacs. She was revealing another aspect of herself to me. She was offering another part of herself to me.

Margaret's real mother had died of cancer some years before. I was introduced to her stepmother, a tall, friendly woman with Midwestern openness and with prominent teeth that reminded me of Eleanor Roosevelt. She referred to Margaret Ann as *Maur-ann,* sliding the two names together.

Margaret's father was a slender, sober man looking somewhat younger than his second wife. He wore thin, wire-rimmed glasses at a time when such rims were considered old-fashioned, and he wore a vested suit. He was the conservative image personified. Neither smiling nor friendly, he reminded me of photographs I had seen of Calvin Coolidge. All during the simple dinner in the dining room he said very little, giving nothing of himself nor attempting to draw me into conversation. I did not feel threatened by Mr. Richardson's coolness. I felt secure in Margaret's love and I was able to study the older man with detachment.

"Maur-ann and Jack," called Mrs. Richardson after dinner, "C'maun out t'kitchen and help warsh the dishes." I was charmed by this plain woman, by her rural, mid-American twang, and by the simplicity and warmth of her welcome to come "out" to the kitchen. I was accustomed to thinking of the kitchen as part of the house, not separate from it. Her usage revealed to me that she'd come from a place where the kitchen was located in a shed outside of the main house, such as one sees on a rural, Midwestern farm, where the heat from the wood-burning cookstove in summer would not heat up the house.

I rolled up my sleeves and helped wash the dishes. I felt very much at home now.

Why *shouldn't* they like me? I thought. I came to Scarsdale as a suitor and I know I can get anyone to like me. I knew I could adapt easily to new ways, even to the new ways of *warshing* dishes *out* in *Maur-ann's* kitchen as I was doing now. The dishes, washed in a dishpan of hot, soapy water, were rinsed, not under running water from the tap, but in a dishpan of clear, hot water. I would even get used to using a bar of regular soap instead of "Rokeach Kosher Soap."

I drove home from Scarsdale much more relaxed than I had been earlier in the evening. I'd faced fears of prejudice. I had confidence in my youth. I knew that my natural ease with people could break down barriers. But I was not asked to return to Scarsdale. And I was never invited to the Richardson home in the Berkshires.

In spite of this cool rebuff, in spite of the stern opposition of my parents our love grew in intensity. At the same time I knew that it was necessary to take some steps, to make some commitment to keep that love alive. Without some plan the love affair would soon lose its precious honesty. I looked into the depth of my being. I weighed against all other considerations the beauty of the love I had for Margaret and of her love for me and I came to a conclusion. I would *not* let her go.

Margaret and I, now in our third year of medical school, began to consider specific places where we would apply for postgraduate training. She was the first to suggest Boston. The idea of our both beginning again in a new place provided enormous inspiration. Margaret would apply for internship and residency in pediatrics at the Boston Children's Hospital and I would apply for training in internal medicine at Boston's Beth Israel Hospital. Now there was a practicable plan for independence and eventually for freedom for us to work out our own destiny.

With this plan I was now willing to fly into the face of all opposition, to break all tradition. I gathered up my strength and made my decision.

"I will marry you in two years," I said to my beloved Margaret Ann.

True this statement implied a long postponement. There was vagueness to it as well. And the words, *I will marry you* (not *Will you marry me?* or *Will you wait for me?*) had a curious ring, perhaps implying, though not intentionally, a condescension to marry.

So the message was delivered. There followed a swift *denouement* that I'd not expected. I had not realized that the words I chose carried so strong a negative implication. But that was precisely the result. Perhaps Margaret had been weighing another offer that I had no knowledge of. Or perhaps she was waiting for a stronger, a more loving, or a more precise re-statement of the proposal. But I failed to produce one. Perhaps she expected me to show a resurgence of fire when she backed away. But that failed to happen. It was as if I had spent myself completely with *I will marry you.* After that I had nothing more to give.

Within months, a relatively short time, Margaret announced that she would marry Brady Benson, a young man she'd met outside of the medical circles that I knew. I was invited to the wedding. I didn't know if the invitation was a general one, one issued to all of our medical school class, or whether it was a special invitation to me. I had the feeling, in either case, she wanted to say *goodbye*, that it was her way of showing a little of herself, a little of the sweetness she'd shown me when she let me see her bedroom in Scarsdale.

I knew I couldn't face it. I didn't respond to the invitation and I didn't go. I felt badly, though, that in not responding in the proper way I might lose the regard of Mrs. Richardson who'd been so kind in Scarsdale to have invited me to *c'maun out t'kitchen* to *warsh the dishes.*

THE MISTLETOE

I.

I tried my best to scrub away the odor of formaldehyde that clung to my hands after the afternoon in the anatomy lab. Then, with a new, freshly laundered white lab coat, and needing to get out into the fresh air, I set out to explore what I could of my new world, that of the Presbyterian Medical Center on Manhattan's upper west side where I had just started medical school a few days before.

I crossed Fort Washington Avenue and entered the Nurses' Residence which, I'd been told, commanded a view of the Hudson River. I found the high-ceilinged dining room, deserted at this hour, with French doors that opened out on to a terrace.

"Good afternoon, Doctor!" It was the janitor who'd come in behind me preparing to mop the dining room floor in preparation for the evening meal.

I don't deserve this, I thought. Not a doctor. Not yet, anyway. I was an officer receiving my first salute.

"Good afternoon," I replied, now floating two inches off the ground. I stepped out onto the terrace. I breathed deeply. I felt an expanded sense of joy as I gazed at the open sky above the river and at the New Jersey Palisades beyond the river.

The air was mild with the first hint of coolness toward summer's end. The trees of Riverside Park below retained their freshness.

It was then that I noticed that the odor of formaldehyde had left my hands.

Not long after that day, still in the first weeks of medical school, I had another uplifting experience. A course in "psychobiology" was a required introductory course. I was pleased that this medical school had taken the firm position that students be exposed to humanizing influences very early in our training. As if to emphasize its importance, the first lectures were given by the Professor and Chairman of the Psychiatry Department himself.

Oskar Denholm, standing tall and slender, his grizzled hair in a brush cut, delivered his message with faintly-accented, Swiss-German severity.

"In dealing with female patients," he warned us (we were an overwhelmingly male class) "One must avoid at all cost any situation that could possibly be interpreted or misinterpreted as seductive behavior. For example," he went on, "One must never sit on a patient's bed. Even though you yourselves may have no conscious thought of misbehavior, you can never tell which woman patient might consider such sitting on her bed as improper or sexually suggestive."

This admonition made sense to me. The Rabbis were perfectly correct in similar warnings.

"Never allow yourself to be alone in a room with a woman. One must avoid a situation where temptation or passion might result in grievous harm. The woman may be an *Aishet ish*, the wife of a man, (the wife of another man.)"

I'd always felt a terrible power in the words, *Aishet ish,* carrying the warning that one must not take away what belongs to another man, that one must not inflict pain on another person in taking away what belongs to him. *Aishet ish* frightened me more than *Lo tin'aff,* the cold words of the Seventh Commandment meaning "Thou shalt not commit adultery."

When I looked beyond the anatomy lab to the time I would be entering medicine, this introduction by Professor Denholm provided a sense of continuity with all that had gone before in my life, with all that was proper and correct and right. Medicine would be "right" for me and I was happy with the prospect of it.

My real introduction to medicine came in the second year, in the course in physical diagnosis. I learned quickly how to cultivate that perfect, polite, semi-detached professional exterior. When I examined the heart of my first female patient, a young woman, I lifted away her soft, smooth and rounded breast. I avoided any contact with the nipple and I placed the stethoscope in contact with the skin over her heart. *Lub-dupp! Lub-dupp! Lub-dupp!* I concentrated on the character of the heart sounds. The first heart sound, the *Lub-* was produced by the closure of the mitral and tricuspid valves. That sound was lower in pitch and it had a longer duration. The second heart sound, the accented *dupp!* was produced by the by the closure of the aortic and pulmonic valves. That sound was higher in pitch and had a shorter duration. My face betrayed no sign of the wonder I felt at the sight and at the touch of that woman's breast.

I was learning. I was on my way to earning the title "Doctor" with which I'd been addressed so prematurely the year before.

II.

Snow lay lightly on the Streets of Boston under dull, gray skies of December. I was now in my first year of residency at the Massachusetts General Hospital. I was in charge of a medical ward with thirty patients in the old Bullfinch Building, and I had under my supervision a medical intern, Jim Bateman. Jim was a graduate of the Harvard Medical School and he was well-regarded, achieving an appointment in this, one of the most prestigious teaching hospitals of the Harvard system.

Jim had an easy grace about him. When he smiled, his eyes would narrow and his face would beam. He was a Southerner with that inexplicable charm, that perfection of courteous manners and that kindly, chivalrous approach that I envied. But Jim would rely on his charm to take short-cuts in his work that caused me some annoyance. His written histories and physical examinations were invariably shorter than mine, those of his supervising resident. The usual arrangement was for the intern's history to record all the details of an illness and for resident to write the more succinct and analytical note. And Jim's handwriting was abominable. Yet I found it impossible to correct his deficiencies. These shortcomings seemed minor when compared to his overall good sense and his considerable knowledge of medicine. So I just worked harder myself. In doing this, I developed a curious, repetitive gnawing sensation in the pit of my stomach.

In the cold and dreary light of that December a young girl became dangerously ill. Angela D'Amato was sixteen, yet she already worked full-time at the Gilette Safety Razor Company in South Boston. A sudden, unexpected headache and an epileptic seizure were the first signs of her disease and she was admitted through the emergency room of the hospital. She had fever and a flushed appearance, but a spinal tap showed no sign of infection.

"What do you make of this?" I asked Jim, whose opinion I respected. "If we're sure she doesn't have meningitis, what else could cause this picture?"

"She could have lupus," Jim suggested, and he showed me a stained smear of her blood. On the slide curious rosettes of immune-type white blood cells clustered around amorphous globs of gray, protein material.

"Those rosettes must be L-E cells," I agreed. "So you're right. She has lupus." The headaches and the seizures were symptoms of the most serious form of the disease, that of lupus cerebritis, and were caused by inflammation of blood vessels in the brain.

The treatment called for A.C.T.H., the adrenocorticotropic hormone. When administered, this hormone stimulates the adrenal gland to produce the hormone cortisol, one of whose most powerful effects is to reduce any inflammation no matter where in the body and no matter what the cause.

I admired Jim's skill in starting the intravenous line and the infusion of A.C.T.H. began. We watched Angela's response during the first few days of treatment and we were relieved to see the first signs of improvement. Her headache and fever diminished. There was only one more seizure and then no more.

The Christmas season was approaching. There was a general lightening of spirits. I felt less strain working with Jim and we completed our daily rounds without the tension I had felt before. I experienced one of those times of exhilaration in which I knew again that medicine was "right" for me.

I returned to the hospital for rounds on a bright Monday morning after a weekend off. My first concern was for Angela and I asked Jim for his report.

"She's doing beautifully. You know she really is a very pretty girl."

I found the change in Angela striking beyond belief. Where there had been a pitiable creature lying curled up on her side in pain and in fear, there now sat, propped up on two pillows, a young woman. She'd put on lipstick and had tied a scarlet ribbon in her hair. There was a mischievous smile on her lovely face. Jim spotted it first, so with perfect grace and with one smooth movement he bent down, went forward, and kissed her.

Kissed her! My fury rose in a wave that stung my face and then settled swiftly as a gnawing, burning pain in the pit of my stomach. Yes, I saw plainly enough what Angela had done. She'd tied a mistletoe to the horizontal bar over the head of her bed.

That was cute enough for a pretty sixteen year old to do, but for a doctor to kiss a patient!

Jim's face, as he came away from that kiss, was wreathed in a merry smile that narrowed his eyes to slits. As I turned away I saw the smile leave Angela's face and a look of confusion came over her. I knew what she was thinking but I could offer no answer to what she was asking:

"Why had only *one* of my doctors read the message of the mistletoe?"

TAOS AND BOSTON

The sky was brilliantly blue that August morning as my wife, Ida, and I drove up the winding road toward Arroyo Seco. We'd been invited to the wedding of "Missy" Comstock's daughter at the little Catholic Church in that narrow valley. "Missy" had a surprise in store for me that marked my day. But that will come later.

After the ceremony, we joined the wedding party that was gathered in front of the church. I knew that the many guests who had come from Boston would be unaccustomed to the power of the midsummer sun at the seven-thousand foot altitude. They would have to shield their eyes from its brightness even more than we did. But the parties from the East would also delight in the thin, crisp air that was so effortless to breathe.

We all felt the excitement as the brass choir, assembled for the occasion, played Baroque airs and as the music soared easily up the canyon toward the ski basin. In less than an hour, however, great billows of grey and black clouds changed the landscape. Here and there curtains of rain blocked out the view of the nearby rounded, shrub-covered hills and of the more distant mountains. The summer mountain rains continued for several hours. But toward five o'clock the sun suddenly burst forth, illuminating in places, the one-hundred miles of the Sangre de Cristo Mountains that stretched far away in both directions. With the sun, the gaiety of the wedding and of the wedding party was restored.

The wedding reception at the inn nearby had started tentatively indoors, but now, with the rain and clouds gone, the guests moved out onto the flagstone patio. They gathered in small groups and gazed with delight at the sunlit mountains, now green again after the rain, or in awe at the vast expanse of the treeless plain to the west where the Rio Grande ran in its deep-cut gorge.

It's been along time, I thought, looking at the cluster of Bostonians against the backdrop of the New Mexico landscape, since I've seen so many white flannel pants, so many white buck shoes, and so many blue seersucker suits. I had left Boston and New York many years before, in the early '50s, after finishing my residency in internal medicine. Just after that I went to work doing tuberculosis research at the Indian Hospital at Fort Defiance, Arizona. In those days, at an evening in town at the "El Rancho" or at the "El Navajo," the finest places in Gallup, it was perfectly proper to appear in blue jeans, denim jacket, and cowboy boots. I came to love the informality of the West. I found Ida there, a Navajo beauty who became my wife, and we settled in New Mexico.

"Missy," a former Bostonian, and a bubbling hostess, grabbed my arm. "Jack," she said, "There's somebody here who wants to meet you. I'm sure you remember Beth. Now she's Beth Reader, but you'll remember her as Beth Auer. She heard you'd be here."

It took me a few minutes to get all the names straight. Of course I remembered Beth. She'd married Jim Reader, another physician, and she, like her husband, had become a psychiatrist and that they'd remained in Boston.

Beth and I had started our internships together at the Massachusetts General Hospital. Of the twelve interns in that group, most were Harvard Medical school graduates who had succeeded in getting that much sought-after appointment. Beth and I were "outsiders." We had come from medical schools in New York. Members of the Harvard group all knew one another. They were very self-assured; they all had brilliant medical school records. They were "known quantities" to the hospital staff. They were expected to perform well and they disappointed no one. Beth and I had to prove ourselves.

On that first day of our internship, we met with the others and with Walter Bauer, the intense, warm, beetle-browed Professor and Chief of the Medical Service in the staff room of the historic Bullfinch Building. That kind of first-day meeting is never forgotten. Members of the same internship never forget one another. We are bound by ties of growing together and of becoming initiated together into a demanding profession. "Missy" Comstock, herself the wife of a physician, knew very well that I would have no trouble remembering Beth.

Beth was the only woman in the intern group, and a pretty one. She had a quiet reserve and dignity about her and she was treated with respect. She was not entirely an outsider in the Massachusetts

General group, it turned out, because her father, Jonas B. Auer, was a distinguished physician who had made major contributions in the field of calcium metabolism and in the treatment of lead poisoning. At the time when we were starting our internship, Dr. Auer was still on the active Attending Physician staff at the hospital. Jonas Auer had come to Boston from Ohio many years before. An outsider and a Jew, he had become a member of the Boston scientific community and he had married the sister of Orville Cabot, a distinguished surgeon.

I found Beth attractive from the very first. After all, I used to say to myself, she is half-Jewish. She had an engaging way of tossing her head when her light brown hair would fall over her forehead. There was a musical quality to her voice that came through even though her speech tended to be rapid and nervous. I remembered her full lips, her straight, short nose, and her shyness. Her large, nearsighted blue eyes had a way of holding me as she would stare through her glasses. She seemed to be asking for protection in some way.

In spite of all that was appealing about her, I had to put a brake on my feelings. I knew I was particularly vulnerable to young women who seemed to "need to be protected." Throughout my second and third medical school years where I'd come from, I'd had a long and wrenching love affair with one of my classmates, Margaret Ann Richardson. My father had been very stern in his disapproval because Margaret was not Jewish. Morris Berkowitz, born in Poland, had been a passionate Zionist and as passionate about preserving Jewish identity. His warning, "You must not do this," stayed with me.

Now, as one of the new group of house officers, dressed in whites, as we used to dress in those days, gathered for our orientation, I would have to "behave myself." This was not the time and place to become involved in any entangling romances. My father's other admonition, crude as it was, stuck with me: "Don't shit where you eat."

There was no opportunity on the medical service of the Massachusetts General Hospital for Beth and me to be thrown together in our work assignments. Interns were paired on the ward service with first year residents, not with other interns. Other interns would be on duty in the emergency room, or on the private service or on a rotation on a specialty service but we would never work together. If Beth had any feelings for me there was little or no opportunity for her to show them. If she *had* sent any signals to me, I must have been too dumb to receive them. But I knew Beth was there, and I sent a feeble message of my own to her, not directly, but stupidly, through her father, Dr. Auer.

Dr. Auer had taken a turn as Attending Physician on the ward service to which I'd been assigned. By this time I was in my second year, and I was more relaxed, I think, and more self confident. I found Dr. Auer charming, mellow, and full of wisdom. When I confided in him that I would be leaving Boston and the Massachusetts General and that I would be returning to New York, he warned me not to appear boastful that I had come from a prestigious institution. He said quietly, "Jack, when you get there, don't tell people where you've been."

I had great admiration for Dr. Auer and we became friends. I felt the kinship of our both being Jewish in the genteel but perhaps aloof, airy, Harvard atmosphere. But if I had any hopes, that by playing the charming, self-confident young man, Dr. Auer might bring home a message that he had found a suitable mate for his daughter, nothing came of it. It was too late. Beth had been going out with Jim Reader. Jim had been a medical student at Harvard, graduating the same year but interning at another hospital. Jim and Beth had known one another before they'd started medical school, before Beth had gone to New York. Now Beth had returned to Boston, their old friendship brought them together again and they would be married.

Now in Taos, thirty-three years later, Beth stood facing me.

"You look just the same," I said. She had the same musical though clipped speech, same full lips and the same blue eyes that seemed to stare impertinently, perhaps challenging, through her glasses. She was the same comfortable height, not too short, not too tall, and she had the same pleasant figure. She was wearing a red dress with a white collar and short sleeves trimmed with white. She wore her hair the same way, full and short. Her hair was all white now, but it made no difference. I liked everything about her.

"You're the same too," she said after a while, "Except nicer." Beth was a psychiatrist, clearly more forthright and more self-confident. She was the mother of three grown children. One of her sons, Jonas, an attorney in his late twenties, was with her now in Taos. I saw that he had the same face, same blue eyes, and the same full lips as did his mother. He had a shyness like that of his mother when she was the same age. But Beth was no longer shy.

I was pleased that she had asked for me. And I was pleased that she'd found me the same, too. Yet I was a little stung that she said I was "nicer" now. Wasn't I nice enough then? I thought. The meaning became clear to me after a while. I became dizzy at the thought of it. Beth was saying, I concluded, that she had liked me more than a little in those days, and that she'd become angry that I had rejected her.

I sought her out a number of times during the evening among the crowds at the wedding reception. I found her warm and kindly each time. We sketched for one another our lives and our careers and how many children each of us had. We were not displeased with our lives. We stood in line together for portions of the wedding cake. When the orchestra struck up we danced together.

When I turned to another couple on the dance floor I explained, "Beth and I have known one another for a long time."

"No," Beth said with a pungency that I was getting used to and that I liked, "We used to know one another a long time *ago*."

When the dance ended — and the evening and this reunion of ours, for we didn't see one another after that — Beth stood up on her toes and kissed me on the cheek, and her glasses and my glasses clicked.

"Who was that woman in red?" Ida, my wife, asked in her way. I didn't know what storm might erupt. I was afraid she wouldn't be satisfied with my reply but I said, "That was somebody I used to know," and then I added what Beth had said, "A long time *ago*."

A FLAW IN THE YOUNG MAN'S CHARACTER

Rose Rachel, our youngest daughter, had just been "stood up." Her newest young man, Dan Klevenger, had promised to call her for a Saturday night at the Swedish Festival to be held at the Civic Plaza. But Saturday morning and Saturday afternoon and Saturday night all passed without a call on the telephone. I saw the pain on Rose Rachel's face while she tried to disguise her feelings with a smile, and with a plunge into activity in the kitchen as she prepared a quiet dinner for herself and for me that weekend that my wife, Ida was away.

I had liked the young man principally because Rose Rachel had liked him so much. He had that "clean-cut" look. At thirty-one he was a quiet achiever, a financial analyst for a utility company. He had those fine features that attract both men and women: a thin face, a somewhat longish nose, blue eyes, and wavy hair. His grandparents were German and Swedish and they'd settled in southern Wisconsin many years before. He was a "melting pot" American and he spoke neither German nor Swedish since his parents spoke only English. He'd married before and had recently been divorced. There'd been no children from that marriage.

The following morning I discussed the situation with Ida on the telephone.

"I feel terribly sorry for Rose Rachel," I said, "But on the other hand it's best that it happened now rather than later. It seems there is a serious flaw in the young man's character."

" I wouldn't be so quick to pass judgement on Dan," was her reply. "You should be more tolerant. After all, you don't know all the circumstances."

I admitted to myself that Ida might be right. Ida always showed good sense in sizing up situations. I would think upon it some more. I took my favorite hoe and I went out into the garden to cultivate the freshly sprouted growth of the three-week corn.

Life is pleasant out here in the garden, I thought. Everything thing is coming up according to plan. The six-week corn on the north end of the garden patch was almost thigh-high, with broad, green leaves rustling in the breeze, hardly a weed or a blade of grass among the healthy corn-stalks. And now the three-week corn has come up, delicate and lighter green. The work of hoeing required only the steady, deliberate, and careful turning of the still-soft earth. There were no painful decisions that had to be made. Now it came to me in a rush of memory. There *was* a painful decision I'd had to make one time many years before and it was a decision that involved the deliberate breaking of a promise.

Nadya was perhaps twenty-seven or twenty-eight and I turned twenty-six that summer. It was my friend, James Feldman, a fellow medical resident at the Massachusetts General Hospital in Boston who told me Nadya's story. Nadya was Russian. Her parents had been killed in the Nazi onslaught in the summer of 1941. Nadya was taken captive and brought to the first of many labor camps in German-held territory. It is easy to imagine how a beautiful girl of fifteen or sixteen could have caught the eye of some of the labor camp guards. She managed to survive somehow. Perhaps she found a touch of kindness in her captors, or perhaps she learned to use her gifts in exchange for food or for being spared from extra work or from punishment. After her liberation by American forces in 1945, Nadya moved westward, learned English quickly, found protectors and sponsors among the Americans, and managed to come to the United States. Within a few years she earned her undergraduate degree and then her master's in social work and then came to the hospital in Boston.

James Feldman presented this mystery woman, this heroine, this survivor of wartime Europe to me. I suspected Jim liked her himself, but he, by this time, was already engaged, and his marriage to Paula, another Social Worker, turned out to be a good one.

Nadya was perfection in her dress and in her manner. In the hospital she wore tailored suits, trim skirts and blouses, and her high-heeled shoes were of patent leather. I learned to recognize Nadya's step as those heels clicked briskly along the hospital corridors. She had a radiant Tartar face, with high cheekbones, dark hair and eyes. Her voice was melody, and her command of English and of all the idiomatic subtleties was complete. Yet her speech was suffused with, and embellished by, the most delicate of Russian accents.

With all these compelling gifts she reached out to others with that sentimentality, with that kindness, and with that touch of sadness that marks the Russian soul.

Nadya had many admirers. I didn't consider myself in her league. I was younger and she more worldly. Yet it was she who invited me to join her and a group of her friends to an outing at Crane's Beach north of Boston one brilliant summer afternoon. In her bathing suit she was smaller and less prepossessing. She seemed more vulnerable, somehow, perhaps in need now of some kindness herself.

I had grown up among aunts and uncles who spoke with a variety of Russian and Yiddish accents. Aunt Henya, Uncle Laibish's wife, had grown up on a country estate in Russia and her accent was the most purely Russian of all. She and my uncle had lost two children to rheumatic fever. It was on me, then, as a small boy, that she lavished all her love, poured out in her richly accented language of affection. I was thus familiar with the rhythm and the melody of Russian speech. Though I learned very few words, what I did learn was the way Russian names could be sweetened with the richest variety of diminutive forms. So when I read the great Russian novels of Tolstoi, Dostoyevsky, and Tugenev, and the plays of Chechov, I was never confused no matter how many different ways a name might appear.

Nadya reached out to me that day and I was vulnerable. We responded to one another in a way I had not thought possible. I made no demands upon her. Unlike her other American suitors and admirers, she found that I was the one most comfortable with her Russian ways. And she chose me because, with perfect ease and with genuine warmth, I knew how to call her by the sweetest of her Russian names, "Nadka," or "Nadyush," or "Nadyushka."

The time for both of us had come to leave Boston. I was to return to Presbyterian Hospital in New York, my alma mater, for a special year in pulmonary disease. But there were other reasons for returning to New York: a vague feeling of a need to return, a possibility I would be needed as my parents became older or ill, and I had made that decision to go home many months before.

I didn't know what plans Nadya had for returning to New York, but when she told me she would be finishing her job at the end of

July, the same time as I would be ending my residency, we decided to drive down together.

We left the great hospital with some feeling of sadness. We had both done well there and we'd been respected by our colleagues. But our spirits rose as we felt the need to move on.

The night of our departure was hot and still, but as the car sped along on the near-empty highway toward the west, a cooling breeze refreshed us. Soon the night began to exert its magic. The woman, Nadya, no longer the exotic, mysterious heroine, sat small and quiet in the seat beside me. We were together and alone, completely comfortable with one another and unafraid. I pulled off to the side of the road in the darkness, my heart racing, and we were soon locked in an embrace and a promise: we would be lovers in New York. I would call her and we would not allow our new lives to lead us apart.

It was near three in the morning when we reached the crowded Manhattan tenement district where Nadya was to stay with a friend.

"Come upstairs with me," she said. I was torn by my desire for her but I feared I would be swept into the abyss.

"The neighborhood is unsafe. I can't leave all my worldly goods packed in the car on the street overnight. I'll call you tomorrow and we will be together."

Now I, the prodigal son, was home. My parents rejoiced that I'd returned from Boston. I would be close to them again. I would take care of them when they became old and ill. I was in pain. Would I "take up" with a "strange" woman and tear myself apart in the process? I'd decided to come home, to do the "right thing." Now I had to stick to my decision.

All that day I imagined I would break away, find a telephone somewhere, find Nadya, love her as we were meant to do. I was certain Nadya was waiting for my call. Many years later Jim and Paula told me it had been true. Nadya *did* wait for me all that day and for many more days. It was my doing. I had cut her off.

Of course I never heard from her or saw her ever again.

A few days later, I moved my belongings to the house staff quarters of the Presbyterian Hospital. My room looked over the broad expanse of the Hudson River. I sought some comfort in gazing out on the water. I had broken my promise. I had thrown Nadya away.

The following day, however, in my starched white uniform, I started my duties on the tuberculosis research floor and my new life began. I was at peace with myself. I'd succeeded pushing Nadya out of my life.

Now, so many years later, Rose Rachel was in pain and my heart was with my daughter. Her young man's call never came, not on the appointed day nor on any day after. Perhaps there *was* a flaw in the young man's character.

Avrum Organick

TWINS

I.

New York Times, June 22, 1985, Sao Paulo, Brazil

SCIENTISTS DECIDE BRAZIL SKELETON IS JOSEPH MENGELE'S

INQUIRY RULES OUT A HOAX

EXPERTS FROM U.S. & 2 OTHER COUNTRIES SAY THEY HAVE "ABSOLUTELY NO DOUBT"

II.

The Nazi doctor, Joseph Mengele, used to take personal charge as he picked out the twins among the crowds of Jews and gypsies coming off the trains at Birkenau and Auschwitz. Their forearms would be branded "Z" for "*zwillings*," their bodies would be measured in every detail, and, when one would die, the other would be killed by an injection of phenol so that their organs could be measured and compared at autopsy.

III.

My wife, Ida, who is Navajo, tells me that among her people twins are at special risk of becoming harmed by witches. Such harm is forestalled by separating the twins at birth and by having them raised in different households. She tells of how Florence Shorty, a member of her clan, the T'senjekinnie clan, and her husband Albert had a set of identical twin girls in 1946. The babies, Lottie and Laura, were strikingly light-skinned, and, as Ida told me, each had a head of thick, blond hair, so different from the usual head of black hair of Indian infants. Because they were doubly conspicuous, twins and blond, Florence gave Laura, the younger twin to Nettie Begay, a T'senjekinnie clan sister, to be raised in Nettie's family near Crystal,

New Mexico. Florence kept Lottie and raised her at Ganado, Arizona.

Ida tells me that when the girls were four or five, they learned they were twins.

"When can I go to play with my little sister," cried Lottie.

"Why can't we be together?"

"Ee-yah!" replied her mother. "We can't let the *Ya n'elgloshi* see you."

The child shuddered at the mention of the evil ones, and she remained silent for a while. But she continued to ask, and her mother just as regularly refused her.

IV.

When the Sabbath services at the B'nai Israel Congregation were over, we joined the rabbi in the traditional Kiddush. A simple table was set out in the social hall with several bottles of Mogen David kosher grape wine, a bottle of whiskey, a shimmering platter of cold pickled herring, and a braided challah sliced on a wooden board. It was a small but a jolly group. There were no more than thirty gathered; attendance at Saturday morning services was often small on a weekend that was not a Jewish holiday, and especially when there was no celebration of a Bar or Bat Mitzvah.

The rabbi, a genial young man with a full head of prematurely grey hair, was given the honor, as is the tradition, of being first to raise his cup filled with wine, and he did so with the words, "Al Cain Bayrach Adonai Es Yom Ha'Shabbos Va'Yikadshayhu. Baruch Atoh Adonai, Elokaynu Melech Ha'Olam, Boray Pree Ha'Gaffen."

The Lord blessed the Sabbath and He made it holy. You are blessed, Lord, for having created the fruit of the vine.

My preference was for the whiskey. A single straight shot of scotch or bourbon is quick to enter my blood, and it is all I need to raise the keenness of my perception. I recited the blessing over whiskey. "Baruch Atoh Adonai, Elokaynu Melech Ha'Olam, Sheh Ha'kol Ni'hiyeh Bi'dvaroh."

You are blessed, Lord, that everything is created according to Your command."

Ahh! The amount of whiskey in the tiny cup was not enough to cause any griping in my empty stomach. Just enough to sharpen my vision. My eyes found in that gathering of older, greying men and women, two strikingly beautiful girls of seventeen or so. I'd never seen them before; they must have been out-of-town guests of one of the synagogue members. They were dressed alike in powder-blue, full-length dresses. Tiny white flowers of the pattern were set off with large fringes of white lace at the neck and collar, at the edges of the quarter-length sleeves, and at the hem. Their honey-brown hair fell in loose curls at their shoulders. Their skin was exquisitely clear, their cheekbones prominent and slightly blushed, and their eyes a perfect blue. They moved about the small gathering with absolute grace and pleasing smiles, speaking softly with the older congregants. I watched them for several minutes when, in one movement, they both turned their faces to me. They were clearly and unmistakably identical twins.

I was stunned with their flawless beauty, the girls now at the peak of their freshness and youth. But more than that, what struck me was the sudden and certain knowledge that these girls could not have been created by accident, by the chance falling together of gene particles. Otherwise, how could each be so perfectly reproduced? There must be some design, some carefully executed plan. I had never been so powerfully moved; I was face- to-face with the force of heredity, of biology, of creation. The words of my forefathers swept before me: Etzbah Elohim He. Sheh Ha'kol Ni'hiyeh Bi'dvoroh.

It is the finger of the Lord. That everything is created according to Your command.

V.

On a bright day in September, with the heat of the summer just past and with the freshness, the color, and the excitement of the Tribal Fair at Window Rock tangible in the air, Ida and I mingled with the crowds approaching the grandstand for the afternoon rodeo. Ida was resplendent in her Navajo costume, returning to the scene where, just the year before, she had been crowned Miss Navajo.

The fair was always a magnet that drew Navajos from all over the Reservation to come to see the rodeos, to see the night performances of Indian dances, and to renew old friendships. The fair was also a chance for some families to set up stands for selling fried bread and mutton stew to earn some extra money.

We passed between the rows of booths where Navajos in great numbers waited their turn to eat before the rodeo began. The men were dressed in jeans, Western shirts, and cowboy hats; the women dressed in long skirts and richly colored velveteen blouses. All wore silver and turquoise.

The booths were not fancy, just roughly put-together boards with canvas tarps above for shade and a wooden counter where the women who served brought bowls of pungent, thin mutton stew. Behind the counter, others were busy pulling dough into soft discs, laying them carefully into the hot, clear lard in black, cast-iron skillets heating on Coleman stoves. The magic of the dough and the hot lard combined to produce the miracle of the rising, brown, softly puffed Navajo frybread.

In front of one of these booths, two little girls of about eight caught our eye. They were in most respects like all other Navajo children, dressed in long, cotton skirts and velveteen blouses, adorned with bits of silver ornaments, brooches, pins, and buttons. Their cheeks were tanned, smudged, and crusted, and they seemed especially happy, chattering merrily in Navajo. The hair of each child was in long braids, but, surprisingly, these little girls were blondes. Sandy blondes, to be sure, but striking in comparison to the jet black hair of other Navajo children. Though not dressed exactly alike, their faces, their smiles, and their pale, hazel eyes were the same. They had to be the twins of Florence and Albert Shorty.

Lottie and Laura had found one another. The booths of their families were but a short distance apart. They were playing together for the first time, each seeing the mirror image of herself. There was nothing that Florence of Nettie could do. It would be cruel to separate them now that chance had brought them together. It would be all right for them to be with one another for a little while.

But if *we* had seen the twins and had taken such delight in the little girls, who else might have spied them?

Two days later, in the Shorty's corral outside of Ganado, a sheep lay dead, its belly cut open and its entrails spilled out on the ground, the shining membranes partly covered with dirt and flies. The same day, Nettie, outside of her hogan in Crystal, found a bone wrapped in canvas wedged among the branches of a juniper tree.

" The *Ya n'elgloshi* have found where the girls live," Ida said. "It didn't take them very long. They probably used their crystal gazers to find the places."

Word of these evil omens spread quickly among the T'sen-jekinnies. Hosteen Tso was summoned to perform a Protection ceremony for the twins.

In the Shorty's hogan that evening with only kerosene lamps and light from the fire in the wood stove illuminating our faces, we waited for Hosteen Tso's arrival.

"Why do the *Ya n'elgloshi* pick out twins for their nasty business?" I asked Ida's father. A kindly, soft-spoken man, Mr. Bird paused for a long time and then replied slowly in English: "Twins are very special. The twin gods, Monster Slayer and Child-of-the-Water, were given the job of killing the monsters and getting rid of all the bad people in the worlds below so that man could come up into this world and live in peace and harmony. But the twins, even though they were very powerful, did not get rid of all the evil in the world. The evil ones are still around here.

"When I was a young man," he went on, "A friend of mine actually saw some of them. He told me this story: 'I was out on the lower slopes of Fuzzy Mountain near Red Lake looking for some lost sheep. I went down into an arroyo, and I followed the arroyo for a while until I came to a place where a log had fallen across. There, in the bank of the arroyo, there was a blanket stretched across what turned out to be the entrance to a cave. When I pulled the blanket aside and found a passageway leading to another blanket. Pulling that blanket aside, I found another passageway leading to yet another blanket. In the dim light coming from somewhere inside, I found a fourth blanket. I was very careful now because I could hear singing going on inside and I could see the light was coming from there. I pulled that fourth blanket just enough to see a circle of men sitting around a campfire. They were singing and praying to a medicine bundle near the fire. Each man was sitting on the folded-up skin of some animal. Some had wolf skins, some had coyote skins, and some had bear skins. The men had red color painted on their chins, then a stripe of black over their cheeks, then a stripe of yellow across their eyes and then white on their forehead. Then the singing stopped and the chief witch stood up and called something into a cave that connected with his. Two skulls came rolling out, the skulls of a pair of twins they had killed, and the skulls started to roll around and around the campfire.

"'Then the men got up, and they vomited, and pissed, and shat on the skulls. When they finished with that, and when they were getting ready to go out, they all leaned forward and started to pull their skins over their heads. At that moment I dashed in from behind the blanket, I grabbed their medicine bundle, and I started to run as fast as I could down the passageway that I had entered through, past the two inner blankets, past the last blanket, and out into the arroyo again. I could hear them shouting and running after me, but I kept on going. I was faster than they were, and I kept on running until I came to my hogan. I stopped there and I turned around. They were still coming after me in their skins. With a stick I drew four lines in the dirt in front of my hogan, and they couldn't cross those lines. I had taken their medicine away from them. Four days later, I found out they were all dead.'

"Witches go after twins," Mr. Bird went on in his explanation, "and they try to kill them. They try to take the whorls from the fingers of the twins or the whorls of hair from the back of the twins' heads. They keep the skulls for their bad medicine. They make a powder out of the fingertips or out of the hair of the twins they kill. They take the powder, and they blow it into the smoke holes on top of the hogans to witch the people inside. Or else they put it on their hands, and they trick you when they shake hands with you."

Hosteen Tso sang the Protectionway over the twins, one at Ganado and one at Crystal. The Shortys were never sure Hosteen Tso's singing would keep the girls safe, so they moved and took Lottie to Phoenix. Nettie and her husband took their children and Laura and moved to Denver. They are very cautious when they come back to the Reservation. They never let the girls be seen together, and they are very careful not to shake hands with anybody they don't know.

VI.

I came away from that Saturday morning worship powerfully moved. It was not so much by the ritual of the service, or by the trappings of the sanctuary, or by the pleasant association with fellow Jews, but by the feeling of elation at having seen, much as Michelangelo had envisioned, "the finger of the Lord." I understood more than ever that little else so powers human emotions as the presence of twins: reverence, fascination, or compulsion to penetrate their meaning. But that fascination with twins can trigger not only reverence for creation, but also evil's imagination.

VII.

You are dead now, Dr. Mengele! You will never see and you will never touch the twin beauties with the honey-colored hair.

Ya n'elgloshi, I hope you will never find Lottie and Laura, the ones with the sandy-colored braids. But I know those twins will have to be very, very careful.

A SLICE OF VENISON

It was now October. For some weeks Jack Berkowitz's Navajo wife, Ida, had felt that curious feeling of emptiness, that ill-defined sadness that told her it was time to get back home. These sensations might occur at any time, in the quiet afternoons when the children were away at school, or even in the commotion of family mealtimes. But the cure for her unease came with a collect call from her sister, Nellie, from the pay phone outside of the office of the new sawmill town of Navajo.

"Our clan sister, Irene, hasn't been feeling well. After the family had a conference we went to a crystal gazer who said Irene needed a *Yei B'chei* ceremony. It will be held at Crystal next week. The Ganado branch of the *Tsenjikinnie* clan are all coming. Also our Uncle Willie from Tsaile. We want you to come, too. And bring your family if you can."

"Jack and I will be there."

It was only a one-day trip down from Denver. The winter route they took to the Reservation ran down Interstate 25 to Walsenberg, over the Front Range of the Rockies at La Veta pass, down through the San Luis valley to Taos, then to Santa Fe, Albuquerque and home. When they were on their way, Ida's brother, Thomas, shot a doe at the summer sheep camp.

"I thought you weren't supposed to shoot does, only bucks," Jack said.

"Look, Jack, don't interfere," Ida said. "We do it our own way. Besides, Thomas shot it on our own land."

Jack wasn't a hunter. He'd never shot an animal and he knew he never would, especially one as large and beautiful as a deer. But if there had to be hunters, he'd accept them. And as for Thomas, he'd always been fond of the man.

Thomas was older than Ida by five years, a ranch hand, a railroad worker and a carpenter. He was always a willing worker around the place, the collection of small wooden houses, a corral, a summer cook shed and two hogans on a rocky slope above the valley. He was a loner, having gone through two wives because of his drinking, his fights, and his stays in jail. When he was at his wildest, just out of his teens, they'd kept him in the older jail at Fort Defiance, but in more recent years, in the new one at Window Rock. He still did some heavy drinking, and it frightened the children to hear his bellowing, his shouting "Godammit!" up at his house on the hill when the family came to visit.

He was tall and slender, tight-muscled in his blue jeans, Western straw hat and cowboy shirts. He had a saddle nose and large, rough hands with fingers stubby and clumsy-looking from his carpentry, which Ida had always complained was too fast and sloppy. But there was goodness about him, too. He always came down the hill to Ida's house to welcome her and the family when they came from the city for a visit. He'd taught Jack how to use a post-hole digger, and how to tighten barbed wire with the wire-stretcher in the Spring when it came time to repair the fences. And he taught Jack to use the fencing tool to pry the rusted horseshoe nails from the old cedar fenceposts. When the two of them worked together their hammers would ring in a series of rising notes as they drove the nails and the tightened wire into the posts. When there were reports of deer running in the high, ponderosa country in the Fall, Thomas took his father's thirty-ought-six and brought down the meat to Ida.

"Now I'll show you how I'll handle this hindquarter," she said to Jack as she prepared to go to work on the venison. "And I know you're going to like it when it's done." She soaked the meat in cold water, washed off the blood, then salted the meat with coarse salt and then placed it on a drainboard to remove more of the blood. Then she washed it thoroughly one more time. "I'm doing it just like your mother taught me, to *kasher* the meat," she said with a wink. Then she splashed dark red wine over it and completed the marinade with aromatic spices, bay leaves, and garlic. "And now it's ready for the *Yei B'chei* tomorrow night."

The ceremony and the chanting had been going on for seven days. Late on Friday afternoon the *Yeis* appeared in their masks for the first time. Everybody wanted to see them. Different family groups had already begun to take their places and to build their own campfire sites along the sides of the quadrangle in front of the prayer hogan. Each family staked out its place; as long as there was somebody to hold it, that place would be theirs for the final night on Saturday.

The blue masks of the *Yeis* with eyes, nose and mouth cut out, were their only costume for this, their afternoon appearance. The rest of their clothes were the usual dress of blue jeans and Western shirts. Their appearance was brief, a foreshadowing of what was to come. The clown among them kept things light-hearted. The children shrank away in mock terror and then laughed and giggled as the clown picked out one group of children and then another feigning an attack, and then whooping away, appearing to be wounded. Then there was laughter as mothers and grandmothers joined with hollering and cat-calling, shooing the clown away.

"That was fun," some of the children shouted. "Will the clown *Yei* be back?"

"Not anymore today," one mother said, "But they'll be back tomorrow night."

On Saturday afternoon Jack stood outside the hogan listening to the singing that was going on inside. He was happy just to stand there. The singing seemed to him to belong where it was. The perfume of the piñons, the gracious shadows of the ponderosas on the nearby rounded hills and the steep cliffs of the mountains in the distance all blended to become part of the scene.

Men, and now and then some women, pushed aside the blanket that covered the east-facing door of the hogan. The sound of the singing became louder as the blanket was pulled aside. There seemed to be no hurry, no urgency. Some of the people entered, some left. They smiled and they greeted one another as they came and went. The women were bringing in enamel-ware pots of steaming coffee that had been prepared in the brush-covered cooking shed behind the hogan. Cooking fires were always going as the *T'senjikinnie* family served coffee, frybread and mutton stew to all who came. The crackle of the fires and the thump of axes wielded by men and boys splitting wood was always heard. The pleasing smell of piñon and cedar was always there. Occasionally there was the tinkle of a sheep bell from the pens behind the cooking shed. Mutton served to the guests was always fresh.

As Jack stood outside the hogan listening to the chanting, a Navajo woman wearing a velveteen blouse, an ankle-length cotton skirt, and a kerchief over head came up to him.

"Don't you remember me? I'm Sarah Goldtooth, Ida's cousin from Sawmill. I remember you from twenty years ago when you were at Fort Defiance. I worked at the cafeteria at the main hospital but we used to deliver food to the sanatorium where you worked. *Yat'eh*, doctor!"

"*Yat'eh*,"Jack answered.

"Well, it's nice to see you again," she said and she moved on.

Jack didn't remember her, but he felt better that somebody knew him. At least I'm recognized as an in-law, he thought. At least I belong here in some way.

A Navajo man of middle age wearing a sport jacket and glasses spoke to him.

"Why don't you go inside?" he asked, speaking perfect English. Jack didn't really feel comfortable with the idea of going inside. This was *their* ceremony, their most solemn and important religious rite. If he were to go inside, his being there might disrupt it. In a way, his being there, like a tourist, might cheapen it. He knew Navajos resent being gawked at and being studied. In spite of the friendly greetings and invitations, Jack knew he was still a white man, a stranger, an outsider. He was content to stand outside, to wander about, to just listen, to feel the magic and the power of it.

"The medicine man says it's all right," Ida said, coming up to him from inside the hogan. "I asked him and he said it's all right for you to come in." Ida took him by the hand, pushed aside the blanket and he was inside.

He stepped to the left in order not to block the doorway. The medicine man had his back to the opposite wall facing the door. Young men who were his assistants sat on either side. Jack knew the etiquette of entering a hogan. He stepped quietly to the left where the men sat and found himself a place on the floor with his back against the south wall.

The center of the hogan was cleared of its usual wood stove. The medicine man's assistants were working quietly making a sandpainting on the smooth floor of the hogan under the light coming through the smoke hole.

The medicine man was dressed casually like the rest of the Navajos in blue jeans and Western shirt but he wore a colorful red bandana tied around his head. He was about fifty-five years old with much thick, iron-gray hair cut short in modern style and he had the rounded belly of a well-fed man. He wore a heavy turquoise necklace, a large silver concho belt, and many silver and turquoise rings. At his side his medicine bundle of soft leather lay open. Its contents, a number of tiny leather pouches, stones of different colors, and the feathers of birds large and small, were laid out. Farther away were little bowls of different colored sands: pure white, black, red, yellow, blue and green.

The medicine man directed the work of his young helpers. They did the work of creating colored figures on the smooth, light brown sand of the background. The young men would take a pinch of color from one of the bowls and, with great skill and patience, roll the pigment out from between their thumb and forefinger. They would draw a straight black line here, a yellow line right next to it there, a green corn stalk and a green angled corn leaf next to it. The medicine man was giving his directions in soft, measured tones. Occasionally he would ask a young helper to make a correction or to lengthen a line. Only now and then would he lean forward, get on his knees, and take a pinch of colored sand and do some of the work of creating or correcting the sandpainting himself.

Jack felt privileged to be able to watch the creation of the sandpainting. The medicine man knew that Jack had sat down in the shadows. He looked in Jack's direction and he nodded his head ever so slightly. That was enough for Jack. He felt he'd been given permission to be there and he relaxed a little more.

There were four assistants. Two of them had long hair tied behind their head in the old Navajo way. One of two with long hair bent his head to the side and whispered something in the medicine man's ear. Jack knew he was being talked about because, a moment before, that same young man had looked in his direction.

Uh, oh, this looks like it might be trouble, Jack thought.

He watched intently as the medicine man touched the young man on the shoulder, nodded his head, and smiled a little in Jack's direction. I guess that means he's telling him it's O.K. for me to be here, Jack thought. But still, maybe it's *not* all right for me to stay here. I don't want there to be any concerns about my being here. Ida told me in the past that the least little disturbance or interruption of a ceremony can break the magic of it. It then might have to be done all over again. All the expense, all the time and effort of so many people might end up being wasted.

Jack had been in the hogan for half an hour. He got up quietly, stepped very carefully around the outstretched legs of the men and boys on the south side of the hogan, pushed aside the blanket, and he was out again into the fresh air.

It was Saturday night. Electric light bulbs had been strung on lines between poles that ranged along the side of the quadrangle. Gasoline-powered generators made a steady, muffled roar, but Jack got used to the sound and heard it less after a while. Loudspeakers mounted on the roof of a Tribal police van boomed out announcements. Some of the elders made speeches which Ida translated for him.

"We want you young men to respect this ceremony," one man said. "We don't want you to get drunk or get into fights." Then he went on to acknowledge the gifts that had been brought. "We understand that Joe Yazzie is the one who trucked in the full tank of water. *Ah shay hay,* Thank you Joe Yazzie. And James Begay, we want to thank you and your boys for bringing in the wood. Stay around. We may need some more. And Albert Shorty, can you hear me? Thank you for bringing in those fat sheep from Ganado."

Ida chose and held on to a spot close to the prayer hogan, just to the right of the hogan door. She set down several little folding chairs around her fire, one of them for her father who was now past eighty-five. She brought the venison rump and started to roast it on a grill fashioned with a long handle. The grill had four short feet that held it over the coals. She set the marinated meat on the heated grill and the juice began to sizzle and bubble. Steam rose from the surface of the meat as it began to cook. Then the outer layers became brown. Drippings from the marinade fell from the grill and exploded into more aroma-filled steam. She turned the roast slowly using a long-handled fork. When the meat began to smoke, the aroma of the roasting venison drifted away, in the direction of the families sitting by their own fires down the line. There was something different, exciting, tantalizing and delicious in that smoke.

"What's that you're cooking?" they asked as they came over in small groups. Ida took a sharp knife and sliced off the outer layer and gave a small portion of the meat to each of the neighboring families.

The meat just exposed was pink. When she turned the roast and cooked the pink part, this side, in turn, sizzled and smoked. The wind shifted. A rising column of smoke now drifted toward the hogan. Each time the blanket was pushed aside the smoke from Ida's roasting venison floated inside.

It had been dark now for several hours. The dancing of the fully-costumed and masked *Yei's* would not begin until shortly before midnight. Everybody was getting hungry. Behind, and off to the side of the quadrangle some families were selling coffee, hamburgers and frybread from little booths or off the tailgates of their pick-ups trucks. But the aroma of Ida's venison drew more and more people to her fire. She continued to slice thin portions from the smoking outer layers and to offer these slices to all who came. They ate with their fingers and they smacked the juice. Ida knew these people. They were relatives, neighbors and old friends from Red Lake, Navajo, Sawmill, Fort Defiance and Tsaile. There was much visiting and chatting and laughing. Ida now became the center of attraction and she continued to slice and to turn and to offer from the goodness of the deer meat that Thomas had brought down from the mountain.

With things well in hand, and Ida holding court, Jack slipped away into the darkness on the way to one of the privies. On his way back, he was threading his way in a narrow space between two parked trucks when he saw the silhouette of man lounging a bit unsteadily against the side of one of the trucks.

"Excuse me," Jack said, "I'd like to get through."

The man turned around. "What are you doin' here?" The light from the fires and from the electric lights fell on Jack's face and on his glasses.

"I'd just like to get through," he said again.

"We don' want you here!" the man said. As he came closer Jack could smell the man's breath. Jack started to back away, to find a way around the rear of the parked trucks when he saw the man swing his fist up toward Jack's face.

"Owuuh!" the man shouted, suddenly in pain. His fist had struck the side mirror of the cab of the truck.

"Get outta here, *a-glani*, you drunk!" another voice shouted. "Don't you start making trouble around here." It was Mrs. Goltooth from Sawmill who'd been resting in the cab of the truck.

"This man," she said pointing to Jack, is *ni hi cha da nih,* our in-law!" She got out of the truck and, with a threatening gesture, shooed the man away. "It didn't used to be this way," she said to Jack, some sadness in her voice.

"Thanks," Jack said. He had the same feeling again, that he shouldn't be here. He went back to Ida's fire and crouched down next to her. He wouldn't tell her about the incident until later. He knew how mad she would get. She would have gone after the man with her long-handled meat fork.

Aroma of the venison now reached the inside of the hogan. At first some of the singers, and then the medicine man himself came out. He squatted on his haunches in front of Ida's fire. Ida was now wreathed in smiles. It was the most distinguished guest of all who had come.

"*Yat-eh, si zaydeh,* (hello, my cousin)" he said. Ida basked in the light of this important man. She now gave him a special honor. She handed him the knife and he cut his own perfect piece and he chewed it right off the knife.

"*A shay hay. D'likan at eh.* (Thank you. It was very good)," he said. Then he reached into his back pocket and pulled out a blue-and-white bandana, wiped his mouth, and went back into the hogan to sing. Those in the hogan noted that he sang with a new burst of energy for the rest of the night. The *Yei b'chei* ceremony was declared a success. Irene, Ida's clan sister, said she was feeling much better.

THE HAMILTON RAILWAY SPECIAL

When I was a boy of ten or eleven growing up in Brooklyn during the Depression, I found great delight in owning, at two different times, two pocket watches. One was an Ingersoll, the other a Wesclox "Baby Ben." They were called "dollar" watches, partly because they cost that much, and partly because they were about the size of a silver dollar although, of course, much thicker. What pleased me so much was that one could own such a substantial and useful piece of machinery (they really did keep pretty good time) for such a reasonable price. The knickers we wore at the time even had a pocket just below the belt line on the right side especially made for those watches.

At the next stage in my life, when I turned thirteen, a Bar-Mitzvah suit was bought for me. This suit, this initiation into manhood, included a jacket and a vest, and the vest had several pockets suitable for one of those pocket watches. It should be added that the Bar-Mitzvah suit came with two pairs of pants. One was a pair of knickers and the other a pair of long pants, a sure sign that I was soon to become a man. And each pair of pants had a watch pocket in the usual position. With all these pockets I had plenty of opportunity to be seen reaching for one of those useful beauties and announcing the time.

Many years later when I was an intern, and the following year an assistant resident, at the Massachusetts General Hospital in Boston, an affectation appeared among my colleagues. This affectation was to sport a pocket watch with a second hand. It was a very physician-like gesture the young physicians liked to display, to look very serious while feeling for the patient's pulse in the wrist with one hand and holding the pocket watch in the other. Such gestures seemed fitting in the hospital's historic Bullfinch building with its Greek-columned portico and its Ether Dome. One of my friends, John K., was in the same year of training as myself. He bought himself a gleaming gold pocket watch and had it engraved with his name and "Resident Physician, The Massachusetts General Hospital."

Where does that show-off get the nerve to call himself "Resident Physician," I thought, when his rank at the time, like mine, was only *assistant* resident. Nevertheless, not having owned a watch since my boyhood, and not being able to afford a gold one, I bought myself another Ingersoll. (The price had gone up to two dollars and fifty cents by that time). I took to assuming the same physician-like gesture, looking very serious, holding the patient's wrist in one hand and holding the Ingersoll in the other.

Two years after leaving Boston, a growing interest of mine in the new drug treatments for tuberculosis sent me west. I became "Chief of Tuberculosis" (actually the only doctor for the one hundred patients) at the tuberculosis sanatorium at the Navajo Medical Center, Fort Defiance, Arizona. The one-story, white-painted wooden building with green shutters and green-shingled roof was modest, to say the least, compared to the grey granite grandeur of the hospital in Boston. I still had my Ingersoll and I still used it in the same physicianly manner. But who was I putting on airs for? Certainly the Navajos didn't care what kind gestures I was performing with my watch or what kind of a watch it was. But somehow I still retained the image of John K. with his gold watch. Vanity impelled me to look for something better than an Ingersoll.

One morning I took the eastbound Santa Fe train from Gallup to Albuquerque. A patient of mine was to have surgery at Albuquerque's Lovelace Clinic and I was asked to assist. It was a welcome break for me to get away from the small reservation town and from the routine of hospital rounds. The train rocked gently as it swept along the wide curves at the base of red sandstone cliffs, and I felt the slowing of the train as the diesel engines strained pulling the train's weight up toward the Continental Divide.

"When we will we get to Albuquerque?" I asked when the blue-coated conductor came down the aisle. From his vest pocket he pulled out his great railroad watch by its silver chain. He announced the time but I didn't hear what he said. All of my senses were focused on the bright, round metal object in the conductor's hand.

I stepped off the train and walked under the arched porches of the Alvarado Hotel. It was a grey stuccoed, Spanish tile-roofed Harvey House, proud symbol of the former great age of railway travel. The aroma of freshly-brewed coffee came from the open doors of the coffee shop that gave out onto the arched porch. For a few moments, savoring the coffee, I imagined that I was living in that leisurely past age. Just behind the hotel, however, lay Second Street, a skid row with its line of cheap hotels, bars and pawn shops.

I was drawn with a mission to one of those dimly-lit, cluttered, last-chance pawn shops. My eyes swept past the guitars, banjos, and hunting rifles hung on the back wall. I was not interested in the glass case that contained old Kodak bellows cameras, Kodak Brownies, or even early German Leicas, Voigtlanders and Rolleiflexes. I found what I wanted among the wrist watches and pocket watches, among the Elgins and the Bulovas. It was a nickel-plated beauty, a Hamilton Railway Special. The bold, black numerals on the watch face spoke with authority. And when the shopkeeper showed me the proper way to open the watch case by screwing off the back (the threads of the screw were so fine and tight) the marvel of the machine came into view. A gleaming, pale ruby sat in the center of the flywheel. All of the flat screw heads reflected light brightly as did all the visible metal parts. Engraved on a metal platform in perfect letters was the legend: "Hamilton Watch Co., Lancaster, Pa., 21 jewels, adjusted 5 positions." The hands could not be set simply by pulling out the stem winder at the top of the watch, a precaution against any accidental moving of the dial when the watch might be dropped into a train conductor's pocket. To set the watch it was necessary first to screw the crystal off the face of the watch, then to find a delicate release lever and then the hands could be moved. Thirty-seven dollars was not too much much to pay for such a beauty.

Now at last I owned a fine pocket watch. Humble as it appeared in its nickel-plated steel case, it was a watch worthy to be used in performing physicianly gestures.

Some years later, still vain, and not any more worthy than that show-off, John K., I found a jeweler in Denver who provided my Hamilton Railway Special with a ten-carat, rolled gold case. Shortly after that, however, the fun of the pocket watch faded for me. My father, for my thirty-fifth birthday, bought me a wrist watch, also a fine Hamilton, in a fourteen-carat gold case. I set the Railway Special in a drawer where it lay for many years. I never did get around to having it engraved.

When I entered into private practice in Albuquerque some years later, I set the watch in a brass stand on the desk in my consultation room. It was a proud ornament and I enjoyed seeing its bold face again. But I was not dependent on it for a time piece and I often forgot to wind it. It became less useful, handsome as it was, and I put it back in a drawer to be used as a spare if my wrist watch was at the jeweler's for cleaning or repair.

It was on one such day, without my wrist watch, that I pulled the pocket watch out of its drawer. I'd been called to see one of my patients in the intensive care unit. Mrs. B. was eighty years old, a retired nurse. The day before, an attempt at coronary angioplasty to dilate a critically narrowed artery had failed. As a complication of the procedure she'd had a heart attack.

When I walked in to the glass-walled, single room, Mrs. B. was awake, alert and frightened. Her arms were tied down and she lay on her back. Several intravenous lines were in place in her arms. Bags of intravenous fluid, 5% dextrose in water, and a heparin solution to prevent blood-clotting, hung on shining steel poles above her head. The rate of infusion of the various fluids was controlled by a boxlike infusion pump. She was receiving oxygen through a two-pronged nasal cannula. A catheter in her bladder led by a tube to a bag hung under the bed to monitor her urine output. On a shelf over the head of her bed a multi-channel cathode ray tube provided continuous display of physiological data. All of these measures had been ordered by the cardiologist who'd taken over her care in the critical phase of her illness. I had to ask to nurse the meaning of all the measurements that were being taken and which moving lines on the monitor measured which function. (The critical care nurse specialist was kind enough to explain them all to me.)

I pulled up a chair and I sat at Mrs. B.'s bedside. I took her hand in mine.

"I'm glad you came," she said, her voice a hoarse whisper but her words still crisp. "What do you think of my chances?" She was a bright lady, a night supervisor in a hospital for many years. I knew she expected the same straight answers I had always given when she asked.

I would be truthful. But I couldn't begin to answer her question, that most important question, until I had a little more time. There was so much data to review, so many laboratory reports, electrocardiograms, and tracings from the monitors to analyze. Although I was an internist, I had to admit to myself that I was a little intimidated by all of the latest technical and electronic gadgetry.

Then I remembered that basic bit of advice that had been given to us when we were interns. It went something like this: when you have a patient who is very ill, and when you have to make sense out of a complicated situation, what will help you most is to get back to basics. You have to start from the beginning. You have to do a physical examination. When I remembered this, I felt my confidence returning.

I took Mrs. B.'s wrist and I placed my left index and middle finger where her radial artery ran in its groove. Then, with my right hand, I drew out the gold-plated Hamilton Railway Special, that symbol of a former mechanical age, and noting the small second hand at the bottom of the watch face, I began my physical examination by counting her pulse.

CECILE COMES WEST

I live now on the Arizona-New Mexico border, land that lies at 7,000 to 7,500 feet in elevation, the coolest and greenest portion of the Navajo Reservation. On the shoulders of the Chuska mountains, whose peaks reach 9,000 feet, three streams flow westward. These are the Whiskey, Wheatfields, and Tsaile Creeks, which, over eons, have carved the underlying red sandstone of the Navajo Formation to form the main branches of the Canyon de Chelly.

It was into this spectacular country that I brought my eighty year-old mother on her first visit to the West. I pass the spot every day where, on that trip many years ago, we left the paved road to cross a cattle guard and entered onto the rutted wagon track to reach my wife's summer sheep camp on the next wooded ridge. I still wonder at the curious juxtaposition of person, time, and place that brought my mother to this wondrous land.

My mother was born in 1894 on New York's Lower East Side, the first American-born child of newly-arrived Jewish immigrants from Poland. On the occasion of that first visit of hers to the West, we drove from Denver, a drive with its own splendid Western scenery, down the eastern face of, and then across the Front Range of the Rockies. It was during that day-long drive that she told me new details of the story of her life that I had never heard before. Those stories still vibrate in my mind as I pass that cattle guard each day and I wonder that in one lifetime a single human being can have lived so long and have traveled so far.

I.

I knew that my mother was the first child to be born in America to a family into whom a number of children had been born in Poland. My mother had spoken many times of her pride that her father, Reb Yitzhak Eliahu Zeitlin, had been a Cohen, a member of the ancient, honored tribe of Priests in Israel and that therefore she herself was a *Bat Cohen,* (the daughter of a Cohen).

"When my mother died, and my father had to remarry..."

"I know what that means, Mom. A holy man such as a Cohen must not cast his seed upon the ground. That means he *must* find a wife." I was enough of a Yeshiva boy to know that.

"And furthermore," my mother went on, "As a Cohen, he couldn't just marry anybody. Certainly not a widow or a divorcee. A Cohen could only marry a virgin."

"I see that could have been a problem," I said. "Where would a man with eight or nine children find a young girl willing to marry him?"

"Well, she didn't have to be a *young* woman. She just had to be a woman who'd not been married before and at the same time one who would be willing enough to be the step-mother to eight or nine brats, some of whom would have been grown or at least half-grown."

"Well, I'm beginning to see what sort of a woman that might be. The good-looking women or girls or even those who at least had a pleasant disposition would have been married off long before. So that would have left an older woman, either a saint, or somebody desperate to marry for some reason."

"That's right, son," my mother said. "The woman my father married was desperate, all right. She was an old, humpbacked witch of a woman, with a big mole on her nose, and a mean disposition to go with it."

I'd never heard my mother speak so unkindly of anyone before. But I couldn't restrain a howl of laughter. "So she was the Wicked Stepmother, right out of the fairy tale!"

"Exactly. Except that it wasn't funny. Although I was only four when my mother died, I missed her terribly. And the new step-mother was, as you imagined, really awful both to me and to my younger sister, Birdie. Things got worse when the step-mother began to have children of her own. (So you see should couldn't have be as old as we'd imagined.)"

"But you still had your father then, didn't you? Didn't he protect you, take care of you?"

"If he was there, it didn't seem to make any difference. As a matter of fact the memory of my father seems to fade when I try to think of him. But I do remember that my older sister, Bessie, was at my side when I was accused of taking too big a portion of food at the table, or when I was rebuked for asking for fruit or candy or something sweet."

"It sounds as if, Mom, misery was mainly a matter of poverty, a large (and growing) family living in a tenement on Rivington Street on New York's Lower East Side as you'd described to me in the past."

"Yes, it's true we were poor, but meanness to a child, unkindness, is what cuts so deeply and that's what is remembered."

"You told me once that you were raised in Canada.. How did that come about."

"It was my older sister, Bessie, who had a lot to do with it. I told you my father was unable to comfort me and my younger sister, Birdie. He just wasn't there. Bessie realized my sister and I couldn't live like that, so she arranged for Birdie and me to taken as foster children by other families, and the family I was sent to moved to Canada."

"How did that turn out, Mom, being taken in by a strange family and then having them move so far away?"

"You're right, son, it was doubly hard in so many ways. The Smiths (that was the name my Jewish foster parents called themselves — how they picked that one I was never told) were poor themselves. They had four children of their own so I was an extra mouth to feed. While I don't recall they were ever as outwardly mean to me as my stepmother, I always had the feeling that I couldn't ask for anything. You know, a child might want a doll or an extra sweet or something. But there was that unspoken and understood, 'You must not!'"

"Was there anyone in the family you managed to get close to?"

"Yes. The next to the youngest child was a girl, Miriam. She was my age or a year or so younger. I remember her serious little face, her jet black hair and eyes. Miriam was a comfort to me and I, I suppose, was a comfort to her in that strained household. There was also a much younger boy, Eddie. He was a sweet thing but he was so little we couldn't really be friends. The two older boys were a bit strange and distant, like their parents."

"And what was it like for you in Canada? Where was it in Canada?"

"It was in Toronto, a city with poor neighborhoods like any other city and we lived in one of the poorest. It was a city crowded with Jewish immigrants and the immigrants always lived in those poor neighborhoods. So Toronto was another Jewish city where the Smiths found they could be feel at home."

"Did you live in crowded tenements like the ones on the Lower East Side of New York?"

"No, son, and for that I was thankful. The Smiths managed to rent a big two-story house, not new or fancy but with plenty of room. There were even a few trees on the street and I liked that."

"It sounds like there were some pluses then in your new life. You were not mistreated, you had in Miriam a little sister and a little friend, and there were trees on the street."

"That's right, son. And there was one more really good thing that happened to me at that time. I was sent to school and I learned English. You may not have realized this, but the only language I knew as a child up until that time was Yiddish. But English opened up a whole new, sweet world to me."

"Why do you say a 'sweet' world to you?"

"I suppose it was because the teachers were so good to me. They spoke to me sweetly in that new language, so I came to imagine, compared to the unhappy things in my life up to that point that had been spoken to me in the old language, that English was part of a new, beautiful world."

"I'll bet you were a good student."

"Yes, I did learn fast. I think at age six or seven, new things come easier. And I suppose I became sort of a teacher's pet."

"I'm not surprised. I'll bet you were a pretty little girl then, too."

"Did you ever see pictures of how little children were dressed then? You must have seen the middy blouse, that sort of sailor's blouse with the broad square collar with the piping on it that falls back over the shoulder, and the contrasting bandana that's tied in the front. I remember being dressed that way for Dominion Day, Canada's national day of celebration, something like the Fourth of July in the United States. Except instead of celebrating independence, we were celebrating our allegiance to Great Britain and to the Queen. You see the year must have been 1902 and Queen Victoria was still on the throne."

"What a bit of history you lived through, Mom."

"What made that day so memorable for me was that my teacher, Miss McCauley, who I loved so much, put her arm over my shoulder and drew me to her. I knew she was proud of me. Then she turned to Miss Brown, one of the other teachers and said, 'This is my little Cecile Smith. Look how prettily she's dressed, the little Kike!'"

"Oh Mom, that must have been devastating for you!"

"Those sweet tongues in those days were so full of hidden hate for us. Yes, it nearly killed me. I've never forgotten it. Even so, it didn't change my love for the English they spoke."

"I know Mom, growing up in Canada instead of New York, your speech is so pleasant, and it doesn't have that awful New York accent. I was always proud to bring my friends to meet you, to hear you speak."

"Well enough of sweet accents. Now your father, he had an accent all right. He came to America when he was sixteen so he was never able to lose his Polish-Yiddish accent. It wasn't as bad as most because he was an intellectual and a medical student when I met him."

"How did you meet him?"

"It was Beenah Sunshine who introduced us. She worked as a sewing machine operator next to me and she'd come from the same little *shtetl* in Poland as you father. It was at a Socialist gathering in one of those Landsmanshaft clubs called the *Yvansker Farband* after *Yvansk,* the little town he'd come from. He was handsome, self-assured, with dark, curly hair. When the political speeches were over and when the music started he came right up to me and said, 'You're an American girl, I can tell. Do you care to dance along with me?' I knew the syntax wasn't right but it didn't matter."

"So it was a romance between an 'American' working-class shop girl and an immigrant medical student."

"Come now, don't oversimplify. Yes it's true. Our both being Jewish had a great deal to do with it, but it was our love of music that drew us together. On my own, in the Smith household, I earned enough to buy a piano, and to take lessons. I learned two pieces, Schubert's 'Moment Musicale Number Three' and Padrewski's 'Minuet.' I think hearing me play is what sold him on me. And we went together to hear Ignace Jan Padrewski play himself."

"Well, there is another bit of history."

"When World War I ended your father had to respond to appeals from his family in Poland for help. He felt the only way he could do this *and* to marry me (he was over thirty at the time and I was twenty-six) was to give up medicine and to get to work earning a living in business. So he proposed asking, 'Will you walk along with me?'"

"Touching. Same error of syntax."

"Exactly. But it worked. When we were to be married we came to New York and I became reacquainted with my sister Bessie and with the rest of my family. 'He's a Socialist and obviously not *Frum* (religiously Orthodox). He probably doesn't even go to *Shul* (synagogue) on Yom Kippur.' But he surprised them all when he sent you and your brothers to the Hebrew Institute of Boro Park, the first Yeshiva in Brooklyn where the language of instruction in the Hebrew classes was all in Hebrew."

II.

My mother fell silent now. We had been talking, I asking questions, she revealing her personal history, which to me revealed bits of world history as well, for many hours. The Front Range of the Rockies, which, in the morning sun had been illuminated from the east, now gave way to interior valleys and then over Wolf Creek Pass. In the afternoon we went down into the valley of the San Juan and finally south into the arid valley of the Navajo Reservation east of the Chuska mountains. Now, in the gathering darkness, we climbed into the green of that mountain range and down into the valleys of Crystal, New Mexico.

I drove my new, 1976 Dodge pick-up slowly as the cattle-guard entry to the summer sheep camp road came into view in the headlights. There I turned off the paved road.

"You did very well, son, driving all the way on the highways, but are you sure you know where you are going now? I didn't see any road sign."

"It's all right, Mom. Once you get off the paved roads there aren't any signs on the Reservation. People just know where they're going. I know this road very well and you'll see I'll get you there." I began to pick my way down the narrow, rutted, sandy track, down off the ridge where we had left the paved highway. Though the headlights revealed mainly the dirt trail ahead, I pointed out to my mother that we were crossing a little valley.

"You can see a little of the sagebrush and dry buffalo grass on the side of the road."

"It looks like the road is washed out just ahead," my mother said suddenly, a little fear in her voice. We'd come to the edge of an arroyo. I slowed down and allowed the truck to nose down before entering a dry stream bed.

"You don't have to worry, Mom," I said, and I shoved the manual transmission into the lowest gear. "The pick-up is the perfect vehicle to negotiate this kind of terrain. Driving across arroyos is standard operating procedure on the Reservation. Hold on, Mom!"

With this I sent the nose of the pick-up down about forty-five degrees and allowed the truck to roll down to the bottom of the stream bed which lay only four or five feet below the level of the valley floor. At the proper moment I gunned the engine and the pick-up climbed easily to the top on the other side.

"This is one of the easier ones. People don't have much trouble with this one unless the rains have been very heavy. But, you don't have to worry. There won't be any more arroyo crossings the rest of the way."

I could sense that my mother was bracing herself against the armrest as I pressed on the accelerator. We started to climb up out of the valley. The first trees we met when we reached the next ridge were the short piñons and through the open windows we could smell the piney perfume they exuded into the night air.

"Ah, now that smells lovely," she said, relaxing a little bit.

"It's the piñion, Mom. It's always a treat."

Suddenly, the headlights caught the flutter of a flying creature crossing the road ahead.

"What was that?"

"It was an owl, Mom. The Navajos believe that seeing an owl at night is a bad omen. But I know you're not superstitious. You've got nothing to worry about."

The road now entered up a steeper climb and I kept the truck in low gear. Now, on a rough, stone-strewn, deeply-rutted road, we were climbing into tall ponderosa pine country. We could only see a narrow strip of night sky filled with stars through the windshield. Straight, dark trees on either side formed a narrow canyon through which the road now ran. At last, the road reached the level of a plateau, and the truck ran more quietly on a soft, sandy surface.

A line of fence posts appeared on the left in the beam of the headlights. When the fence line suddenly ceased, I slowed the truck and drove off to the left on a still less-traveled track.

"Are you sure you know where you're going, son?" my mother asked.

"Of course I know, Mom. We're very close. In a few minutes you'll see the camp."

"I never dreamed that you, a boy from Brooklyn, would be able to guide me through a forest at night like this," she said.

"Oh Mom, things change. I'm a long way from Brooklyn now and you're a long way from Rivington Street."

A short drive up the new track, and I guided the truck across a meadow of tall, rich grass. Then, with a turn to the left, down across a very shallow, dry-stream bed, up again to gain a rise, we entered among the tall trees again. Then, off to the left, we saw the welcoming orange glow of a friendly fire lighting the rosy trunks of the ponderosas. We had reached the summer sheep camp at last.

"There they are, Mom," I said as my Navajo wife and dark-eyed children came running to greet us.

"We were worried about you," My wife, Ida, said. "You did well to find a place like this in the dark."

"Yes, we were nearly lost," I teased. "But a friendly owl showed us the way."

Ida looked at me darkly, but a smile soon came over her face.

"Come, I'll help you get down off that truck," she said helping my mother down. "I'll bet it was a rough ride."

"It was, especially the last few miles. Your fire and your camp look so beautiful. I'm so glad to be here," she said as her grandchildren came running to embrace her, drawing her toward the warmth of the fire.

FORT DEFIANCE REVISITED

I walked down the main street of Fort Defiance the other day. The great cottonwoods still form a gentle canopy that shades the street from Arizona's summer sun. The powerhouse with its tall smokestack, the gothic stone Catholic church, and the post office still stand at the south end of the street, but the two trading posts, the Fort Defiance Trading Company and Griswold's, are no longer there. The three-story, red sandstone hospital with its bit of greenery, its little strip of lawn, dominates the east side of the street. What is new is the outpatient and emergency room addition, a squat, square, stuccoed, one-story, ugly affair that has been added to the south side end of the hospital. It's too bad they couldn't have made some attempt to match the addition with the pleasant, rough-hewn, native stone of the main building. What had been the wooden tuberculosis sanatorium with its front lawn of grass and trees on the west side of the street opposite the hospital is gone. That has now been replaced by a paved parking lot.

Most days, in the middle of the day, and especially on weekends, the street is pretty quiet. A few Navajos are usually waiting to go into the hospital or driving down the street. The men still dress in blue jeans, Western shirts, and cowboy hats, and the women, especially the older ones, in traditional velveteen blouses and ankle-length skirts. But the younger women and girls may be seen in Levi's or shorts and wearing Nike jackets.

Chevy, Ford, and GMC pick-ups are still the principal vehicles, but these days minivans, conversion vans, and four-wheel drive, extended cab pick-ups cruise the street as well. The old, green, horse-drawn Studebaker farm wagons with their rubber-tired wheels and the people sitting on the driver's bench or in the bed of the wagon that used to be so colorful all disappeared a long time ago.

But the changes aren't that great considering that forty years have passed. Fort Defiance is still pretty much the same place. I had no difficulty recognizing it.

My assignment as pediatrician at the Fort Defiance Hospital was my first job, my first adventure after I finished my residency in Indianapolis. I was ready for the West, for a chance to see Indian country, for a chance to do some really good medical work where it was needed, and for a chance to get away from Indiana and the middle west where, frankly, I'd never been happy.

Why had I been unhappy? Well, being shy didn't help matters, but what really made me unhappy was that I was looked upon as a kind of freak. It wasn't that I was horrible to look at. My face was O.K.: plain, with glasses, but not ugly. My hair was dull-colored, straw, or light brown; my nose was acceptable, my eyes a nice mid-American, Anglo-European blue. What made me different was that I was small. Tiny. Four eleven and eighty-five pounds. Flat-chested.

"She must have an infantile uterus, or ovarian agenesis," I used to hear the smart-ass medical students say. Or, "She's just totally undeveloped; no life, no juice, no sex in her." Or, "She's hypothyroid; she doesn't radiate any heat." It just went on and on like that. Maybe I didn't really hear them say those things but I know that's what they thought.

They didn't know what was inside of me. It was just plain cruelty. It's true I didn't menstruate until I was seventeen, but I did menstruate, so it couldn't have been ovarian agenesis or anything like that. It is true I didn't have anything in the way of breasts, but I did have nipples, and I did have feelings in them.

I didn't wear make-up. I was just too angry. I wasn't going to do anything to please them. That's the way it was through high school, college, medical school, and hospital training. I was never asked out. No one ever made a pass at me. No one ever came on to me. I was never grabbed or held or kissed. I was cold in my virginity.

When I came to Fort Defiance it was the same thing.

"There's no *life* in her. She's dull. She's a *nothing*," the other doctors would say. There was a group of Jewish doctors in Fort Defiance at the time I came there. They were all specialists of one kind or another. The chief surgeon, Ben Kaplan, the chief pediatrician, Barry Margolin, the ophthalmologist, Sheldon Ziff, the dentist, Martin Blumenfeld were all married and formed their little clique. Jack Berkowitz was head of tuberculosis. He was single but he was busy sparking a Navajo girl (a beauty, actually, and a former Miss Navajo). I never got any feeling of warmth from any of them. And it *was* disappointing because I had expected more. After all I was a professional colleague.

But the Navajos, especially the patients, the children and their parents, were wonderful. They were the ones who radiated warmth, and they brought some warmth out of me. They had a name for me. Not out of derision, but out of love: 'Ason Yazzie,' (Little Woman).

In the summer of my second year James Kobiashi, a medical student from California, arrived in Fort Defiance to spend an externship, one month each on pediatrics and on surgery.

"Hi, I'm James, Dr. Bowman. I'll be your scut boy for the next month," he said when he showed up for duty on my floor.

"You won't have to do any scut work here. We have a pretty good lab. You won't even have to draw bloods," I said in my most professional manner. "But I do expect you to be on time for rounds with me every morning, to take the histories and to do the physical examinations, to write preliminary orders on all new admissions, and to take first call for pediatric emergencies on the nights I'm on call."

James Kobiashi was muscular, of medium height, (but, of course, taller than I) with a merriment about his black eyes that made it hard for me to maintain my official attitude for long. He radiated self-confidence, but he knew how not to be overbearing. There was richness in his voice and melody in his cultured speech. His appearance was as Japanese as his name, but he was refreshing, open, and enthusiastic.

Within a very few days of his arrival, he caught on to Navajo words of greeting. "Yat'eh ah'bin," (Good Morning) he would say every morning to all the little children on the ward.

The older girls would giggle and call back to him, "Yat'eh, azay'ich'inn" (Good morning, doctor). He would tease the older boys and give them Navajo names, "Ashki de Jollie" (Round Boy)or "Hosteen T'la pahe," (Tan Man) if they were fat or lightly complected. They would tease him in return and call out to him familiarly, "Yat'eh sik'ess" (Hello, pal, or Hello, buddy).

Is it a wonder that Jim's skill in breaking down barriers worked on me, too?

"I've heard there's a great spot for a cookout called 'Natural Bridge,' just three or four miles from here. How about it? I'll get the steaks."

Just like that! The first invitation I'd had to anything since I'd come to Fort Defiance. It was easy to say yes. It was summertime. The daylight lasted until almost nine o'clock. The chance to get away from the hospital for a change, to breathe the cool, piñon-scented air as the shadows lengthened, all these added to the appeal of Jim himself. Yes.

I was somehow completely at ease in spite of the newness of the situation for me. A man asking me out? He was just a boy. Jim was only twenty-three. I was twenty-eight, almost twenty-nine. I was his teacher. This wasn't a date. It was, as Jim said, just a cookout. Of course I would go. Nothing to it.

But there was a subtle change in myself. I would be gay, light-hearted. I washed my hair and I let it fluff out a bit. I didn't wear perfume, but the soap I showered with had a light, lavender scent. I put on a white, peasant-type blouse with short, puffy sleeves and a wide ruffle around the neck. I didn't care if I was flat. It was sick how those women used to worry about their boobs, how they used to pad their bras, how they subjected themselves to breast-augmentation surgery. Well, maybe I shouldn't be so hard on women for being vain, I said to myself, as I tried on a pair of silver and turquoise earrings I found in my top drawer. I'd bought them for my sister at the Navajo Arts and Crafts shop in Window Rock. They were pretty. I swept out of my room with a whoosh of my long, Navajo-type skirt, and I left my glasses behind.

Jim was right. It was just a short drive down along the valley of the Black Creek Wash on the old dirt road going south toward St. Michael's. About a mile past the black, volcanic dyke that sticks up like a wall across the valley, Jim turned right and up about a quarter of a mile along an old wagon track. The track climbed the lower part of the gentle up-slope of the green Defiance Plateau. The sun had already dipped behind the brow of the mountain ahead and to the west, but looking back toward the east, the valley was flooded with soft, late-afternoon sunlight. Cottonwoods sprung up here and there along the meandering wash, and Navajo houses, hogans, little corrals and cornfields lay scattered about. Three miles across the valley a line of smooth, rounded, orange-pink sandstone cliffs caught the full sunlight, and beyond them, the clear brightness of the sky.

"You were right, Jim. It's absolutely beautiful here. I never knew there was so much loveliness so close to Fort Defiance."

Jim parked the car at the edge of a narrow arroyo that was all that was left of a small canyon that carried runoff from the plateau. A slab of flat, lichen-covered, gray rock about eighteen feet long and three feet thick lay across the top of the arroyo, deposited there by a flood that had come down the canyon some time in the past. The Navajos called it "Navajo Bridge."

Jim set about gathering wood for the fire.

"Gather up some of those small flat rocks," he said. "We'll use them to support the grill."

Jim returned from a little excursion he made up the slope, out from under the branches of the juniper and the first of the piñon at that elevation, and he piled an armful of twigs and branches on the ground.

"Here. Make four flat piles of the flat stones in a square about a foot apart."

I did as he said and he lit the fire. The dried wood flashed up into flames in an instant. None of the damp, moldy sticks you find back in Indiana that smoulder and stink and never burn right, I thought. Wow! Look at that fire. I had to back away from the heat, but as I did so, I felt the cool air on my back. It was getting dark quickly in the shadow of the mountain.

The flame died down quickly. Jim was clever enough to use only small sticks and twigs at first, adding the larger chunks of wood later. He placed a flat steel grill he'd brought with him and he laid it across the stone supports I'd made for him. Then he waited until the grill became hot from the glowing coals.

I leaned back and watched the shadow of the mountain behind us creep across the valley. The color of the sandstone cliffs grew a deeper orange, and then, as the light faded further, the rocks took on a phosphorescent glow.

"In some ways," Jim said, "the color of those cliffs reminds me of the last of the sunlight on the windows of Oakland when you see them from San Francisco. The open valley here is a little like the open space of San Francisco Bay."

"You sound like you're lonesome for home," I said.

"Not a bit. It's just the space and the light. But the people, that's another matter. I'm glad to be away from there."

"I've heard that the West coast and San Francisco in particular is a very friendly place."

"Not if you're Japanese. When you're on the street, in a bus, or on a street car you can feel the eyes of Caucasians looking at you. You know they're tying to figure out what kind of an Oriental you are, Chinese or Japanese or Filipino or something else. Out here, very frankly, I feel much more comfortable. I guess I look enough like a Navajo that nobody thinks of trying to figure me out."

I felt a sudden rush of warmth for Jim. I'd thought he was so self-confident, so comfortable with himself. Here he'd opened himself up to me. I didn't say anything for a while. I didn't want to encourage him to go on bringing up painful memories. It was too lovely where we were.

Jim put on the steaks and the embers burst into flames and smoke when the fat dripped in the fire. He was in no hurry to turn the meat over. He liked the steaks with the fat black and crisp on the outside, just like I did. He stared into the fire for a while and then went on.

"They hauled my father right out of the Moffat, right out of his internship at the University of California Hospital. Can you imagine that? He was sent off with the rest of the Japanese to the internment camp in Idaho in 1942. They paid him twelve dollars a month to be one of the doctors in the camp."

The wind began to blow a little harder down the mountain. The smoke from the fire was getting into Jim's face, so he moved around to where I was sitting. He leaned forward to turn the steaks over, and when he sat back down again his arm brushed against mine.

They were wrong, I thought. There *is* life in me. I can feel it in my arm. Next to his arm.

The sky above the cliffs to the east now darkened. The bright star, Vega, appeared, and not long after that, the Swan rose on its side, flying down the stream of the Milky Way.

"Yat'eh abin," I said to the children when I walked on to the ward the next morning. What was that, a chirp? I asked myself. An evening cook-out shouldn't make you chirp, you silly woman! Dr. Bowman, a silly woman? And that tingling of your face when Jim came in, was that a flush? Or a blush?

"There's a squaw dance on the divide on the road to Ganado," Jim said. He'd learned more about where things were going on in two weeks than I learned in a year. "I'll pick you up a little after six on Saturday." There was that confidence again, I thought. He didn't even ask me if I wanted to go.

I threw off my glasses the minute I got back to my room that Saturday evening. I looked at myself in the mirror. You know with just a little bit of a smile and a little bit of color in your cheeks, you're not half bad, really, I said to myself. He'd notice if I started wearing lipstick, I thought. What the hell. One of these days I'll pick some with just a little bit of color. Nothing flaming red, of course. I'm sure I'll find something just right in Gallup. No perfume. That would be too obvious. Just a little cologne. Cologne is more subtle and it doesn't hang on as long.

We swept southward on the east side of the valley on the highway toward Window Rock. The sandstone cliffs rose on our left. Across the valley to the west, on the lower slope of the mountain, I tried to find the canyon at the outlet of which lay the Natural Bridge. The bridge between the sexes. The bridge between the races.

"No, it's too far away and too small to see from here," Jim said when I asked him. "But it was a perfect spot, a perfect evening, wasn't it?"

The road west of Window Rock took us across the valley, past the fair grounds, and then on the way up the mountain. The juniper bushes on the lower slopes gave way to the piñons and, still higher, the ponderosa forest began. I sat quietly next to Jim, our shoulders almost touching.

"This is so much different from Indiana, Jim," I said. "Out here you can tell how high you are just by looking at the trees."

"It's that way in California, too. Only there, when you climb to a certain elevation out of the Central Valley, you run into the redwoods. The giant sequoias. I'd love to show them to you some day."

I got a little dizzy. He's thinking about me. He's connecting with me, I thought.

We drove several miles at the top of the plateau with scattered ponderosa pines and open meadows stretching in all directions.

"So this is what the top of the mountain looks like," I said. "The folks back home would never believe this was Arizona. Even I thought Arizona was all desert, heat, and cactus."

"Wait till you see the Tuolomne valley in Yosemite," Jim said. "Even though you think you know what it will look like from pictures, when you actually see it, you will never believe how beautiful it is."

A crude wooden sign attached to a fence post pointed to the left. Jim slowed down and turned onto a dirt road leading south. It was nearly dark now. In the rearview mirror we could see the headlights of several pickup trucks that had turned off the highway after us. Those headlights were shining through the dust we had kicked up.

"It looks like I found the right road. Everybody seems to be following us in."

Soon, through the dust, we caught up with the taillights of a pickup turning off to the right onto a less-traveled track.

"Looks like that fellow's going where we want to go." Our headlights caught the glow of the cinnamon-colored bark of an old ponderosa pine when we turned. Further ahead we saw a cluster of taillights, the rear ends of trucks that were parked in a circle in a meadow among the trees. Crowds of Navajos wandered about in the semi-darkness, light coming from a huge fire of logs in the center of a large circle.

We found a place to park and Jim took me by the hand. He pulled me as he threaded his way between the trucks and through the groups of Navajos. The Navajos moved about gaily, chatting and greeting one another as they came and went.

We stood quietly inside the circle. Our faces felt the heat of the great fire which churned smoke and spewed sparks into the night sky. On the other side of the circle a cluster of men and boys and an occasional woman had already begun to sing, loudly and in unison, accompanied by the beat of a small drum held by one of the men. Jim folded his arms around me from behind and I could feel his happiness and my happiness.

"We're going north this time," Jim announced. "We're going to the canyon."

"Which canyon?"

"Canyon de Chelly, the red rock canyon, the one with the Anasazi ruins. Be prepared for a half day's drive. I haven't seen it myself yet but I hear it's marvelous."

On an early Saturday afternoon, after rounds and after giving a report to the weekend duty doctor, I rushed back to my room. I put on the same peasant blouse with the ruffles around the neck, the same ankle-length Navajo skirt, a different set of earrings, coral this time, a pale blush of lipstick, and a touch, just a touch of Chanel Number Five.

We climbed the same forested plateau going straight up out of Fort Defiance, the day brilliant and blue with fluffs of white clouds accompanying us. At the higher elevation the air was cool in spite of the August sun.

"There's never been any clear-cutting on the Defiance Plateau," Jim said when we passed the sawmill town. "Hosteen Begay, whose little boy we had on the ward last week, works for the Tribe. He told me that the Navajos were among the first to practice scientific harvesting of trees. The largest trees, the ones with the cinnamon-colored bark, had never been cut. Some of those were always left standing for seed. The slender, smaller trees with the dark-colored bark are the new growth."

Past the sawmill town the road ran northwest and then north. After a steady climb we dipped down into a broad and open meadow. Just ahead of us, a vertical gray cliff rose about three-hundred feet high. It extended about a quarter mile east and west and it was made up of compact vertical columns.

"It's just as Hosteen Begay described it. He said the Navajos call it 'Tsilth-da-sa-ahn,' which means simply 'The Rock That's There.' It's a volcanic formation where the rock cooled and crystallized to give it that fluted appearance."

The road curved to the left around the rock formation, then ran straight through the forest along a somewhat improved logging road for about twenty miles. When we began to descend, suddenly a vast space opened up before us.

"Look," Jim exclaimed, and pointed to the northeast. "Those must be the Lukachukais!" In the late afternoon sun the light fell on a line of deep red, sandstone benches, each bench separated by a small canyon. And mounted on top of each bench was a towering, gray, ragged peak of volcanic rock, the whole complex extending twenty or thirty miles in a south to north direction.

"'Like stout Cortes/Silent on a peak in Darien.'" I said.

"It's much grander than I imagined," he said. "Let's get out of the car and stand here for a while. I need time to let this sink in."

We stood side by side and held hands. I leaned my head against his shoulder and he kissed the hair on the top of my head.

We drove down the mountain in the gathering dusk, down through the piñon, then the juniper, then across a brush-covered plain where the penetrating aroma of sage greeted us through the open windows. We reached the paved road of the South Rim Drive and soon found the sign that said "To Spider Rock Overlook."

"This is a must. They say it's the grandest view of the Canyon. Are you ready for it?"

"I'm ready," I said.

It took us longer to reach the overlook than I expected. There were only one or two cars in the paved parking area and the light was fading. Jim took my hand as we got out of the car, and we walked to the stone wall that marked the edge of the overlook. The gulf, the depth, and the darkness nearly swallowed me. The parapet was too low. I went down on my knees and pressed the solid stone against my chest. Only then did I dare to look into the canyon again.

"It's at least a thousand feet deep at this point," Jim announced. He stood his full height and leaned over the parapet.

"Don't! Get Down!" I shouted, and I crouched myself down still lower.

"You've got to look. It's the most spectacular sight in the West."

"Not until you get down a little yourself. It just scares me too much."

"O.K.," he said kneeling beside me. "Now take a good look before the light fades altogether."

Spider Rock, the column, a shaft of deep red sandstone perhaps seventy feet wide at the base and thirty feet wide at the top, rose nearly a thousand feet from the darkness at the bottom of the canyon almost to the level of the overlook. Perched at the top of the column and catching the last of the light of the day was a thin layer of cap rock, much lighter in color than the rest of the shaft.

"The Navajo legend says the cap of light rock is what is left of the bleached bones of the victims of Spider Woman after she devoured them. How do you like that for a gruesome tale?"

I held on a little tighter to the stones at the top of the parapet and gazed once again into the depths. Canyon de Chelly was wider where Spider Rock rose up than at other places because, in fact, three canyons came together there. Once more I felt the enormous power of the dark depth below. It was as if the gulf was drawing me into it.

"Thanks, Jim. I've had enough.' I wasn't ashamed at all to crawl on my hands and knees, back away from the wall, far enough back to where I felt safe.

"But you haven't seen the companion shaft, Talking Woman, on the other side of the canyon. Talking Woman is the one who tells Spider Woman which victims to choose," and with that Jim followed a path that led away from the protecting parapet and further out onto the promontory, further toward the edge.

"No, I don't want to see Talking Woman. Jim, I'm frightened. Get back here!"

Jim didn't answer but disappeared into the near darkness. I got up and ran back to the car, and then beyond the paved parking area that was as far away from either edge of the promontory as I could get. I threw myself down under the protecting, low branches of a juniper and flattened myself onto the flat rock from which it took root.

Jim could trip and fall in the darkness. He has no fear, no sense. The worst of all possible thoughts came to me. I hugged the ground, pressing myself against the rock as earlier I had pressed myself against the parapet.

"I won't do that to you again, Marion. I'm sorry"

"Jim, you're back! Thank God!" I jumped up and threw my arms around his waist. I pulled him down beside me and I held on to him. I wanted him all over me. I wanted his hands on my breasts. I pulled his hands down over me and I cupped his hands over my nipples. I pressed my mouth against his mouth and his arms tightened around me. I felt his rising and I pressed myself against him. This was the moment that was right for me, for us. That surge of heat rose within me, that aching within me and I pressed against him. I saw that he was struggling to free one of his hands as he reached into his pocket. A condom. That's O.K. if he wants it. I don't care. I just want him. I watched him roll over on his side to pull down his pants and I did the same. I helped him. I tilted myself so he could get to me, to get into me. And he did. Not gently, but he did and I struggled now to wrap myself around him and I held on to him as he came. Too soon but I wanted him and I didn't care. He laughed and I was happy for him that he came and I held him in me because I loved him and I wanted him. Then I laughed too. And he kissed me and I kissed him and we held each other as the wind blew across the promontory and across his sweaty brow and mine.

"I'll cook you a Japanese dinner," he offered two days later. He'd brought all his paraphernalia, his little electric cooker, his Teriyaki sauce, his Saki cups and warmer and the clear rice wine. He tossed the bits of skinned chicken breast, the cauliflower, and cashew nuts into the peanut oil, added a dash of sesame oil, and threw them into the electric pan.

"Now for the chopsticks. You hold the lower one against the middle finger and the upper one lightly under your thumb. And you don't use them like pincers; you use them like a shovel. Don't try too hard or you'll get a cramp in your hand."

I sat back and watched him work. He wore a bandana around his head to catch the sweat and a sash around his waist to fasten his kimono. His short, stiff, black hair glistened, and his epicanthal folds, when he smiled and laughed, caused his eyes to narrow to a slit. It must have been the whole cultural thing, the dinner, his dress, that made me more aware now of his Oriental features.

"You don't mind me being a Jap?" he asked, as if he'd read my thoughts.

"I don't mind, Slant Eyes. I love you. You don't mind that I'm so tiny?"

"You know what they say, don't you?"

"No, what do they say?"

"Big girl, big cunt; little girl, all cunt!"

"You bastard!" I shouted and I jumped up and pulled him down I ripped open his kimono and my mouth found his nipples. We wrestled and laughed and shouted and stumbled into the bedroom where we loved again, forgetting until afterward the cauliflower, the cashews, and the Teriyaki chicken.

We felt each other's presence during the days, so full were our nights. I watched with joy as Jim worked with the children on the pediatric ward.

"Deetch'eh, (Open your mouth) and take a deep breath," Jim instructed as he listened with his stethoscope to the lungs of the fat boy. "We'll have you out of here in no time, Ashki de Jollie." The child smiled that he'd pleased his doctor.

"Ee'zinn, (Stand up). Let me look at that leg of yours, Hosteen T'la pahe," he said when he came to the boy with the spider bite on his leg. The shy, tan boy stood up and let himself be examined.

Jim moved with that sort of skill from child to child and from bed to bed making his rounds. But our days together came to an end when the time came for Jim to move on to the surgical service.

"Well, how is it over there, Mr. Blood-and-Guts?" I teased after he'd been on the surgical service a few days.

"I like, I love it, I'm sorry to say. I don't want to hurt your feelings, but in surgery you *do* things. You find a woman complaining of abdominal pain. You find she has right upper quadrant tenderness. Her white count is elevated. You make the correct diagnosis: acute cholecystitis. You take out an inflamed gallbladder, you sew her up. She gets better, she's cured, and you're done. I gives you a tremendous sense of accomplishment."

"It doesn't hurt my feelings when you tell me this, Jim. Surgery is part of medicine. Being a caring person as you treat patients is what counts, and I know you're that kind of person. I'm happy for you if you're happy."

Boy, that was some speech, I thought. The great professor oration. I confess to myself I was jealous that he'd found such joy doing something away from me, not connected with me. But I tried not to let him see that. He had to be free. We still had our nights. We still had our time off together on weekends.

We had our nights. We were finding new ways to do it. Wild. Fun. Shouting and laughing. We had our world together. Nobody could take that away from us.

We had our weekends. We strolled together under the gaudy lights of the midway at the Navajo Tribal Fair at Window Rock. We ate the spongy, freshly-made frybread, dipping it into the thin, clear mutton stew that we bought at the Navajos' stands. From the grandstand at the rodeo grounds we admired the Navajo girls as they leaned into their horses careening around the barrels in the barrel race. We cheered the tough, wiry Navajo boys with their sweaty, determined faces as they clung to the rope and to the backs of wild broncos and massive, churning bulls. We shouted encouragement at the team-work of the lean cowboys at the calf-roping: the swift running down of the calves, the lassoing of the feet, the quick flipping over of the young animal, the tying of the legs, and then we cheered the cowboy when he flung his arms up for the timer in triumph.

At night, with the Navajo audience, we watched the Grand Entry of the costumed tribal dancers: the feathered headdresses of the Plains

Indians, the buffalo skins and the eagle wings of the Pueblo dancers, the flat, black headdresses of the Apache devil dancers, and the twin-feathered, blue *Yei B'chei* masks of the Navajos. Then one-by-one, tribe-by-tribe, group-by-group, illuminated by small fires on the sandy floor of the great arena, we watched their pride as each group danced to their respective drumbeat, chanted their song, stamped their feet, and threw themselves into the magic of their ancient rituals.

In the darkness where we sat, I reached for Jim's hand to hold in mine, and his dark, smiling, almost Navajo face, with his narrow, Asian eyes, looked back at me.

Our weekends took us eastward, over the forested Chuskas into New Mexico, across the tan, barren plains to Crownpoint, and then north to the ancient city at Chaco Canyon. We stood side by side in amazement at the smooth, rounded outer wall and at the tight masonry of the great house. We entered the giant, roofless kiva and I could imagine the shuffling feet and the chanting and the masks of long-dead dancers.

The trumpets, the fat, base guitars and the squeaky violins of the mariachis at Santa Fe at Fiesta brought us other delights. We danced to their music in the bricked courtyard of the old De Vargas Hotel while the little boys and girls of the old Spanish families pranced around us. The children were dressed in their finest communion suits and white dresses while their parents and grandparents, seated at tables around the courtyard, smiled and plotted family contracts for the future.

"The Zozobra! It's time for the burning of the Zozobra!" someone shouted. Old and young rushed for the passageway to the street and the courtyard was emptied. We followed the crowds outside. The throngs in the plaza were in motion too, out to the park where the paper and wood monster loomed in the darkness. The torch-bearers approached and applied their flames to the giant effigy of gloom. The flames licked slowly at the base of the figure, then exploded in a giant roar. Loudspeakers at the base of the Zozobra blared the forth simulated moans and groans of the creature and the crowd rose in shouts and cheers. With one great flash of light, and with a burst of flames and sparks rising in the night sky, the monster was consumed, while the people applauded and raised their voices in peals of laughter.

"C'mon, let's get out here. I'm hungry for you," Jim said. We rushed back to our room upstairs at the La Fonda, undressed in a moment and soon, like the effigy of gloom, we too were consumed.

I had known she was there since I arrived at the hospital at Fort Defiance. Perhaps it is just in retrospect that I perceived her as the coldest of all the cold, distant, and aloof members of the hospital staff. She had always ignored me, looked past me when I went by, failed to recognize that I existed. Angela Thibault was a member of the establishment, the nurse anaesthetist. She had been there for seven or eight years and, in that time, had seen as many as three or four changes of doctors at the hospital.

"It doesn't really matter who you are," she seemed to say the few times she cast her hard, gray eyes in my direction. "You'll be gone like the others soon enough."

I never heard anyone say a good word about her. She was an Indian in an Indian hospital so she had a right, I suppose, to claim her position there if she liked, but she was not a Navajo. She was a member of some Oklahoma tribe, a light-skinned, light-eyed, mixed-blood.

I had to admit she commanded a certain amount of respect for what she did. I used to see her through the small glass window of the operating room door. It was her eyes mainly that I saw since, in the operating room, her face was always covered with a surgical mask, her head covered with a surgical cap, and her muscular body always swathed in a surgical gown.

"You'll have to come and watch me later today," Jim said. "I'll be assisting Dr. Kaplan doing the appendectomy on your patient, Ellen Tsosie. Dr. Kaplan agreed with your diagnosis of appendicitis."

Typical James Kobiashi, I thought. That boyish confidence, that I would have some thrill watching a medical student assist at a routine appendectomy!

But Ellen Tsosie was not a routine patient. I had only seen this eleven year-old once, earlier that morning, when she'd been brought to the emergency room with nausea and vomiting. The doctor downstairs had admitted her with a diagnosis of gastroenteritis, but when I examined her, though she did not complain, I found she had tenderness in her lower abdomen. That's when I called for a surgical consultation with Dr. Kaplan. What I loved about this child was her stoicism and her bravery. The ambulance driver had told me that during the ride over from the outlying clinic at Chinle when Ellen felt she was about to vomit, she just opened up her little cardboard suitcase and she vomited into it rather than mess up the ambulance.

"Of course I'll come to watch you assist at surgery today. Ellen is very special to me." So I scrubbed and gowned up and I entered the operating room.

I have to admit that Jim looked very much the professional, the surgeon, gloved, gowned, with cap and mask, standing opposite Dr. Kaplan, holding the retractors. I watched his dark eyes move quickly, from Dr. Kaplan, to the scrub nurse, to Angela. Angela, at the head of the sleeping child, worked the dials of the anaesthesia machine, checked the rate of the intravenous infusion, and squeezed the Ambu bag with a steady, deliberate rhythm. I was happy for Jim. If surgery was what he wanted, that was O.K. with me.

"I saw Jim and Angela Thibault in Gallup on Saturday." This casual remark by Annie Notah, chief nurse of my pediatric unit, sent an electric charge through my chest.

Why is she telling me this? Is it to deflate me somehow, to drag me down to some common level? For the moment my anger was with Annie but soon enough I directed it at Jim.

"I heard you spent a little time with Angela in Gallup, Jim."

I could tell by the swift rising of color in his face that he was angry, too, and that I'd caught him so suddenly the moment I saw him.

"Look, Marion, I just ran into her. I was shopping for some Navajo jewelry. She said she had some gifts to buy too and she was on her way to the best places. So I followed her to Tobe Turpen's and to Richardson's Pawn."

"Is that all?"

"Of course that's all. Come on, don't do that to me, give me the third degree."

"I'm not grilling you for the fun of it. I just don't want you to hurt me, that's all," and I turned away so he wouldn't see that I was beginning to cry.

"I'll never hurt you, Marion. I love you. Let me see you tonight. I've got to get back to surgery now." He reached for my hand but I wouldn't let him, and when he disappeared down the hall, I ran into the staff bathroom and let the water stream from my eyes.

I was in a calmer mood that night. It was my turn to cook, just a simple roast chicken, wine, candles. It was patch-up time after our first lovers' quarrel.

"So what is she like?" I wasn't going to shove the thing under the rug. I needed to know something about the enemy.

"I can't tell you much about her. She doesn't say much about herself. What I know about her I heard from others: that she'd had a hard life in Oklahoma, part Indian, part white, never comfortable in either world."

"Yeah, so you've got a lot of sympathy for her, right?"

"Come on, Marion, don't be so sarcastic. We both know what it's like to be 'off-center.'"

"So what are you now, a sociologist?"

I was sorry I said that. The conversation was turning sour. I didn't want to start another fight. I thought I would just engage in a little gentle mockery.

"You know she's old enough to be your mother."

"Yeah, and you're small enough to be my daughter!"

"Bastard, bastard!" I said and we were both laughing, jumping at each other, our mouths together, rolling on the bed, hands in each other's shirt, the sex exploding, the fire blazing again, wild again, sweet again.

The rains came every afternoon that early fall, and with the rains, the chill winds that came with them. Bah Salt, age three, was brought in by a horse-drawn wagon from Piñon, Arizona with pneumonia. Why this previously healthy child became so suddenly, gravely ill with the X-ray showing infiltrate in both lungs, struggling to breathe, was a puzzle, so frighteningly swift it was. Her parents, bronze of skin, silent, polite, stood at my side watching as the girl coughed, strained, turned blue with coughing, with crowing respirations. With each drawn breath she made a crowing sound, and the notch at the top of her sternum and the spaces between her ribs were drawn inward. The full flow of oxygen and humidification in the croup tent, and the intravenous antibiotics didn't help. I was on the point of calling in Dr. Kaplan to do a tracheostomy. The tracheostomy might make it easier to suction the thick secretions from her windpipe, but the shock of surgery might push her over the brink. Her respirations became more rapid, her eyelids failed to close completely and only the whites of her eyes showed between her lids.

"The parents want to find a medicine man to sing over the child," Annie Notah said coming up to me.

"That would be fine but the child cannot be taken out from here."

"They understand that. The sing can be done over an article of the child's clothing. The parents have relatives in town here, the Tabahas. The prayer can be done in the Tabahas' hogan."

I prayed too as I reached into the croup tent for one of the child's undershirts and I handed it to Annie.

The rain and thunder, the splashing of water on the windows, and the rushing of water in the arroyo behind the hospital continued through the night. Toward morning the wind pushed the rain-laden clouds to the east and then the wind stopped.

In the morning Bah's respirations became quieter, coughing less frequent. The crowing quality when she inhaled, ceased.

The child would live.

The Salts came up to me, pressed my hand gently and said over and over again, "A*shay*-hay, Ashay-hay," (Thank you, Thank you!) When I was preparing to leave that evening, confident because the child had made steady progress during the day, the Salts followed me out of the building. Mrs. Salt tugged at my sleeve and pulled me toward their green-painted wagon. She reached under a tarp that covered the bed of the wagon and pulled out a package about the size of a pillow that had been freshly wrapped in brown paper. She handed the package to me and gestured to me that I should open it. I was reluctant to accept it, knowing how poor they were, but I had to oblige them. When I tore open the wrapping paper the tears came. The gift was a Pendleton shawl, brilliant in its stripes of purple, blue, and red, fringed with a border of deep purple tassels, and soft and warm to the touch. My voice thickened but I was able to say the word of thanks that I'd learned.

"A*shay*-hay, A*shay*-hay." I held the package under one arm and threw the other around Mrs. Salt's neck. She pressed her wind-thickened face against mine, hugged me in turn, and we held on to each other.

"A*shay*-hay, Azay ich *inn*, A*shay*-hay, Ason Yazzie."

I ran toward Jim's apartment with the package under my arm. I was giddy from the fatigue of staying up the whole of the night before and all of the day with the sick child, giddy with the emotion and the embrace of the Navajo mother whose child would live. I stumbled once or twice running up the stairs, fumbled for the key and opened the door.

I wasn't sure at first if I heard the sound because of the pounding in my chest from running up the stairs. I stopped and I knew what I heard. It was coming from the bedroom, the grunting, the breathing, the rocking. Fucking! It was her! Angela was on top, pushing and straining to reach her orgasm, and underneath, from below her hanging breasts, that laugh, Jim's laugh, the laugh that I knew and that belonged to me.

I'll try to describe what happened in the next two hours, the images of frantic flight, swift, uncontrollable, inevitable. I spun around, out the door, down the stairs, out the outer door, onto the paved parking lot. I reached for the keys to my car and in doing so I dropped the paper-wrapped shawl, the Pendleton, the striped, the fringed, the soft, the warm. I didn't care that it fell into a puddle from the rains of the night before. The trunk key, the ignition key, which is which? The one that works. The car started up quickly, the engine raced, the tires squealed as I reversed onto the street, then lunged forward on the road that lead north, out of Fort Defiance, up the mountain toward the saw mill town. The headlights led me on. The arms on the steering wheel, the foot on the accelerator were not my own.

Beyond the town the road pulled me west, uphill between the ponderosas, car lights falling on cinnamon-colored bark, north to the palisade of 'Tzilth-da-sa-ahn,' halfway there. Gravel clattered against the underside of the fenders as the car turned to the left, around Fluted Rock, then up the straight graded road north, getting closer. Lukachukais somewhere out there in the dark, who could care now? Now spinning through the twisted road on the sage-scented plain, to the paved South Rim Drive, and to the sign, 'To Spider Rock Overlook.' The car door opened at the now-deserted overlook parking lot. There the parapet, over the parapet toward the rocky ledge, the edge itself. I heard the soles of my shoes scraping the pebbles of the flat rock of the edge. I stopped. A faint, waning force of life held me, caused me to hesitate at the brink. The great, black gulf hung before me. The shaft of Spider Rock rose from the depths. In the star-light the faint whiteness of the cap rock glowed dimly, the bones of the victims of Spider Woman.

I stood at the very edge when the darkness and the great dark depths sucked me forward.

They say when a person falls from a great height they die before they hit the ground. That's not true. As I fell into the blackness of the canyon, as my speed increased, as I felt the pressure of the wind in my face, I found I was struggling to keep my body in an upright position. I reached out with my arms to grab onto any tree tree or bush that might help to break my fall, but I was now rushing past too fast for that. Suddenly fear exploded within me. When my head struck the rock nearly a thousand feet down, a one millisecond —a ten-kiloton — a sunburst — of pain — then the blackness and the silence.

I can't explain why I chose to come back after nearly forty years to enter into somebody's dream, or why I chose Jack Berkowitz who had always despised my plainness, or what he thought was the absence of life or passion within me. Maybe I chose him as an act of forgiveness, arriving myself at a more charitable view of him. Perhaps he'd been too busy with his Navajo girlfriend to shed any of his warmth and kindness (which people said he had an abundance of) in my direction. Or perhaps I know, since he married the girl and that they've had children and grandchildren, that he would visit Fort Defiance and that he would think of me and remember me.

I had tried to enter Jim's dreams in the past, but I'd succeeded only in the first few years when the memory of my suicide was fresh. I understand he is now a distinguished transplant surgeon, professor and chairman of a department of cardiac surgery at a medical school in California, that he married a Caucasian girl, that they, too, have had children and grandchildren. I'm told that he is still handsome and that his short-cropped, bristly hair is now largely gray. It has taken me many years to forgive his betrayal of me, his theft of my life, but I still love him, that he did open my short life to me.

SQUIRREL'S EARS

We moved Grandpa Bird to the Red Rocks Nursing Home in Gallup last year. He'd not been happy in the nursing home in Rio Rancho even though Ida was faithful in driving up the hill from Corrales to see him nearly every day. I was faithful myself in taking him out every Saturday morning, helping him from the wheelchair to the front seat of the car, then driving him down the hill to our place in Corrales for the day. There he could talk to Ida and there he could see some of his grandchildren and great-grandchildren.

"Now, in Gallup, at least he's closer to the Reservation," I said to Ida. "Almost all of the nurses and aides are Navajo and he has someone to talk to in Navajo whenever he wants to." I didn't have to tell Ida, because she knew as well as I, that most of the residents in the nursing home, though Navajo too, were so far gone, so demented, that they were no company for him. It was no comfort for him to see those old shriveled faces and those blank, staring eyes. But Grandpa's mind and his memory were still good, as they are to this very day.

"I know I am going to live to one hundred and four," Grandpa has said many times. He's probably right.

From the large, east-facing window of his room he can see the cars and trucks on Highway 66 and the Santa Fe trains rolling in and out of Gallup. A little to the north of that he can see the continuous flow of traffic on the Interstate which runs in the new cut in the hogback.

His ability to see all this came about just within the last year, when he was ninety-eight. Dr. Arthur Weinstein took out the cataracts he had in both eyes and replaced those old, clouded lenses with new, plastic implants.

So he's closer to home now, being in Gallup. When Ida takes him out for an afternoon or for an overnight pass, as she will at corn-planting time, she can take him home to Red Lake. That's where his home has been for nearly sixty years. From the front porch of his cabin he can look down upon the valley to see the fields he had fenced and irrigated, and he can look across the valley to the pink sandstone cliffs that turn to gold at the end of the day.

Grandpa has said that he would live to be a hundred and four. He was still herding sheep when he was eighty. I had difficulty keeping up with him then when I was forty-five.

Of course, things happen to a man in the course of a long lifetime. Grandpa had his gallbladder taken out at the Indian Hospital at Fort Defiance when he was seventy-five. He did just fine. I took care of him when, in his eighties, he had a very painful case of the "shingles" and I had to give him injections of Demerol. Another time I admitted him to the hospital under my own care when he had a case of severe inflammation of the face. I thought it was a case of erysipelas which required intravenous antibiotics. Then, when he was having repeated infections of his urinary bladder, we arranged for him to have prostate surgery. Again, his strong constitution helped him through.

But he was getting older. In the winter of his ninety-seventh year he became ill with cough and weakness. I brought him to my office where an x-ray showed that he had pneumonia and where an electrocardiogram showed a rapid, irregular heartbeat. I treated him with antibiotics and with digitalis to slow down his rapid heart rate and to strengthen his heart. Again he recovered.

This time we knew we would have to keep Grandpa Bird with us. He was getting too old and too weak to stay by himself in his cabin at Red Lake. This was especially true for the wintertime. He had only a wood stove for heat and the cabin would get cold if the fire went out or if he ran out of wood or coal. And then he might trip or fall on the ice and snow on the way to the privy. Often there was no food in the house and nobody to cook for him.

So we brought Grandpa to stay with us in Corrales. He had a room of his own, the bathroom was just down the hall, and when the weather was warm he could sit out on the patio and sun himself.

"Dad, come here!" our son, Joseph, called to me with some urgency one Sunday morning. "Grandpa asked me to help him but he can't get up." I rushed in to see what was wrong.

"Something happened to my leg," Grandpa said. "It's cold and I have no feeling in it." I felt his legs and his feet. The left foot was cold and it had no pulse in it.

"Phil," I said on the phone to my friend, Dr. Jacob, a vascular surgeon. "It looks like my father-in-law has thrown an embolus to his left leg."

"Get him down here to the hospital right away. I'll have my technician meet you there and I'll see him right after that." We found a wheelbarrow to get Grandpa out of the house and into the car to the hospital. Dr. Jacob took him to the operating room and he saved Grandpa's leg that day.

So now Grandpa is comfortable and safe in the nursing home in Gallup. Even his eyes are better. And he can get home now and then, and at the end of the day he can see the cliffs across the valley when they turn to gold.

Grandpa is half Hopi but neither he nor anybody has any stories about his Hopi father, or how that Hopi man happened to meet his mother, a Navajo of the T'a chini clan from Canyon de Chelly. Ida remembers her grandmother's peach orchard in what was then called "Wild Cherry Canyon," a box canyon that opens into the Canyon de Chelly from the south, and the wagon trips from Red Lake each summer. Grandpa would drive the wagon up past Old Sawmill, through the ponderosa forest, past Fluted Rock, then down to Chinle at the mouth of the Canyon. From there he drove back up into the Canyon on its sandy bottom, past White House ruin, to his mother's place. They would return with the wagon bed full of peaches. Ida's mother would then pit them, dry them in the sun under a cheese cloth and store them in a gunny sack in the root cellar for the winter.

Grandpa used to tell his own story.

"I didn't start school or learn English until I was fifteen. The only boarding school was at Fort Defiance then and it was more than sixty miles away from Canyon de Chelly where I was born. The *silah-o,* the Navajo policemen, used to round up the children to send them to school, but I didn't want to go to school. I just wanted to stay in the canyon and to be able to go when I felt like it to all the places I liked and that I knew so well.

"I knew of special places in the big canyon and in the little side canyons. I knew where all the springs were and where the grass grew damp and rich. The spring I liked best was back in Wild Cherry Canyon where my mother had her hogan and a peach orchard. When I would get to the spot I would spread the tall grass aside and there was the cool water coming up from the ground at the base of the cliff. I would brush away the water striders and the dead leaves from the surface of the water and I would put my whole head in it. How cool and fresh the water was after a hot climb to that place! I would feel the cool water soak right through my hair and it would feel so good trickling down the back of my neck. After that I would climb the slope a little way and I would lie on my back while the sheep came to drink and to eat the grass. I would let my eyes climb up the red cliffs that rose straight up to the sky.

"I would find the place where my mother and I used to climb up the trail to the top when we wanted to get out of the canyon. It was a very steep trail, almost straight up a big crack in the canyon wall. There were toe-holds and hand-holds that were cut into the rock by the Anasazis, the 'Old People,' when they lived in the Canyon. Half way up there was a place where my uncle propped up a log and where he had cut notches so you could climb straight up.

"But most of the time I just wanted to stay down in the Canyon. I wanted to feel the sun on my back and to feel its heat on my face. Some of the side-canyons were cool and narrow. If you looked straight up to the sky in one of those narrow canyons you could see the moon in the middle of the day.

"I loved the quiet of the canyon, but if you listened carefully, you could always hear something. There was the sound of the sheep bells and the bleating of my own sheep. You could also hear the sound of a neighbor's sheep in the distance. Sometimes you could hear the strange sound of the braying of a donkey as it echoed off the cliff walls even if the donkey was far away. The grasshoppers and the cicadas would fill the canyon floor with their humming and thrumming. From somewhere up the side of the cliff, the canyon wrens would call, their high notes followed by a trickle down of lower notes. In the air high above, the black crows would circle and make their sound, "*Gah-gee!*" and that's what we Navajos use as their name. And then "Tsip-tsip-tsip!" would be the short cries of the swifts as they make their crazy turns and dives in the air.

"I also began to explore the caves and the houses of the Anasazi, the Old People, even though I knew I wasn't really supposed to go into those places. I'll tell you more about how I started to go into those caves later. But those caves were just the right places to hide in because I knew the Navajo policemen wouldn't go there to look for me. I used to hide in my secret places in one or another of the Anasazi caves, never the same one each time. The *silah-o* came back one time and said they had caught Grey Eyes, and they had sent him off. They said if my mother wouldn't hand me over, they would send *her* off, to the jail at Fort Defiance.

"So they caught Grey Eyes! He had been to school at Fort Defiance before and he said he would never go back. It looked like things were getting pretty serious. Grey Eyes wasn't the kind of boy who could be caught very easily. Let me tell you about him.

"Grey Eyes was my cousin, about a year younger than me, and a little shorter, and not as strong as I was. He was related to me through my mother's side of the family. He was the son of my mother's brother, so he was not of my clan, the T'a chini clan. He belonged to my uncle's *wife's* clan, so he was of the Black Goat clan.

"Anyway, besides being my cousin, Grey Eyes was my best friend. He was just a little bit crazy, but that's why he was so much fun. He was always thinking up crazy things to do. I would usually go along with him, but sometimes I had to say, 'Look, *sik'ess,* my friend, that's enough!' Then he would listen to me because I was older.

"He didn't really have grey eyes. He got his English name when he was sent to boarding school at Fort Defiance the first time. He was sent to school by my uncle's wife's brother.

"'You're just growing up wild,' Hosteen Black Rock told him.

'I've heard about the crazy things you've been doing with your ropes and lassoes. Just because I taught you to weave a rope and how to throw it doesn't mean you have to have yourself killed. It's a lucky thing your cousin Joe Bird was with you when you tried to lasso that mountain lion. Now you're almost thirteen,' Hosteen Black

Rock went on. 'You've got to learn English so you can help your mother. That way, when she goes to the trading post you'll be able to speak for her. Those white traders don't always understand Navajo. And sometimes they'll try to trick you if they think you don't understand English.'

"Well, the first day Grey Eyes got to the boarding school the head of the boys' dormitory asked him his name.

"'*B'nah t'lpahe,*' my friend said.

"That white man thought he knew Navajo but he really didn't. He thought *B'nah t'lpahe* meant 'His Eyes are Grey.' Us Navajos use the same word, *t'lapahe,* for both light brown or tan and also for grey. So that's how my friend got the name `Grey Eyes.'

"He used that name until he was an old man and he died with that name. But when he was a boy his eyes, those crazy eyes, were really light tan, almost yellow, like a cat's.

"But do you know what? When he was beginning to get real old, like I said, and he lived to be ninety, he began to get that grey ring around his eyes the way old people get. Pretty soon that grey ring got thicker and thicker and it covered up all the tan color. So all the white people who got to know him when he was an old man thought 'Grey Eyes' was the right name for him.

"Grey Eyes hated the boarding school from the very first day. He told me about it later.

"'The teachers talk *mean* to you. They make you get up in front of the room and they *yell* at you. They tell you to say a word over and over again. If you keep on getting it wrong, all the girls, and even some of the boys, laugh at you. They make you wear those stiff shoes that hurt your ankles and they make you tie the strings so tight. They hit you if they hear you talking Navajo to your friends. And they make you go to church. You have to sing all those songs about Jesus.

"'Anyway, I figured out a way to get out of that place. One of the janitors in the dormitory, Kee Tsosie, was a member my clan, the Black Goat clan. I told him that the pillow they gave me was too hard and that I wanted to stuff it with yucca leaves. I told him to get me a whole pile of yucca leaves and to hide them in my foot locker when I went to class. That night, after the lights went out, I started to weave a rope like my uncle Hosteen Black Rock taught me. But there wasn't enough. I stuffed some of the yucca leaves in my pillow so Kee Tsosie would think I was really using the yucca for pillow stuffing. The next day I told him some of the other boys wanted yucca for their pillows and I told him to bring me some more. So he kept on bringing more and every night I kept on weaving my rope. Finally, on the fourth night I had enough.

"'When it got real still, and when I didn't hear any more footsteps in the hall or any sound of horses in the street, I tied the rope to the head of my iron bed. Then I let myself down out the window. I hid in the shadows until I was sure nobody was still up or walking around. Nobody saw me. They didn't see the rope until the next morning.

"'I headed west through Bonito Canyon and I ran until it got light. I hid under a juniper bush all day. In the afternoon I heard the sound of slow hoof beats. It was Hosteen Yazzie, an old man I knew from Chinle. He was taking some goods on a string of burros and he was leading them from Fort Defiance to the trading post at Chinle. I told him my mother was sick and that I would go back to school as soon as I got a medicine man for her. I would even help with the burros if he would take me with him.

"'So that's how I got away from Fort Defiance. If I can help it, I will never go back there again.'

"Now I'll tell the story of how Grey Eyes tried to rope the mountain lion.

"Grey Eyes' mother had a burro and she let Grey Eyes herd the sheep and goats that belonged to her. In the fall and winter Grey Eyes' family lived on the north rim of Canyon del Muerto. But with a burro you can travel long distances. Grey Eyes would ride his mother's burro all around Chinle, at the mouth of the Canyon de Chelly (that's what *Chinle* means: 'the mouth of the canyon') and then come up on the south rim to where my mother had our winter sheep camp.

"I was always happy to see Grey Eyes come around the canyon that way. Both of us could ride on the back of the burro together and we would ride all over. The south rim of the Canyon de Chelly is covered with tall sage brushes and they have big, knotty roots. On the burro you don't have to worry about getting your feet caught in those roots. And you can go farther and faster.

"Well, one day Grey Eyes and I were riding the burro on the south rim. He was helping me find a mother goat and her kid that were missing. We searched for the lost goats all afternoon and we had gone many miles to the south and east, almost to the foot of the mountain. The wind was starting to come up from the east. The burro, (us Navajos call burros *Tyelli*) was starting to walk slower and slower. We could tell he was getting tired so we let him rest in the shade of a cedar tree while we just sat on his back. The sun was getting lower and, at that time of the year, it cast long shadows on the ground. We knew we would have to be getting back soon. My mother would be disappointed that we couldn't find her goats.

"Just then we heard a loud scream, 'EEEEeeee!' just like a little boy crying. The hair stood up on the back of my neck. Just then *Tyelli* pointed his ears straight ahead. We didn't see anything at first, but when a burro points his ears, you know something is in that direction. My heart was pounding. Grey Eyes, who was sitting behind me, began to fidget, and I could feel him reaching down to grab his rope.

"She came around from behind one of the big sage brushes, very slowly, a long, tan, smooth mountain lion. We saw her head first. She was carrying the dead, white, fluffy kid in her mouth like a limp rag. She didn't see us because the sun was throwing its long rays into her yellow eyes and because we were standing still in the shadow of the cedar tree. She couldn't smell us either because the wind was coming from her direction.

"The big cat kept on moving slowly. More and more of her body kept on coming out from behind the sage brush. *Tyelli* kept absolutely still all this time and his ears just kept pointing straight ahead like two arrows. Pretty soon we saw the rest of the lion, first her big, floppy, front paws, then her shoulders rippling up and down as she walked. Then we saw the curve of her back, and then her haunches, and then her rear paws. Then, like in slow motion, hanging down at first and then curving up near the end, we saw that long, thick, tan tail, just as long as her body.

"I held my breath. The lion didn't even know we were looking at her. We were lucky so far. I was waiting for the lion to keep on going her way. I was just beginning to breathe a little easier when I saw Grey Eyes reach down and grab his rope. Then, with his rope in his hand, he raised his arm and started to swing it slowly in a smooth, steady motion.

"*Ch'indi!* I hissed, just loud enough, I thought, for Grey Eyes to hear. 'What the *devil* do you think you're doing! Don't even *think* about it!'

"The lion must have seen the movement of Grey Eyes' arm or maybe she heard the sound I made. She turned away from us and, in a flash, her hind end and her tail rose up in the air, and she bounded away. We heard the crash of dried, broken twigs as the lion disappeared behind the thick sagebrushes and then she was gone. Finally we could only hear the rising moan of the wind coming down from the mountain.

"'Crazy, crazy, crazy!' I kept on yelling at Grey Eyes and I kept on yelling because I was still so scared. 'You can't just try to rope a lion like that. Don't you have any *sense*? You need a *gun* and *dogs*! You've got to know what you're *doing*!'

"Grey Eyes slunk down a little bit. 'I was just going to lasso her to a tree,' he said. He knew he almost did a stupid thing.

"*Tyelli* was glad we turned around. We headed back into the setting sun with the cold, pine-scented wind behind us, back to my mother's winter sheep camp.

"Navajos aren't supposed to touch dead people or anything that belonged to dead people. Us Navajos who live in the Canyon in the summertime know that all around us, in the caves in the cliffs, or in some places right on the ground, there are the square stone houses of the Anasazi, the Old People. They used to live in those places but they are now all dead. So we herd our sheep, we grow our corn, we plant our peach trees, and we build our hogans on the soft, level ground in the bottom of the canyon. Navajos never go up into the places where the Old People once lived. *Most* Navajos, that is. But every now and then some Navajos *do* climb up into those ruins. I was one of them.

"Right across Canyon de Chelly from Wild Cherry Canyon, there's a cave with a tumbled down ruin in it. And on the ceiling of that cave, the Old People painted the sky and the moon and the stars. You could see the dark blue paint from far away, but if you got closer, as I did when I herded sheep that way, you could see the moon and some stars in it. I wanted to get a closer look at the painting, but when I was little, my mother warned me not to go up in there. It would have been easy to climb up to that cave because of the tumbled down rocks at the base of the cliff.

"One time when I got older, one of our goats started climbing up the slope that led to the entrance of the cave. I followed the goat and I tried to chase it down. Before I knew it I was standing right on the floor of the cave. I was panting from the climb and I was a little scared to be there. I was careful not to touch anything. But when I looked up at the ceiling I saw what I never saw from below. The big, round, white ball in the middle of the dark blue ceiling was the moon, all right, and the smaller white spots were the stars. But the stars were scattered here and there. I tried to make out any of the constellations I knew, but the painting didn't seem to be a very good picture of the sky at night. But deeper into the cave, where the ceiling sloped down to meet the back wall, there I saw it, a cluster of many stars together. It was a painting of the *Dilye'eh*, the Pleiades. The Old People really *did* know the stars. They knew the *Dilye'eh* just like us Navajos know the *Dilye'eh.*

"There, in that quiet cave, the long dead Anasazi were talking to me. They were saying, 'We, too, knew the *Dilye'eh.* Those are the stars that come up in the east before the sun in the late summer, that are high in the sky in the middle of the night in the winter, and that go down in the west right after the sun in the very early spring.'

"I didn't tell my mother that time that I was up in that cave. I didn't want her to worry about me. I was a little worried myself that something might happen to me because I stood there with the ghosts of the Old People. Pretty soon I realized that I was still all right, that nothing happened to me. So I wasn't afraid anymore. Maybe the ghosts of the Old People couldn't hurt you after all. But I still wasn't going to do anything foolish either.

"The summer after Grey Eyes ran away from school he told me that some white men were digging in the ruins of Antelope House in the Canyon del Muerto. They called it Antelope House because the Old People painted a stick figure of an antelope on the cliff above where they used to live. Later a Navajo artist came along and painted a better picture of an antelope right next to it.

"'The white men dug out a lot of sand,' Grey Eyes said, 'and they found a round room. It was just below the square tower of Antelope house that is still standing.'

"'What do you mean, 'a round room,' I asked.

"'Well, it's like a kiva that the Hopis have and that they pray in. Maybe the Anasazis were like the Hopis.'

"I didn't know the Hopis prayed in round rooms under the ground. Us Navajos pray in our hogans or out under the sky. I was curious because my father was Hopi. I never knew him but I wanted to know more about my father's people.

"From where my mother's hogan was at the mouth of Wild Cherry Canyon it didn't take too long to walk to Antelope House. If you didn't have sheep to herd you could walk there in about two hours. You head out into the main Canyon de Chelly and you go downstream to the west. You pass White House ruin and you go on down to where that big canyon, the Canyon del Muerto, joins the Canyon de Chelly from the north. Then you turn upstream into the Canyon del Muerto for about another two miles. The walls of the Canyon del Muerto are just as tall as those of the Canyon de Chelly, about a thousand feet, and red, red, red, just like the walls of the Canyon de Chelly. There are some trails up to the north rim of the Canyon del Muerto that Grey Eyes' people, the Black Goat clan, use but I've never gone up those trails.

"Antelope House has a two-story stone tower that stands under an overhang of the cliff, and the house stands at the level of the sandy floor of the canyon so it is very easy to get to. I came up to Antelope House one day when none of the white men who dig were there. It must have been a Sunday. It was a little scary to be there all by myself. Even though I had been in the cave with the stars on the ceiling, this was different. The square stone tower was so straight it almost seemed like somebody could still be living there. I looked up into the doorway of the tower that was at ground level. The roof of the tower was gone so there was plenty of light to see inside. The walls still had white plaster or paint on them. There were some square windows at the upper level of the tower. The wooden lintels of the windows and of the door were still sound.

"All over the ground there were bits of broken pottery, even piles of broken jars and dishes. You could still see what were parts of pretty designs on the outside of almost every piece. Usually the designs were in red or black on tan, or else black on white. Even though they were pretty I didn't pick any of them up. They could still be *ch'indi.* If you are Navajo you still have to be careful.

"When I came around the south end of the tower I looked down and there it was, the kiva. There was no roof or ceiling on the room but you could tell the top came up just about to ground level. It was smaller than I thought it would be, just about twelve or fifteen feet across. The walls were lined with stones that were all cut the same size and they were laid down in perfect circular rows. Just above the floor there was a low, stone bench that went all around the room.

"So that was it, the kiva! That was where the Old People prayed and danced and had their ceremonies. I wondered if my father used to climb down into a kiva like this one in his Hopi village. I wondered why he left his people to come almost two-hundred miles, to marry and to live with a Navajo woman. I wondered if he ever knew about this kiva, or the Anasazis, or whether his people had once lived in these canyons. And I wondered whether some of *my* blood had come from a place like this, or maybe even from this very same place.

"I was glad Grey Eyes wasn't with me this time. I just wanted to be alone to wonder about these things.

"After a while I started to walk around the rim of the kiva. I was very careful not to get too close to the edge. I certainly didn't want to fall into the holy place of the Old People. When I'd gone nearly all the way around, I saw what looked like a small bundle lying on the ground. When I got closer, I saw that the bundle was partly unwrapped and some of the old, dry, brown cloth had been pulled away. Someone had been careless to leave the bundle just lying on the ground like that. It must have been the white men who had been digging in the ruin. They would probably come back for it later.

"I came up to have a closer look. I caught my breath when I saw what it was. It was a cradle board, very old and brown and dry, and on the cradle board with the wrapping partly unwound, were the bones of a very young baby! The skull was nearly all gone, but the jawbone was there, and one shoulder blade, and the tiny, tiny ribs.

"I was not afraid somehow to be looking at the bones of a dead person. They were the bones of a *baby.* How can you be scared of a baby? A big lump began to grow in my throat. These ruins that I was starting to go into were not just stone houses or kivas or paintings on the ceilings of caves. These were the places where real people once lived. Maybe they were even my own people. These people had babies, and some of those babies got sick and died, like this one, like the baby of my uncle's first wife, Bah Yazzie. I remembered how that baby died, how it was so tiny, and how it was so still and cold, and how Bah Yazzie wrapped the dead baby on a board and put it into the ground. When I remembered that, and when I saw the tiny bones of the Anasazi baby, I cried, and I ran away from that place.

"I was beginning to get more interested in what the white men were finding in the caves and ruins around Canyon de Chelly. And I was becoming less and less afraid to go into those ruins. But it was Grey Eyes who helped me with my greatest adventure.

"A number of miles south of where the Canyon de Chelly opens into the plain to the west, there is another small and narrow canyon. It runs in the same direction as the Canyon de Chelly, from east to west, and it makes a cut in the same plateau. But it widens out in the west so that people traveling from Ganado in the south going to Chinle hardly notice it.

"Grey Eyes used to hang around Chinle a lot and that's where he heard there was a ruin in that canyon called *Tra Trahzi B'kin* or 'Three Turkey House' ruin.

"'It's very hard to find the mouth of the canyon,' Grey Eyes told me, 'But if you trust me, I'll show you how you can get into the ruin from the top and I'll help you.'

"It sounded like it would be great fun and I wanted to hear more about it. As I told you, Grey Eyes was a little crazy, but if you didn't let him get too far, you would be able to do things you never thought could be done, and yet you could get away with it.

"Grey Eyes was getting better at weaving the strongest ropes. He really thought his rope was strong enough to hold that lion that time. It probably *was* strong enough. I didn't let him that time because he didn't plan for it right. This time he seemed to know what he was doing.

"'I checked out all the bushes at the rim of Three Turkey Canyon just above where the ruin is. None of those bushes is strong enough to hold you. But about thirty feet back, there's an old piñon tree about a foot and a half thick. That's where I'll tie the rope. From there I'll run the rope to the rim and then I'll lower you down.'

"I knew I could trust Grey Eyes to weave a good strong rope but I didn't know how much of an overhang there was. I didn't know if I would be able to swing into the cave once I was lowered down. I might be left hanging in the middle of the air with yet another drop to the bottom of the narrow canyon. But I knew I was going to try it.

"After Grey Eyes tied the rope to the piñon tree, he tied it to my waist and he started to lower me down. After I was let down about forty feet I was able to look into the biggest cave I had ever seen. The ceiling of the cave was smooth and curved. It was about seventy feet from the ceiling to the floor of the cave and it was more than a hundred feet wide. Inside the cave were many, many small houses, maybe ten or fifteen of them. I had never seen so many houses all in one cave like that. It was like a little town. Yet there was nobody there.

"When Grey Eyes lowered me to the level of the floor of the cave, I found I was hanging in mid-air about eight feet away from the rim of the cave. There was no way I could get my foot on solid ground and no way I could climb in.

"So the straight drop to the cave that way wouldn't work. I signaled to Grey Eyes to hoist me back up. But nothing happened! Then I realized that Grey Eyes just wasn't strong enough to do that.

"I shouldn't have listened to that crazy Grey Eyes, I thought. Now it's too late!

"Just then I looked down and I saw the branch of a juniper tree that was growing out from a ledge of rock about six feet below where I was hanging. I hollered to Grey Eyes to lower me down another little bit. I could tell he was scared too, but he let me down until my feet reached the branch. Then I kicked the branch and I started to swing, first away from, and then back to the branch. I kept on kicking and I kept on swinging closer and closer to the rock. I hollered to Grey Eyes to let me down another few feet so I could grab the branch with my hands. He followed my directions and soon I was hanging on to the tree. It bent under my weight and I thought it would break but it didn't. I just hung there for a while as my heart pounded and I tried to figure out what to do next. For a long time I didn't dare to look down. Finally I did look down and saw that, while I still held onto the branch, I could get my feet on a ledge just below where my feet were. I leaned forward and was able to touch the rock with one of my hands and I held on long enough to know I could lean forward and that I would not fall. I was able to let go of the branch now and I crept along the ledge holding on to the rock with my bare hands. A few feet away there was a crack that led up to the cave. I inched along the ledge until I reached the crack, and from there it was an easy climb into the cave. When I got to the level floor of the cave I just stayed on my hands and knees for a long time. I wasn't afraid to touch the dust of the cave where the ghosts of the Old People might be. All I knew was that I was safe.

"I just rested there for a while until I my heart slowed and I could calm down. When I looked up, I saw what I hadn't seen before. Way at the back of the cave there was one large house, larger than all the others, and it had three turkeys painted on the front of it. I had plenty of time to take a good look at how the Old People painted those turkeys. The turkeys had small heads and long necks, and long tails that hung down. Two of the turkeys had white heads, necks and breasts with brown bodies and tails, and one had a brown head, neck and breast with a white body and tail.

"Before I could spend any more time looking at the ruins I had to figure out a way to get out of there and to get home. I looked over the edge of the cave and I tried to guess how far down it was to the bottom of the canyon. It was pretty far, maybe about a hundred feet, but there was a rocky slope about halfway down. I knew Grey Eyes had a long enough length of rope for me to reach that rocky slope. I called to Grey Eyes to release the rope so I could use it. I pulled the rope into the cave and I told Grey Eyes to wait for me at the mouth of the canyon.

"I was still shaking from the scary struggle I had. It's a good thing I didn't look all the way down when I was creeping along that ledge.

"When I looked around I realized that the white men hadn't started digging in this cave yet. I had it all to myself. It was quiet except for the wind and the 'tsip-tsip-tsip' of the swifts and for the fluttering of their wings as they flew in and out of the cave.

"I started to explore a room in the first of the stone houses. When I walked inside, my feet stirred up the dry dust that lay on the floor and the dry dust stung my nostrils. The light was dim inside the room but I could see that the walls in one corner of the room were black and there was some burned-out wood in the corner. A large clay pot with a pointed, black bottom stood almost upright in the middle of what had been a fire. It was as if the Anasazi had just got up and left, and they left the stew pot just where it had always been. I thought they might be back any minute and find me there and say 'What are you doing here in our house?'

"There was a smaller room that I had to crawl to get into. Inside there were some large, clay jars with stones on top of them. When I looked inside one of the jars there were ears of dried corn, but the ears were tiny, no bigger than my thumb. In another jar I found the dried seeds of either pumpkin or squash.

I took handful of these and I stuck them in my pocket.

"It was getting late. The wind began to pick up and it made a moaning sound that was a little scary. I figured it was time for me to get out Three Turkey House ruin and get home. I tied Grey Eyes' rope to a corner of the stone house that was closest to the front of the cave. I looped it through the open door, through one of the open windows and then back to the door where I tied a good, strong knot. Then I started to let myself down off the front ledge of the cave. For the first fifty feet or more I dangled and I swayed a little in the wind. Finally my feet reached the steep slope with many large boulders, and I let go of the rope. My feet started slipping and I set many large rocks loose. Soon, some of the rocks that I loosened on my way down began to roll after me. One big boulder went whizzing by and just missed me. A smaller rock hit me on the ankle. I kept slipping and sliding. The canyon was getting darker and darker and it was harder for me to see where I was going. What a relief it was when I got my feet on the sandy bottom.

" I still had to pick my way around boulders and dead trees that were scattered here and there on the canyon floor. I tripped a few times and landed on my hands but I felt happy to feel the smooth, solid ground under me.

"It was almost night when I reached the mouth of the canyon. Many miles across the valley I could barely see the dim outline of Black Mesa set off by the last red glow of the setting sun. I whistled for Grey Eyes and he whistled back. I suppose he was glad to see me and that I was safe. I thought he would begin to ask me how I got into the cave, what I found there, and how I managed to get out. But all he asked me was, 'Did you bring back my rope?'

"The next spring my mother planted the pumpkin seeds. The seeds sprouted, first the little round seed leaves, then the large pointy leaves. I was excited to see the vines start to grow out over the ground. Soon the blossoms came out, large and fresh and yellow. But the pumpkins that came after the flowers hardly grew and the fruit had no flavor or sweetness. It was if the ghosts of the Anasazi were saying. 'You stole into our storehouse and took what didn't belong to you. Now we'll take away some of the pleasure you thought you would have from us Old People.'

The *silah-o* came back one time saying they'd found my friend, Grey Eyes, and they had sent him off the second time. They said if my mother wouldn't hand me over, they would send *her* off to jail.

"That time I stayed away for two days and two nights. When I came back my mother was crying, 'I thought you fell down somewhere, that maybe you'd broken a leg.'

"I felt sorry for her, that she'd worried so much about me. I felt bad that I was so stubborn, that she might have to go to jail because of me. 'The last wagon-load of children left for Fort Defiance two days ago,' she went on. 'I know the *silah-o* will be coming for me soon. I would have asked your uncle to take you there on his horse but he's away in Utah and won't be back until next month. Now there's no way to get you to school even if you wanted to go.'

"I felt a lump growing in my throat but I wouldn't cry.

"'All right, *Shi'-mah,*' I said. 'I really want to stay here in the canyon with you. I know how hard it will be for you if I go. But it looks like I can't stay. So I'll tell you what I'll do. I'll *walk* to Fort Defiance.'

"*'Shi-yahzh!'* she cried. 'It's over sixty miles to Fort Defiance. And it's dangerous to walk through the forest.'

"'I'll do it,' I said. My mother knew I'd made up my mind.. She didn't argue any further.

"That evening, my mother made up a big batch of corn tortillas and she threw them into a sack with some peaches from her trees. She took her little pouch of white cornmeal for herself and a pouch of yellow corn pollen for me. We hiked up toward the head of Wild Cherry Canyon, but we stopped on the way to fill a clay jug of water from the spring. At the head of the canyon we rested for a while and we looked straight up thc steep trail that went to the top. I wondered how we would manage the climb with the extra load of food and water, but she just slung the load in the shawl on her back and she started up step by step. 'Be sure you don't look down or look back,' she warned me. Then up we went with hands and toes in hand-holds and toe-holds, all the way to the top.

"We rested there on the rim until our hearts stopped pounding and until we caught our breath. I looked down for a last time at my beautiful canyon, now deep in the shadows. I could still see my mother's hogan and the peach trees and the sheep corral. They all looked so tiny, so far down and so far away.

"It was nearly dark now and we camped for the night. 'What are you going to do now, *Shi-mah?*' I called after her when I saw her wandering off toward a clump of cedar trees. She said nothing but she started to strip bark off some of the trees. When she had an armful of bark she sat down and quickly wove the bark into two pairs of sandals for my feet. 'It's a long and rough road to Fort Defiance,' she said, 'And you'll need these.' When the stars came out we could see the Swan coming up on its side. Later in the night the Swan began to turn and to head down to the west. Still later, before the first light in the east, we could see the *Dilye'eh,* the Pleiades, rise above the horizon. 'The summer's nearly over, *Shi-yahzh,*' my mother said, pointing to the cluster of stars with her chin.

"Early the next morning, before the sun was up, my mother stood up and sprinkled the white corn meal in the four directions and said her prayer for me. I hugged her goodbye, and I started out at a run, south and east across the sagebrush-covered plateau. I headed in the direction of the dark green mountain, but it was over twenty miles away. I sang my morning song as I ran and I felt the cool, morning breezes in my face. I turned back now and then to be sure of my direction. Black Rock rose out of the plain on the other side of the Canyon de Chelly to the north. Way off to the west, the sun's rays were beginning to light up the sides of Black Mesa on the other side of the Chinle Wash.

"But I couldn't just keep looking all around. My foot almost got caught on the roots of one of the giant sagebrushes and the ground was getting rocky. It was getting hot on the open plain when the sun rose higher, but I kept on going. After a while the going got even tougher. I entered in to an arroyo that I knew would lead me up to the mountain. But I had to be careful to avoid the boulders and the branches of trees that had been washed down by the rains and that were all over the floor of the arroyo.

"I followed the arroyo for a long way, going uphill all the time. Sometimes the arroyo was so deep I couldn't see over the top of it. One time, when my head was level with the ground above the arroyo, I saw a shadow moving along and following me. I tried to see what it was but it kept on ducking behind the sagebrush that was thick along the way. Finally I saw that it was running on four legs and that it was covered with fur. A *ya n'elgloshi!*, a Skinwalker! I could feel the hairs stand up on the back of my neck. I grabbed a rock and I threw it with all my might. I was good at throwing rocks; with my first rock I hit him. I heard the rock go 'thump' on his chest. He let out a howl and then I saw him run off with his tail between his legs. It was just a *mah-ee yahzha,* a coyote, but a big one. I was happy that I got a good look at him and that he was just a coyote and not a witch in an animal's skin. I was also glad that I saw him run off to the side and that he didn't cross in front of me. That would have been almost as much bad luck as if he'd been a real skinwalker witching me.

"Finally I got to where the forest began. First the piñon trees gave me a little shade here and there on the lower slopes of the mountain. The air was fresher with the smell of the piñon. Later, the air became cooler also from the breezes blowing downhill from the shade of the tall ponderosas.

"My heart was pounding now after the brush with the coyote and with the hard running I'd been doing for nearly four hours. I rested at the foot of one of those great ponderosas and I took my first bite of food. How good my mother's corn tortilla tasted! The peach was hot from the sun and its sweet, sticky juice ran down between my fingers but I didn't care. I took a long drink from the water that had come from the spring in my canyon. It was warm, too, but its taste was pure and it reminded me of home.

"I looked off to the north. Now that I was higher, I could see in the midday haze the red cliffs at the base of the Lukachukai mountains, and on top of them, the gray peaks of the Lukachukais themselves. And off to the northwest, the light fell on Round Rock, that big, round, flat-topped rock that stands in the broad valley of the Chinle Wash.

"I must have fallen asleep for a while, because when I woke up, the sun had swung around to the west. I got up then, stretched, and started out again at a trot south and east into the ponderosa forest. The floor was covered with pine needles and that made it much easier on my feet. I ran along in the cool shade and I felt the cooling breeze in my face once again. Overhead, I heard the wind coming up in the treetops.

"It was all so peaceful, running along like that when, suddenly, I heard a crash behind me. Then there was another crash beyond the trees to my left. I was frightened. I began to think that maybe the animal I had seen near the arroyo *was* a *ya n'elgloshi* after all, and that maybe he and his friends, once they got me in the forest, would try to get even with me. Maybe they were throwing their witching bones at me. But after a while I saw that the crashing noises were just from the big pine cones coming down from those tall, tall trees.

"It was pretty easy heading south and east along the forest floor. I could see where I was going because the forest floor was flat and because there were no large boulders or thick underbrush to block the way. Every now and then there was a clump of oak trees I would have to go around.

"As long as there was enough daylight I was able to keep right on going, but when it was beginning to get dark, I knew I had to find me a safe place to camp. By this time I had been running or walking about fourteen hours. I hadn't seen another person (except maybe that skinwalker, if it *was* a skinwalker) all that time. My feet were getting sore. I'd almost worn out the first pair of cedar-bark sandals my mother had made me but I figured they might last another half-day.

"I found a nice place to lie down. It was in one of those clumps of oak trees. It was a real protected place. Any animal or person or skinwalker couldn't get in without making a noise. It didn't take me long to fall asleep. You can imagine how tired I was. Even when the wind was blowing in the trees making a sound like a person moaning or sighing, it didn't scare me or keep me awake.

"I was stiff and sore all over when I woke up. It was barely light then. I stepped out of my hiding place and I took out my corn pollen to pray. 'Beauty before you, beauty behind you, beauty above you, beauty below you, beauty all around you.' Just as I was raising my arm to sprinkle the corn pollen all around me, I saw somebody standing there about a hundred feet away on the other side of a little grassy meadow. I the dim light I could see he was tall and heavy and that he was wearing something dark.

"'*Yat'eh, sik'ess,*' (Hello my friend), I called out to him. '*Chad ish ahn b'ana nah.*' (What are you doing here?).

"He didn't answer. He turned his head. In the dim light I could see there was something funny about his head. It was too small for his body. He didn't have any neck, and his nose and his chin all came together in a point.

"'EE yah!' I shouted in alarm. '*Shash at eh!*' (It's a *bear*!) When I yelled like that, the bear let out a kind of yell of his own, his front paws flew up and he fell right on his back. Then he scrambled to his feet, let out a big shit, ran off on all fours, and disappeared into the darkness.

"It took me a long time to get over my fright. I was relived that the bear was frightened, too, and that I didn't run into him again.

"When it became lighter I could see that the light was coming from the east and I was more sure of my direction. I headed off again to the south and east. I made as much time as I could while it was still cool. After I ran for a few hours I came to a place where the forest floor dropped off to a lower level and I crossed a large, open meadow. When I looked back over my shoulder, I saw a tall, gray cliff that had ridges on its face from top to bottom. The Navajos call that cliff *Dsilth dah sah ahn,* and the white men call it 'Fluted Rock.' I knew from what my uncle used to say, that if you see that rock, you know you're more than half-way to Fort Defiance.

"I camped out again in an oak tree grove that second night. My first pair of cedar-bark sandals was completely in shreds. I was thankful that my mother had made me a second pair for the rest of my journey.

"When I started out the next day I noticed that the land was sloping down. The tall ponderosas were giving way to piñon, cedar and juniper, but it was still a high plateau. I came to place where, through the trees, I could see a deep, open valley that lay to the east of the plateau I'd been traveling on. A line of pink sandstone cliffs ran along the east side of that valley and the valley ran for many miles from north to south. There were some places where black rocks came up from the floor of the valley. My uncle said one time that the white men told him that those black rocks were once hot liquid that came out of the earth and then cooled and turned hard. Where there was a line of black rock like a wall that ran from east to west, my uncle told me, and where I would see a small canyon with red rock walls where it cuts through the mountain, there I would find Fort Defiance.

"At last I came to the place where I saw that wall of black rock and that red rock canyon. That's where I came down from the mountain. In a narrow valley near the opening of the red rock canyon, I found a two-story building made of red sandstone. Many, many small children were out playing in front of the building. The little girls wore short, cotton dresses, and the little boys wore short pants and long stockings and high-topped shoes. I suppose they were white man's clothes.

"Among the little boys there was a tall boy about my age. It was Grey Eyes! I ran up to him and we threw our arms around each other and we jumped up and down and we laughed. It wouldn't be so lonesome for me after all. Now I was at school at last. I would learn English and my mother wouldn't have to go to jail. As it turned out later, I stayed at Fort Defiance for many years, until I was a fully-grown young man.

"Later I worked for Lorenzo Hubbell at his trading post at Ganado. I hear it's a famous place now, but at that time it was just a little trading post like many others on the Reservation. I was pretty good with horses and mules at that time and that came in handy because we were sent to pick up supplies in Gallup with a wagon drawn by a team of four mules. The roads weren't good enough for the trucks they had in those days so we took the team. It took us two days to get to Gallup and, of course, we had to camp out on the way. Coming back, with the wagon loaded with flour, sugar, coffee, canned goods and hardware it was real hard work going back over the divide. It took us an extra day for the trip back.

"When they were building the new dam at Red Lake, I went to work with the white men from the Bureau of Indian Affairs. We had to level the land below the dam and we had to set out the plan and dig the irrigation ditches. Then we had to distribute the land to different families. The Clevelands, who used to have the whole valley for their sheep, didn't like to have newcomers taking some of their land. They didn't like the T'senjikinnies. They said the T'senjikinnies had plenty of land of their own to the north, at Star Mountain, and to the south and west, at Ganado. But they went along with the project when they were told they would get some of the irrigated land, too. They even made me president of the Red Lake Chapter even though I was married to a T'senjikinnie. We had forty acres of irrigated land in the valley. We built our hogan and our cabin on the slopes above the valley and that's where we herded our sheep, too."

When Grandpa told that part of his story I had a question for him.

"When you fenced those forty acres, how did you dig the post-holes?" When Ida and I first came to Corrales about fifteen years ago, and when we were fencing the gardens behind out house, I learned to use a post-hole digger. With a post-hole digger you could dig a round hole straight down two and a half or more feet into the dirt.

"Grandpa, did you have a post-hole digger? (You see, though Brooklyn-born, I now considered myself something of an expert on life in the West.)

"No," said Grandpa, "We just used a crowbar and a spade. And we cut the cedar posts ourselves and we hauled them down from the mountain." Those fences with their sturdy cedar posts are still there and they mark the work that Grandpa had done nearly sixty years ago.

"I would be home at Red Lake in the spring for planting and irrigating, and in the fall for harvesting," Grandpa continued. "For a good part of the year I was away working on the railroad, the Santa Fe and the Union Pacific, as a section gang foreman. Most of the Navajos on the work gangs didn't speak English, but I would be able to help them and to explain how the work was to be done. The railroad work took me all over the West and the Southwest, from Wyoming to California and from Texas to Arizona."

Grandpa is ninety-nine years old now. He's seen the seasons change with the wheel of time, from the peach orchards and the Anasazi ruins in the Canyon de Chelly, from the ponderosa forests of the Defiance Plateau, from the irrigated fields below Red Lake, and from the grand sweep of the mountains and plains of the West. We still ask for his advice.

"Grandpa, when is time to plant the corn?"

Grandpa Bird always takes a little while but then he answers in his steady measured way, "After the time when you can no longer see the 'Dilyeh'eh,' the Pleiades, go down in the west in the evening, and when the leaves on the cottonwood trees are the size of a squirrel's ears."

BLIND

I.

The air was soft and heavy with perfume of honeysuckle in the Ozark summer night. Cicadas were everywhere and, in the distance, in the dark trees, a mockingbird sang. And into such a magical night Jack Berkowitz, M.D. stepped out of the Fort Leonard Wood hospital laboratory. His senses were keenly tuned to the beauty that now greeted him. He was feeling great joy for what he had accomplished in the microbiology laboratory that day and now he was rewarded by the soft air that brushed his cheek.

The tasks Jack was learning to perform were simple ones. They were, in fact, the techniques of Louis Pasteur of the previous century. But Jack was an optimist. Given the smallest start, the smallest concrete symbol of a new departure and a new future, his spirits soared. He was thankful for the time afforded him in his two weeks of active duty with his Army Reserve unit, the 452nd General Hospital out of Milwaukee, Wisconsin. Here he was able to concentrate on learning what he needed to know to become a research microbiologist.

The first technique he learned was how to seal the top of a sterile glass ampule that contained living organisms using a gas torch. To protect the contained microbes from the extreme heat of the melting tip, the bottom end of the ampule was kept cold by holding it in a beaker that contained a mixture of dry ice and alcohol. This was done in one operation, using the fingers of his left hand to grasp a pair of forceps that held the narrow neck of the ampule, tip up to the flame, while the bottom end remained in the cold bath. Then, with his right hand to hold the torch, he was able to flame the tip. Once sealed and frozen, a specimen could be stored in a dry-ice chest or a freezer for an indefinite period of time.

Next he learned how to make basic nutrient broth and agar from prepared powders and water. He learned how to place the solutions in screw-capped bottles or test tubes and how to sterilize the media in the autoclave. He learned not to fear the hissing of the steam valves, how to operate the ponderous doors of the autoclave, how to read the pressure gauge and to set the timer to assure the sterilization process, and how to vent the autoclave before removing the metal baskets that held the sterilized media.

The next steps were to learn how to enrich the media and how to pour the agar. The melted agar was poured into shallow Petri dishes and covered while waiting for the agar to harden. Jack's early efforts were disheartening. Instead of a perfectly smooth surface so necessary for identifying colonies of microbes or for picking them off the surface of the agar, his first pourings resulted in a surface that was lumpy or irregular, the agar having cooled too much before it was poured. It was the addition of nutrient horse-serum and yeast extract (which contained growth factors for the fastidious organisms he was about to culture) and of the penicillin (to inhibit the growth of competing bacteria) that caused the problem of early cooling. After repeated trials he learned how to add the necessary ingredients to the melted agar at just the right time and at just the right temperature. The agar plates, when cooled, were perfectly smooth. And Jack's happiness carried him out into the night.

Jack had decided to seek a career in academic medicine. He knew he was a good clinician. He'd spent some six years after completing his residency in internal medicine in clinical assignments. These included two years studying new drugs for the treatment of tuberculosis on the Navajo Reservation, two years on the tuberculosis service at Denver General Hospital, and two years on active duty at Brooke General Hospital at Fort Sam Houston, Texas. He knew that now he must select a field of laboratory research. There were challenging problems in certain newly described pulmonary infections. He saw his future as an investigator in these diseases.

While Jack was assigned at Fort Sam Houston he'd become fascinated with cases of non-bacterial pneumonia in young soldiers. Some of these pneumonias were due to viruses. Techniques for isolating these viruses in tissue culture were being developed in special laboratories, but these techniques were difficult, expensive and required long periods of training to master. Other pneumonias were due to a different type of microbe, a microbe of the type that caused a disease in cattle called "pleuropneumonia." Pleuropneumonia-like organisms, were, like viruses, small enough to pass through fine-pore filters, but, unlike viruses, capable of being cultivated outside of living cells on specially enriched culture media. The problem was to identify which cases of non-bacterial pneumonia were due to these tiny microbes and which antibiotics might be available to treat them. Jack felt drawn to doing research in this field. He was challenged with the task of isolating these organisms from patients ill with disease and then later of studying the disease process in detail in a suitable laboratory animal host.

His spirits were high after he was discharged from active duty in Texas. He hoped to return to Denver and to find support for doing this research in the Warren Research Laboratory at the University of Colorado.

"I regret to tell you, Jack," said Robert Wilkins, Jack's former clinical chief and director of the research laboratory, "That you lack the qualifications for appointment here. You've simply spent too much time in clinical medicine."

Since when was it a mistake to spend "too much time" in clinical medicine? Jack thought. Hadn't Robert Koch, the discoverer of the cause of tuberculosis, been a country practitioner? And hadn't Edward Jenner, the man who described vaccination to prevent the dreaded smallpox, been a doctor among people and cows in rural England?

But Jack was unable to bring up these lofty arguments with his former chief. He was too modest to think of himself as one to be compared with such great men. Jack took a teaching position, then, at another university. He was determined to develop whatever research techniques were necessary to pursue his own goal. Now, a few years later, at the modest laboratory at Fort Leonard Wood, Jack felt he was accomplishing what he had set out to do. And so his spirits were high as he stepped out into the beauty of the summer night.

But when Jack returned to the barracks he found them empty. There was no one with whom he could share his happiness. He realized it was a Friday night, the first evening of the first weekend at camp. Members of his unit, the 452nd, had reserved one of the gymnasiums on the base, decorated it, and made it ready for a dance. He heard the music coming from the open doors of the hall and he was drawn to it. He found it brilliantly lit and filled with the familiar faces of the doctors, nurses and enlisted men of his outfit.

"Where have you been all these days?" someone asked. "We've missed you. What have you been doing?"

Jack had been a recluse in the laboratory. His heart was full now. He was happy again.

The music started up. Jack didn't feel he had to talk or to explain what he'd been doing. He simply wished to express his joy in dance. Margaret, the brightest, the most out-going of the nurses was there, smartly dressed and in uniform, with dark eyes, broad smile and high cheekbones. Jack extended his arms to her in a wordless invitation to the dance and she accepted. Jack had learned to be bold at a dance, to be among the first on the dance floor, and to start with prettiest girl.

And so the evening began. The music and the companionship, the easy exchange of greetings and of pleasantries filled the hours. Jack danced with each of the six nurses in the unit. All were good dancers. But Marilyn was perfection.

Marilyn was not strikingly pretty like Margaret but she had a softness and a pleasantness about her and a soft voice, too, though she did not speak much. In the waltz position in the dance, she would position herself very close, raise her left arm high, place the bend of her elbow on Jack's right shoulder, and let her hand fall lightly on his chest. She moved with exceptional ease and she followed Jack's gentlest lead without error.

The doors of the improvised dance hall were open to the night breezes, "Moon River" was the song and Marilyn was Jack's partner with her matchless grace.

II.

During the second week at Fort Leonard Wood Jack stepped out of the laboratory to assume, for a time, his role as a physician. He had the chance to examine a number of young soldiers who'd become ill with pneumonia. The experience here at the army base in Missouri was similar to what he had seen at Fort Sam Houston in Texas. These patients had non-bacterial pneumonia. When he examined their lungs he found they had rales but they did not have the physical signs of lobar consolidation. The x-rays showed patchy infiltration in the lower parts of their lungs on one or both sides.

Pneumococci or other bacterial pathogens were not found in the sputum and the fever did not respond to penicillin. Jack recorded the names of those patients with a brief description of their symptoms and he drew a sketch of their x-rays in a bound notebook as he'd always done in his clinical work. These were the very patients he was looking for. This time he was prepared to capture and to identify the elusive organisms that caused their disease.

The microbes would be found in secretions in the throat and in the sputum. Jack took pains to swab the soldiers' throats himself and to take samples of their freshly coughed-up sputum. So that there would be no loss of viability of the organisms, he innoculated the material directly into the enriched broth that he'd prepared and brought to the bedside. He knew he would succeed.

His spirits rose as went back to the laboratory with his specimens. Here he placed the broth cultures in the incubator. After forty-eight hours, allowing time for the organisms to multiply in the broth, he pipetted the broth cultures into sterile ampules. He looked forward to the next step. With the skill he had so recently mastered, he sealed the ampules. Now the microbes were captured and preserved. He would take them with him when he returned to his laboratory in Milwaukee. Jack also took samples of serum from the same patients, and these too were labeled, frozen and stored.

It was all falling into place, just as Jack had predicted. He'd learned the laboratory skills to match his interest in a certain type of pneumonia. He was happy now with what he'd accomplished.

III.

As the days passed and as the end of the two-week tour of duty came near, the spirit of camaraderie of the staff of the 452nd General Hospital increased. There were more dances the second week of the tour and there was to be a final dance the evening before the unit was to break up and to return home. Jack went to those dances where he knew he would find Marilyn and where he knew she would be waiting for him. That calm spirit, that perfect touch, that faultless movement would be his for a few hours.

Members of the 452nd were accustomed now to see the two as nearly constant partners at the dances. If there were any who suspected a developing, entangling affair, they did not say so. If there were any rumors, or hints, or jests about Jack's dancing with Marilyn, Jack heard of none.

At the dance on the final night at Fort Leonard Wood, a perfect night like all the rest, Marilyn motioned to Jack. A balding, middle-aged man with a pleasant manner was standing at her side.

"Jack, I want you to meet my husband."

Her *husband!* Jack was unable to understand the fierceness of the emotion that came over him. How could she have given so much of herself *knowing* that she was married? He felt betrayed. He could not bear to look at her. Several times during the evening he sensed that Marilyn was trying to catch his eye. He found in her face, when he looked in her direction for the last time, that same soft look that was her invitation to dance. But as he turned away, Jack saw her face change. Now he saw a look of dismay, of entreaty, and of pain.

There was no sense to it all. Jack was *blind!* It hadn't entered his head that *he* was married, that his beautiful wife, Ida, had just given birth to their third daughter, the perfect Rose Rachel, that their oldest child, Yanabah Yonah was a blooming six, that their second daughter, Alice was a sparkling four, that he and his wife were admired as the perfect couple, and that they had just bought a two-story brick colonial house on a quiet, tree-lined street. For all his optimism and enthusiasm for his own work, Jack was blind!

The little world, the encampment of the 452nd General Hospital at Fort Leonard Wood, was about to dissolve. It was the morning that the group would be leaving. In their smart uniforms the doctors and the nurses, the administrative officers and the enlisted technicians lined up in their last formation, the last roll call before boarding the buses that would carry them back to civilian life.

Jack was still blind. Marilyn was standing in line with the other nurses. All but she appeared high-spirited with the prospect of going home. Jack allowed himself a glance in her direction. He found that she, too, was trying to find him, trying to extract from him one last look of kindness. He could not forgive her. He could not erase that expression of cold anger from his face. Blind!

ELIHU'S DEATH

My brother Elihu was only seventeen months older than I was. We were close enough in size when we were little to be thought of as twins. In an old photograph I remember we sat side-by-side in a wide, twin size wicker stroller dressed alike in 1920's style leather aviator helmets while our mother, Cecile Berkowitz, in a "cloche" hat, stood proudly behind us.

We were particularly close companions again after we moved from Brooklyn to Washington Heights. I missed the tree-lined streets of the Boro Park neighborhood we'd come from, but there were compensations living in the upper reaches of Manhattan. At the level of 162nd Street, Manhattan was only a slender plateau just a few blocks wide. Wooded parks along the slope leading down to the Hudson River on the west, and down the steeper slope to the Harlem River on the east provided for us open views of a different sort and opportunities for exploration and adventure.

During that first winter in Manhattan we took the Flexible Flyer sled we'd brought from Brooklyn and we pushed northward along the level, snow-packed, wooded trail that ran halfway between the edge of the plateau, the street level above, and the Harlem River below. We imagined we were in a northern wilderness, one or the other of us running and pushing from behind, or sitting on the sled and being pushed. We headed north into the wind. The frigid air seared our lungs. Our cheeks smarted, and our fingertips, in spite of the gloves we were wearing, burned with the cold. We soon came to High Bridge, a high-level aqueduct of Roman design with a foot-path along the top that brought us across the river to the Bronx. On steep-sloping, snow-covered streets we spent the late afternoon belly-whopping down the hills until the sun dipped low in the west. Then, tired and happy, we dragged the sled behind us and walked back across the bridge. We looked down from the tall, stone arches on the Bronx side and hoped to catch sight of a train running north from Grand Central Station along the tacks of the main line of the New York Central Railroad below. Then, over the cold, gray river that was spanned by the bridge's central steel-arch, we reached the trail on the Manhattan side that led us home.

When our childhood and our boyhood ended we went our separate ways. Elihu was brilliant in mathematics. He followed our older brother, Howard, to the University of Michigan and Elihu entered the College of Engineering. The first year he was away, I was so absorbed in senior class activities in my last year in high school, I had no reason to be envious of Elihu's new life in the Middle West or to miss him. There could be no thought of following him there, because, within the next year I became ill. First there was fatigue, fever, and cough. Then x-rays of my lungs showed a cavity that was clearly due to tuberculosis. I was forced to take to my bed at home, and received, at that time, what was considered to be good treatment, artificial pneumothorax, designed to put the lung at rest and to promote healing. When I was better, I was able to go to school at City College but it was necessary for me to remain in New York to continue my treatment. From City College, I went on to medical school in the city.

My brother chose chemical engineering. When he found that the computer could assist in calculations in chemical engineering in one of his early jobs in Louisiana the early 1950's, he seized upon a new career in computer science. By 1953 he was called upon to develop a new department of computer science at the University of Houston. He became an early expert and educator in the field, writing textbooks on the FORTRAN computer language. Soon he become editor of one of the new journals in the rapidly developing field. As his reputation grew he was invited to spend sabbaticals at the Massachusetts Institute of Technology and at Stanford and to give papers at international conferences abroad. After some twenty years he was recruited as a senior professor of computer science at the University of Utah in Salt Lake City.

I stood in awe of my now-illustrious brother, but at the same time I loved him. Elihu looked at my own career in medicine. My interest in new developments in the treatment of tuberculosis, then to research in atypical pneumonia, led me to become director of the University of Colorado's teaching medical service at Denver General Hospital.

"I wonder how you do it, Jack," he would say. "You seem to have such peace of mind." This was an expression of his old rivalry with me, his younger sibling. But I know he loved me as I loved him.

Elihu's work in Louisiana led him to meet and marry Betty Beauchamp from Shreveport and they had two sons. My studies in tuberculosis led me to the Navajo Reservation in Arizona. There I found an exotic culture and an exotic Navajo beauty, Ida Bird. We married and have three daughters and a son.

Quite unexpectedly, when he was fifty-one, a periodic physical examination and a routine blood count showed that Elihu now had chronic lymphatic leukemia. My heart sank when he told me this. I'd been attending a meeting in Salt Lake City. To shake off the shock of it, I walked many miles one night from the central part of the city along South Temple with its once-magnificent mansions, to where my brother lived near the foothills.

During the first years of his illness Elihu had no symptoms but he knew the disease would manifest itself in time.

"I know I will not live a normal life-span," he said in his matter-of-fact, uncomplaining way, wishing not to cause me pain or sorrow. But in time he began to have increasingly frequent infections, then progressive loss of weight. In spite of these signs of the advance of his disease he continued in his work. He helped to design more powerful computer chips and a way to join individual computers into networks, the Nexus system.

Before long, telephone calls from Elihu's wife, Betty, became more frequent. Elihu was suffering more serious infections. These telephone calls would cause me great anxiety and I would offer what advice I could. When my brother became sick enough to require going into the hospital, I would fly to Salt Lake City, to consult with Elihu's doctors, to review the hospital chart, and to help Betty just by being there. Betty was brave.

"I feel better knowing what the exact facts are," she would say.

Elihu than had another very serious infection, the "shingles" in widespread form, disseminated herpes zoster. He was left this time with such severe pain from neuritis that he was unable to eat. His weight fell to one-hundred fifteen pounds. His doctor, Dr. Rothstein, arranged for Elihu to be fed intravenously.

Elihu's time was short now in the eighth year of his disease. I arranged for a visit in the summer at what might be a happier time, not one of those forced emergency trips when Elihu was in the hospital. With my family and our first grandson we drove from Albuquerque where we had settled and where I had gone into private practice.

We drove over the changing Western landscape, through miles of sculptured red rock country with its backdrop of green, snow-capped mountains, to Moab. There we crossed the brown and roiling Colorado River, and on to an ashen desert where we crossed the Green whose waters made green the melon fields.

We needed this distraction before seeing the sick man, my brother. We followed the railroad across more desert, then up winding canyons to the cool summit of the Wasatch Mountains and then down into the Utah Valley. Our reward were pleasant hours with Elihu in the shaded patio of his home. Though thin and drawn, he took delight with our visit and he smiled at the bright toddler, the grandnephew we brought to see him.

The final series of events were periods of high, recurring fever. We thought at first the fevers were due to infections in the sinuses or to abscesses in the liver. The fevers were, in fact, due to the rapid progress of the leukemia itself. Elihu's disease was in its pre-terminal phase. He'd been making increasingly frequent trips to the hospital. He was weary of the painful needles, of the endless blood tests, and finally of the biopsy of the liver that was complicated by bleeding. Near the end, his platelet count dropped to such dangerously low levels that spontaneous bleeding occurred. Elihu refused any further blood or platelet transfusions. In spite of daily elevations of his temperature and growing weakness such that he could hardly stand he continued to teach his classes. Finally, no longer able to go on, he took to his bed at home.

He called for his sons, Allen and Joseph, for his friends on the faculty, and for his friends from the synagogue he'd helped to found to bid his goodbyes. On the telephone he described to me the gathering around his bed.

"Everybody's so serious it's almost funny!" It was if he was disembodied, already looking on in curious, detached amusement.

The next day he became progressively weaker and a hemorrhagic rash appeared. When I called that night to ask Betty how he was, Elihu himself reached for the phone.

"Jack," he said hoarsely, and then, no more. He'd dropped the phone out of his hand.

The next day, our oldest daughter, Yanabah, and I flew to Salt Lake City. Allen met us at the airport.

"I didn't think he would make it through the night," was his report.

In the upstairs bedroom, his eyes closed, Elihu lay near death. He moaned periodically, unable to speak. He moved his gray, pitifully thin arms about aimlessly. Betty and Joseph were at the bedside.

"Elihu," Betty said, "Jack is here."

Elihu gave no word or sign of recognition.

I turned away into the next room and I wept.

He's separating himself from us already! He just *wants* to hurt us by his dying, I thought as my tears flowed. Then, when my pain subsided at last, I understood, and I understand it to this day. The dying do not intend to cause us pain. It is the *separation* from us that causes the pain. *That* is the cause of the pain of death after all.

When I was calmer I went back to the bedroom where Elihu lay. It was possible for me to be more clear-headed. Elihu, by raising his arms, seemed to be asking for someone to pull him up. And this meant that he was probably short of breath. I ordered oxygen and he didn't object when I placed the prongs of the nasal cannula in his nostrils.

I sat at Elihu's bedside for many hours without his making any effort to communicate with me. When darkness came, my spirits waned once again. I needed some relief, some diversion. I dressed in warm clothing and I went out into the snow-covered streets that night. It was December, and Salt Lake City had had a heavy snowfall several days before. Fog had settled over the valley for many days excluding the sun and the snow lay about without melting. When I returned to the house I was happy to find that Rose Rachel, our youngest daughter, had flown in to Salt Lake City that same winter night and there was comfort in that.

After a night of more restlessness and moaning, Elihu appeared even weaker.

"How long can he go on like this?" Betty asked.

"One can never tell; he might go on for another day or two," I said.

"I feel so helpless," she said and she wept.

I saw now that Dr. Rothstein had left an indwelling intravenous needle in Elihu's arm.

"We can give him some morphine," I said. "That might relieve some restlessness and shortness of breath."

Joseph and I drove to the hospital pharmacy and picked up a prescription that Dr. Rothstein had left for four vials of morphine. Now I was physician as well as brother and comforter. I drew up the contents of one of the morphine vials into a syringe and I trembled a bit as I injected it through the rubber cap of the needle.

"What are you doing?" Elihu asked in a very weak, hoarse voice.

Elihu had spoken!

"We're giving you something to help you," Betty said.

I remained at the bedside and I counted the respirations. I was hoping I'd not given too much. After a while Elihu spoke again and he said,

"Thanks, Jack. That helped."

Elihu knew I was there! I'd never experienced such joy in the setting of such sadness. The pain of separation I'd felt so keenly the day before was gone.

'Did you hear that?" I asked Betty, and she said yes, she'd heard Elihu say it.

The relief the morphine gave didn't last long. Within an hour or two I gave two more doses but there was no apparent response to these injections. Elihu spoke no more. He showed signs of still more restlessness, motioning for someone to help him sit up.

"Can we give more oxygen?" Joseph asked, and I turned up the dial on the tank to four liters.

I noticed that the pulse at the wrist would disappear when Elihu was sitting up but that it would return when he would lie down again. After the last time Elihu was helped up and then helped to lie down again, I could no longer feel the pulse at the wrist but I could still feel a pulse in his arm. This had to mean that Elihu's blood pressure was falling; I could tell this even without a blood pressure cuff.

Elihu was getting more restless now. He was gesturing to be helped to sit up more often. There was only one dose of morphine left.

Betty and I were at the downstairs kitchen telephone trying to reach Dr. Rothstein at the hospital for more morphine when, from the upstairs bedroom we heard a sudden, hoarse cry, and then the sound of sobbing. We rushed upstairs, both of us thinking for a moment that it was Elihu who had cried out. When we came to the door we found it was Joseph sobbing, his father in his arms. Elihu had stopped breathing. The anguished cry had been his son's.

Joseph and I set Elihu's lifeless, gray body down on the bed. I gathered Elihu's two sons, his wife, and my daughters at the foot of the bed and I led them in reciting the *Kaddish: "Yisgadal v'yiskadash sh'may rabboh."* "May the great name (of the Allmighty) be magnified and sanctified." Elihu's suffering had ended.

I embraced them all and we wept some, but mixed with the sadness we experienced a sense of relief. The tears were now ending. There were important telephone calls to make: to the mortuary, to the rabbi, to other members of the family, and to colleagues at the university. Later in the day there was a call from the mortuary to come to make arrangements for the funeral. The mortuary building was once one of the grand houses on South Temple, that broad street of proud mansions that ranges up the hill from Temple Square, the same street I had walked when I first learned of Elihu's fate nine years before. The funeral directors handled Jewish burials among all others. A plain pine coffin was Elihu's wish and we chose one of those.

The next day the mortician called to say the "washers," (the *chevra kedusha,* or the ritual burial preparation committee from the synagogue, whose function it is to wash, dress, and prepare the body for Jewish burial) had completed their work. The family could now view Elihu for the last time since the coffin would be closed for the funeral service. Elihu lay in a clean, unstained pine casket dressed in a white *kittel,* or shroud, with a *tallis,* or prayer shawl over his shoulders and a *yarmulke,* or skull cap on his head. In death his nose was thin and aristocratic. In his life he had come the full circle. Now, as he'd wished, he would be buried as a Jew. Betty, Allen and Joseph, and my daughters, Yanabah and Rose Rachel and I made our goodbyes in silence and then we came away without tears.

I felt the gloom and the sadness ebb away as the house filled with close relatives. Betty insisted that everyone stay together, that none stay away in a motel. Allen and Joseph were busy driving to the airport to bring home new arrivals. Betty's mother, Mary Beauchamp, a grand lady from Shreveport walked with a cane but she knew everybody's first name and we called her "Grandmary." Betty's sister, Barbara, came with her husband, Sam. Yanabah and Rose Rachel took over many of the household chores, preparing meals and straightening up. I helped in meeting with the rabbi and in writing the obituary for the newspaper.

A fire in the fireplace brought more comfort and we gathered round it, telling family stories and stories about Elihu without pain. Betty's two sisters-in-law, my wife, Ida, and my older brother, Howard's, wife, Basha, arrived the following day and so there was more comfort, more conversation, and more help.

The funeral service two days later was attended by some two-hundred friends, members of the faculty and students from the university and by friends of Betty and members of her church. The rabbi's eulogy described Elihu's work; he had no hobbies. He was devoted to his family and he wished to be identified with the Jewish community.

Elihu was buried on a cold, gray day when snow and ice lay on the ground in the B'nai Israel Cemetery, a portion of Calvary Cemetery at the foot of the rounded, treeless hills north and east of Salt Lake City. In the latter half of the last century the Mormons had provided a place for burial of Jews who lived in their community. The rabbi recited the "*El Moleh Rachamim,*" ("The Lord is full of compassion.") My throat tightened and tears came again as I felt the power of those words in the ancient language that Elihu and I had known since our childhood. Then the rabbi led us in the "*Kaddish,*" and we recited the responses in words that do not mention death or pain but which call upon us to praise the great name of the Almighty. The rabbi threw a handful of earth on the unstained, pine coffin, and then Elihu was lowered into the grave.

Out of the cold once more, the house was warm with friends, neighbors, colleagues and students. Neighbors brought in platters of turkey, kosher salami, cheese, bread and cake. I visited with many who had known and loved my brother and it helped to ease the pain of death and the loneliness. Many of them said I looked like Elihu, that my manner, speech, and gestures were much like his. (After all, we were almost twins.) They said it gave them comfort that something of Elihu still lived.

The rabbi returned with several members of the "*Kol Ami,*" ("Voice of my People") Congregation of which Elihu had been a founding member, and with a minyan, a quorum of ten, he led the evening service. The rabbi read the Twenty-third Psalm in Hebrew and in English and he led the mourners once more in the "*Kaddish.*"

That night the cousins, Allan and Joseph, and Yanabah and Rose Rachel, bedded down in sleeping bags on the living room rug in front of the fire. I was still too moved by the emotions of the day for any further conversation, so I dressed warmly and went out again to find comfort in the night. I trudged for more than an hour through the snowy streets of the neighborhood, the houses decorated now with Christmas lights for the approaching holiday.

EPILOGUE

Everyone flying into Salt Lake City that season experienced it. The whole of western United States lay under a dome of high pressure, with clear, cold air above trapping fog in the mountain valleys below. At night and in the early morning the moisture of the fog would precipitate as fine ice crystals on the metal surfaces of parked cars and on the iron railing that lead up to the house. Though fog lay over the valley for many days, nearby ski areas at higher elevations were enjoying sunny weather.

We'd been house-bound for many days and we longed to see something of the sun. The families at Elihu's house piled into two automobiles. Joseph and Allen, who knew and loved the mountains and the countryside, drove the cars and they took us up out of the fog-bound valley. We climbed up Emigration Canyon, the route by which Brigham Young had led his followers down from the Wasatch Mountains into the Salt Lake Valley one hundred forty years before. After we climbed some two-thousand feet we saw the sky at last, at first veiled by a thinning mist, then clearly the deepest, most stunning blue. On a snow-packed, sunlit hill, on sleds, inflated inner tubes or on flattened pasteboard cartons children came sliding down in greatest merriment. Then we drove through the broad, snow-covered upland valley past farms and mountain farming communities drenched in the sunlight. But the December sun began its early descent, and sinking, illuminated the west-facing hills with pink.

Sam, Barbara's husband, was unaccustomed to such sights of mountain landscape. He asked to stop the car so he could take a picture of the sunlit hills. At that moment, my cleared-eyed wife, Ida, saw a very large, black bird approaching with slow, measured wing beats. It was followed by a quarrelsome pair of magpies. The great bird wheeled as if in disdain, and as he turned, he showed white on his head, neck, and tail. It was a bald eagle! We were all excited to see such a majestic bird. Binoculars which Betty brought were passed around so that all of us could see the great eagle. He landed on the upper branches of a small juniper tree, his weight causing the branches to bend, and then his large body was carried up again with the rebound. Through the binoculars I was able to see clearly his giant yellow beak. I had seen a bald eagle once before in the wild, flying high over a mountain valley in Colorado, but never close enough to see the beak, that powerful destroyer of flesh. At last the eagle lifted his folded wings, jumped off his perch, and with powerful downstrokes of those wings, now fully extended, he flew off.

We followed the eagle's flight until he disappeared behind a promontory of the mesa, flying into a nearby side-canyon. We hurried into the automobiles and set out in pursuit, hoping to catch one more glimpse of the great bird. We were happy to find him again, flying in the side-canyon. The eagle then came closer, crossing our path as it flew to the west across the broad valley. Confident and powerful, it was clear that he *owned* the valley and air above the valley. Near the high ground on the other side of the valley, the first eagle was joined by a second eagle and the two flew to the north in the gathering darkness.

Our spirits remained uplifted even after we went down into the gloom of the fog-shrouded city. For many days after we carried with us the memory of the flight of the eagle.

MY REAL NAME

Jack Berkowitz submitted a short story under a pseudonym to the *Hudson Valley Literary Review.* Jack's story was not accepted for publication, but Maureen Bray, the founder, editor and publisher of the *Review* invited Jack to a social afternoon at her home, Apple Hill House, at Croton-on Hudson to meet with her and with a group of writers (contributors and would other would-be-contributors) like himself.

So on a breezy, late-summer afternoon, with dryness and heat in the air and just before the leaves began to turn, Jack took the train north from Manhattan. How good it had sounded to Jack to get out of the City. It should have been a relaxing ride as the train sped along the eastern shore of the Hudson River. The gentle swaying of the rail coach and the double clicking of the wheels were soothing to the few scattered passengers on the nearly-empty car. As the train raced north, the river widened, presenting the pleasant prospect of the sun's reflection on the broad expanse of the Tappan Zee. But Jack was becoming increasingly nervous. He had decided to introduce himself to Maureen, whom he had never met, using the name he'd used in his correspondence, his pseudonym, "Bernard Moiseivitch." But there was no joy in this plan for him. Intentional deception was not his style.

Meeting new people had never been particularly easy for Jack when he was younger, but as he made progress in his career as a biologist, he became more self-assured. He had done graduate work at Harvard. The name, Jack Berkowitz, M.D., was now recognized as that of a solid contributor in biomedical science. Jack was co-author of a series of studies developing a model of respiratory disease due to mycoplasma in gnotobiotic mice.

Jack was able to face the world as "Jack Berkowitz." With his later work using electron microscopy and immunofluorescence to localized the mycoplasma organisms at the surface of the bronchial epithelium, Jack became a regular speaker at the annual meetings of several scientific societies. His early fears of rejection because of his Jewishness and his Jewish name melted away. At Harvard he learned to wear only blue oxford cloth, button down shirts, plaid bow-ties, Harris tweed sport jackets with suede elbow patches, light beige chino trousers, Argyle socks, and comfortable brown leather loafers. But he would go no further than this in adopting protective coloration. He would not change his name.

Jack had seen many Jews change their last names to get on in a hostile world where "Restricted" meant "No Jews or Negroes Allowed." But Jack held such Jews in contempt. He thought it pitiable when a Weinstein changed his name to "Winstin," or a Silverstein to "Sterling." Jack found it ludicrous that those who changed their last names still clung to their identity by holding on to their first names, Melvin "Fowler" from Melvin Feinberg, Stanley "Wardlow" from Stanley Warshower, Aaron "Curtis" from Aaron Cohen. To hold on to those first names was a dead giveaway. Jack would have none of it.

But when Jack began to write fiction, basing his tales on his youthful romances, he decided to use a pseudonym because his wife, a fiercely proud but jealous woman, objected to the idea of his writing that kind of story in the first place. One early piece that she got to see galled her in particular.

"Why are you writing about that woman? She must be an old grandma by now," forgetting that she was a grandmother of five herself. "And besides, she jilted you, yet you still go on pining for her!"

In his using a pseudonym, Jack wanted to project something of himself, using a name as Jewish as his own and perhaps even more foreign-sounding. It was if he was starting all over again saying, "Take me for what I am or not at all." The name would be a kind of code name for himself, like a puzzle or a joke that only those who really knew him could figure out. His real name, the one by which he had been called up to the Torah at his Bar-Mitzvah, was "Yaakov Dov-Bear ben Moishe." So "Dov-Bear" became "Bernard," (a name that many Jewish boys were given at the time Jack was growing up) and "Moiseivitch," Russian for "Moishe's son."

When the train pulled in to the suburban station at Croton-on-Hudson, Jack felt he was about to step into that "Restricted" world he'd imagined as boy. It seemed that the train station itself with its gabled roof, its neat platform, its perfectly trimmed lawn, its shrub-bordered, small parking lot, now empty on the week-end, hadn't changed since the turn of the century. A taxi took Jack through the town which, it seemed, stood unchanged by time. Tall, pleasant elms shaded the greenery that surrounded turreted Victorian houses with their open porches all across the front and sides. Gracious, two-story carriage-houses stood further back from the street, the upper story for the servants' quarters. Solid coarse stone graced the outside of the Romanesque-style Methodist church. A polished corner-stone bore the marking, "Founded 1906," and Jack thought, That's the year my father Moishe arrived in America from Poland. The Presbyterian church on the next block was of red brick with pointed Gothic windows and a square cathedral tower. The Episcopal church nestled close to the ground, surrounded by dense, well-trimmed shrubbery and it had the finest slate roof that would last a thousand years.

The cab brought Jack to the western edge of the town where Apple Hill House stood on a rise. From below, all Jack could see of the view was the bright sky beyond the house. The tall, three-story, red brick home with its period Mansard roof cast a long shadow as Jack climbed the hill. Only a few cars had arrived. It was early but Jack was able to see several figures on the lawn above the driveway. He heard the clinking of glasses and the murmuring, polite sounds of the guests greeting one another. Jack didn't feel he was ready to make a frontal assault up the steps to the main entrance, so he entered the house through the rear, kitchen door.

He tried to appear nonchalant when he came face-to-face with the first person he met, a short, middle aged lady with glasses.

"Hi, I'm Bernard." He'd broken the ice. Here he was with his false name. He heard himself pronounce the name "Ber*nard*" with the accent on the second syllable. It didn't sound quite right. Maybe I should have rehearsed it, he thought. Maybe it would go down better if I'd pronounced it "*Bern*ard." Whichever way, it was a lie. He felt sorry he'd deceived the lady. He was so preoccupied with his deception that he couldn't think of anything meaningful to say by way of conversation. He was suffocating. He escaped by way of the front door and out onto the west-facing lawn. Here at last there was a fresh breeze, the smell of newly-cut grass and a pungent hint of open water. The house commanded a view of the shimmering

Hudson River, of the rounded, tree-covered hills of the opposite shore and of the open expanse of the Tappan Zee to the south.

For a few moments he felt liberated from the fix he'd gotten himself into. He found a place on a bench on a great porch that looked out to the west where several other guests had also decided that was the best place to be.

"Hi, Im *Bern*ard," Jack said to a young man on his left. (Still doesn't sound right, he thought). Richard (that was the young man's name, and Jack was sure that *was* his name) was talking the kind of talk one hears at that sort of gathering.

" I submitted my proposal to forty different publishers," Richard said, "and six of them responded positively. The book is an environmentalist's tour guide to the rain forest of Belize. You know how important it is to get that book done before the rain forests are all gone."

Wow, Jack thought. *That's* a subject that is bound somehow to click. It's not just a dressed-up personal memoir like my story.

A tall, willowy woman, Joan, with a pleasant, strong face, deep-set eyes and a prominent chin sat on the porch railing. Her long, slightly grey-streaked hair was haloed in the low-lying sun.

"I travel to different cities for the Bureau of Housing and Urban Development, and New Orleans was my most recent stop. It just breaks your heart to see the Blacks displaced from their homes because of the gentrification of their neighborhood beyond the Vieux Carre."

"Hi, I'm Ber*nard Mohsay*ivitch," Jack said, finding Joan a woman of charm, intelligence, and character. Things are *happening* in this world that people *want* to read about, he thought, not just old love stories. And here I've messed it up again. First I couldn't decide between *Ber*nard and Ber*nard.* And then at the last minute I couldn't decide how to pronounce the last name. Nobody would pronounce a Russian name '*Mohsay*ivitch' when it should be pronounced '*Moysay*ivitch' like the Russian pianist Benno Moiseivitch.

Jack wandered back into the house where many rooms on the ground floor were filling up with more guests. He decided he would do better not to introduce himself to anyone else.

A woman behind him stood on her toes and waved to a slender young woman entering the living room from the kitchen.

"Maureen!" she shouted.

Jack found it difficult to believe that the founder, editor, and publisher of the *Hudson Valley Literary Review* would be so young and beautiful. She was of medium height, and had her light-colored hair bobbed in the style of the twenties. She wore a simple white blouse and a long, mid-calf length grey skirt. She had eyes of the palest blue, almost white, and an earnest smile that showed as much gum as teeth. She couldn't have been more than thirty-eight or forty.

"Maureen Bray! I'm so glad to meet you at last," he said, avoiding the false name and feeling the confidence he would have had as Jack.

"I'm Ber*nard*," he said, finally introducing himself.

" I've read your story," Maureen said. "I want to know more of what Anne, the girl from Arizona, felt when she got to New York."

Jack's head swam. Maureen had remembered every detail of his story. And she'd picked out the very weakness in it that had troubled him. He determined in his mind to fix the deficiency in the story immediately.

"Ber*nard*, how do you pronounce your last name?" Maureen asked with a smile that nearly melted Jack to the floor.

*"Moysay*ivitch," he answered, switching this time to the correct Russian pronunciation. Lies, lies, lies, he exclaimed to himself, and he made some pretense to move away.

Jack mingled with the crowd without pleasure and he headed for the table with wine, crackers, and cheese. A soft, leather-bound guest book lay on the table. When he opened it he found that several signatures were there already. He reached for his pen and wrote "One day I'll tell you my real name." and he signed it "Bernard Moiseivitch."

Maureen Bray proved to be a skilled and perceptive editor. Jack's second story dealt with myths and devils. After some correspondence and Maureen's suggestions for re-writing, Jack's story was accepted for publication in the *Hudson Valley Literary Review.*

At the last minute Jack decided he would have his story published under his real name and he told this to Maureen in his correspondence. She accepted this without comment at the time.

They met again several months later at a restaurant in the Roosevelt Hotel in New York where she came to present Jack with the (customary) author's five free copies of the issue of the *Review* that contained his story.

Maureen looked a little different this time. She had let her hair grow out and had let it become darker. Jack felt it much easier to talk with her now since he was not using a false name.

"Did you ever read what I wrote in your guest book last summer?" Jack asked.

"Yes, I read it that very day. And I knew it for what it was, an appeal of some sort. And that is what drew me to you."

IN SEARCH OF THREE TURKEY HOUSE RUIN

The celebrated Canyon de Chelly lies just a few miles north of the place where I became lost. But I will tell about that later. A paved road on the south rim of that famous canyon leads to well-marked turn-offs and to overlooks where visitors can look into the canyon's depths. Visitors marvel at the sheer, red rock walls nearly one thousand feet in some places. The ancient Anasazi stone houses that cling to narrow ledges or that lie protected in the overhang of shallow caves bring to those visitors a sense of the passage of time, to the many centuries before, that people once lived there.

By contrast, the Three Turkey Canyon that lies about five miles south of the Canyon de Chelly, is not accessible by paved road. There is a graded road south of this smaller canyon that roughly parallels it but there are no markings to the trails that lead to its south rim. There are no signs to identify points where the principal attraction of this canyon, the Three Turkey House ruin, can be viewed. The ruin called by this name is a cluster of many stone house houses in a large cave in the south-facing wall of this canyon. It takes its name from a pictograph of three turkeys painted on the wall of one of the houses at the rear of the cave.

It is the inaccessibility of this site which adds to its mystery and for some years I wanted to see it with my own eyes. My wife's father had told of his finding that ruin as a young boy and of his entering that ruin by having lowered himself down into it from the rim. So that ruin held particular fascination for me and I was determined to find it and to photograph it.

I had made several unsuccessful attempts to find it by myself but I didn't succeed. One time I was able to identify a dry stream bed as the beginning of Three Turkey Canyon where it crossed the graded parallel road. With my camera and tripod I started to hike down the canyon going west, confident that I would find the ruin a short way further downstream. Making my way was somewhat difficult because of the many boulders and shallow pools of water along the bottom, but I knew I was headed in the right direction since the walls of the canyon on either side were becoming progressively higher. When the canyon made a sharp turn to the northeast I was certain I would find the cave and the ruin right around the bend but I was mistaken. The canyon took another turn to the west and then another to the north. I was certain that with each new turn Three Turkey House would come into view but I was repeatedly disappointed. I had walked now more than two hours and it was getting hot. I'd not taken the precaution of carrying water nor had I left word, in case I became injured, (twisted an ankle or broken a leg) of where I was headed and where I might be found. Since I was carrying the camera and tripod in one hand (I hadn't thought to carry them in a backpack) that left me somewhat unbalanced walking over the uneven ground and increased the likelihood of a fall. When I realized all these potential dangers, I turned back. Good sense prevailed. I was happy to find my truck where I'd left it where the stream crossed the road.

The Three Turkey House ruin continued its hold on me. I was determined to find it and to see it. On the next opportunity I had to search for it, I hired a guide at the headquarters of the Canyon de Chelly National Monument a few miles away. Alice Anagal, a forty-year veteran guide knew every inch of Canyon de Chelly, but she confessed she was not as familiar with Three Turkey Canyon. She'd been there only once many years before.

We piled into my truck nevertheless and found the graded road that runs west toward the community of Nazlini and that lies south of the openings of both the Canyon de Chelly and Three Turkey Canyon. In the distance across the plateau to the north we could see what we were certain was the top of the north wall of the canyon we were looking for. But which of several unmarked smaller dirt trails would lead us to the canyon rim? Which one of them might lead us to where we could get a glimpse of the ruin we were looking for?

My guide chose one track which seemed to be heading in the right direction but that road did not lead us to the canyon rim. She suggested we stop at a place where the land was beginning to slope downward. From there we hiked down an arroyo which led us at last to the bottom of the Three Turkey Canyon. My guess was that we were at a point somewhat to the west of the place where I had abandoned my search several weeks before. I was certain now that if we continued downstream in a generally westward direction we would find the ruins.

The Turkey Canyon here was about three hundred feet deep and a mere thirty to fifty yards wide. Its walls were of wind-deposited sandstone, yellowish pink in color, and the canyon continued a twisting and turning course. With my guide, Alice, this time, we rounded each turn in hopes of finding the ruin before us. After over an hour, however, and after many turns, the ruin did not appear. It was getting late and Alice suggested we turn back. But I insisted we keep on going, knowing that surely we would find the cave after the next turn or the one after that. I had a smaller, digital camera with me this time and I was determined to record our success when we got there. Alice went on ahead and rounded yet another turn. I heard a shout. "It's here!"

The large cave, nearer the bottom than the top of the cliff, faced a very narrow turn of the canyon. From the vantage point of the stream bed where we stood, I was in a much better position to photograph the structures within the cave than would have been possible from the top of the opposite cliff. As many as fifteen or twenty stone houses occupied the floor of the cave, all, with but one exception, with remarkably intact straight walls and with wooden lintels still present over the door and window openings. The curved outer wall of one of the structures at the east end of the complex must have been that of the kiva, the ceremonial chamber. And on the front wall of a building at the back of the cave, the turkey paintings! There were three of them. The turkeys had small heads and long necks, and long tails that hung down. Two of the turkeys had white heads, necks and breasts with brown bodies and tails, and one had a brown head, neck and breast with a white body and tail. With the telephoto lens of my digital camera, I brought the images close enough to see that the painted pictures, somewhat chipped at the edges, were those indeed that gave their unique name to the ruin and to the canyon.

It was with mixed emotion that I took my series of photographs of the ruin. I was exhilarated that I was able to get close-in pictures of the famous turkeys themselves, wider shots of the complex of houses and kiva, and vertical shots to show the height of the cliff and the position of the cave in the rock face. At the same time I felt humbled and quiet at the silence, the stillness of the great scene before me, knowing that the people who once lived there, who'd concealed themselves in the safety of their homes in the cave, were so long gone.

My guide and I turned back, confident that by retracing our steps we should find our way to the place where we had entered the canyon. It was a long walk back up the canyon. In addition to the general uphill course we now had to take, we had to climb out of the dry stream bed to its banks and down back again into the bottom to make the otherwise tortuous route as straight as possible.

After more than an hour of this moderate effort, Alice recognized the arroyo through which we entered the canyon and the climb became steeper. I called ahead to my guide to tell her that I was stopping to rest. When I followed the course she'd taken and reached a higher level, I saw no sign of her. I climbed a bit more and found that I could see a long way across the top of a level, juniper-studded plateau. I expected that I should soon see my truck in the place where I'd parked it but it wasn't there. I then remembered with some alarm that in my excitement with coming near the place I'd been looking for so many months, I'd jumped out of the truck and had left the windows open and the door unlocked.

I was afraid now that by some unlucky chance a thief had come upon the truck, had managed to get it started (I'd taken the keys with me) and had driven it away leaving us stranded. I climbed further to the top of a small hill nearby to get a better view. I searched in vain for the truck on areas of level ground, the points between adjacent arroyos. I realized now also that I had left my pair of binoculars in the open truck and they might have helped.

The day had become progressively cloudy, and without the sun or the shadows it cast, I was now unsure of directions, east or west. But from my position on the top of the hill, I was able to locate the top of the canyon's south-facing cliff, the feature we had seen when I parked the car. I found tire tracks (which I thought were those my own truck) on a road leading in that direction (which I assumed to be north). I marched off down that road for perhaps twenty minutes. Then I found along that road an abandoned trash heap that I knew we'd not seen on our way when we'd driven up. So this could not be the way.

The clouds now thickened and it began to rain. I looked for any sign of the graded road that had taken us to the area but I could not find it. It was from a track north of that road that we'd seen the cliff-tops that I still had in view, but I saw no sign of the road.

I traced my steps back along the road I'd taken. I was determined to remain on as high a ground as I could so that I could continue my search in another direction. The brief rain had stopped but the light was fading and it was getting later on that fall afternoon. I had not seen my guide now for nearly an hour. If she had turned back to find me, she'd certainly lost me as I had lost sight of her.

I realized now that I was lost. Night might soon fall and with it total darkness. Perhaps a bear or wolves might be about. I had with me neither flashlight nor matches, nor a warm hat nor a jacket. It was not too early in the season at this elevation for snow. Yet somehow, since I am optimistic by nature, and since I was still happy at my success at finding the Three Turkey House ruin, I seemed to experience no fear.

At last a thought occurred to me. I would find a ranch or a house somehow, tell people there of my predicament, then they would help me find my truck. Although in my scanning over the plateau I'd seen no sight of a settlement of any kind, I now heard what sounded like the cries of children at play. I strained my ears to catch the direction the sounds were coming from but I was unable to do so. Then the sounds stopped. The voices had seemed like a way I might find help, but now I had to continue my visual search which was to be increasingly hard in the gathering darkness.

I came now to the edge of the high ground I'd been on to find that I was looking into an arroyo, the kind I'd been reluctant all this time to go down into for fear of losing my vantage point. A figure appeared, climbing up to where I'd been standing. It was Alice, my guide. She'd come back to find me.

I was certain she was lost as well as I was, that we were both lost. There was comfort in seeing her, but I was still not sure we would find our way out.

"Did you find the truck?" I asked. She didn't answer my question, but instead explained, "I saw you up on top. I used the binoculars that I found in the truck. I kept calling you but you didn't answer. Then I started to climb up here after you."

Now I was greatly relieved. We were not lost after all. And the high-pitched cries I'd heard were not children at all but those of Alice, calling for me, perhaps using words that I did not understand.

"The truck is right there," she went on, "just on the other side of this arroyo." I looked in the direction she was pointing to but I couldn't see it. I still wasn't convinced we would find our way home.

"It's there, behind that bush. Don't you see its shining metal toolbox on the back?" At last. It was there, the truck pointing not in the direction I'd remembered, but with the rear of the truck facing me. And the truck, forest green in color and difficult to see in the fading light, was partially hidden behind a giant juniper bush.

We rushed down into the arroyo and up the other side. My optimism was confirmed. I'd been lost but not for long. My spirits high, the day a success, we climbed into the truck, and I navigated the rutted track out of the wilderness.

LOST IN WILTSHIRE

Imagine a perfect June day in England. My wife, Ida, and our daughter, Shoshana, decided to stay in London — to shop at Herrod's and at Selfridge's. They allowed me freedom of the whole day which included, for the evening, a performance of Andrew Lloyd Weber's *Cats,* and for the day, a trip to see the great cathedral at Salisbury.

My interest in the Salisbury cathedral dated back to some twenty years earlier. Our son, Benjamin, and I were visiting the Metropolitan Museum of Art in New York City. We were struck by two works of the English painter, John Constable. Side by side were two of his paintings of famous cathedral, one a sketch, and the other, the finished, detailed picture. The sketch was the fresher, more exciting view. Set on a broad, green plain, the vision stayed with me, that of the classic gothic structure with its towering, needle-like spire, the tallest in England, and I was determined that I would see it one day.

An opportunity to do so occurred a year before that summer's day. I was on my own in London with a day free on a Sunday, the day before I was to meet with our Daughter, Aliza (who'd been staying in Dublin) at Heathrow for a return flight to the United States. With that one day free, I planned to make the quick rail trip to Salisbury. It was in early January, the time of year with the shortest days, but I was still determined to do it. But a chance to meet an old friend on that day took priority. John Batten had been a Pulmonary Disease Fellow in the United States in the nineteen fifties and he and his wife, Anne, had visited me in Arizona at that time. When he called me at the bed-and-breakfast I was staying at, it was too precious an opportunity to miss, to meet again after forty years and across the span of five thousand miles of ocean and a continent!

The Battens were gracious in every way showing me the warmth of their friendship and inviting me to join them for a day in London. We had luncheon at the Oxford and Cambridge Club on the Pall Mall and visited the Tate Gallery. There an exhibit of the works of the American painter, Whistler, was being held, and, in the permanent collection, we studied the evolution of the style of the English painter, J.M.W. Turner. So the short day was consumed in the good company of my friends but the Salisbury Cathedral was not on the agenda for that day.

But now, a year and a half later, my chance to see the Salisbury Cathedral had come round again. I left the ladies to their shopping and I set out confidently by way of the London Underground for the Waterloo Station. There was time before my train was to leave for me to explore the famous station. I found, on its special platform, the sleek, new Euro train ready for its run to the Continent through the newly completed cross-channel tunnel. Though I was not (myself) a passenger on my way Brussels or to Paris, I felt the thrill of being close to the modern marvel of the "Chunnel" that had been so long dreamed of and completed at last.

When I boarded my train, I was whisked through some of the industrial suburbs to the west of London, but I did not see the trash one sees on railroad rights-of-way in American cities. Soon we were in the country and I was delighted to see fields of incredible bright yellow, a crop I was unfamiliar with and had never seen in the United States. I learned later that the crop was rapeseed, used in the production of cooking oil.

When I got off the train at Salisbury, it was a short walk from the station to a medieval arched gate that led to a narrow street of shops and then to a view of the great cathedral itself. Although the structure was set in a generous green lawn, the lawn was not the vast plain I had had in my mind from the John Constable painting. But I was not disappointed in the soaring view of the tower nor in the grand dimensions of the nave that I soon entered through the west portal. As I looked down the long distance of the nave to the transept, I saw a large number of people seated up front and I partially heard the voice of a speaker addressing those congregated. It was clear that some sort of service was in progress. I did not wish to get too close so I took a seat at one of the rear-most pews.

I strained to listen to what the nature of the service was, clearly not an ordinary worship service since it was a weekday. I soon realized that the speaker, a man of middle age, was delivering a eulogy. Soon a number of younger speakers were invited to speak, teenaged boys and girls, and these were introduced as schoolmates of the person being memorialized. I realized that I had come upon a funeral service for a young boy, the son, I gathered, of one of the masters at the cathedral school. Several well-dressed men and women, the men in suits and ties, the women in suits or dresses and wearing stockings and high heels, arriving late, took their seats near me. They were members of the community, perhaps parents of classmates of the dead boy. I suddenly felt quite out of place, an intruder in my tourist attire of athletic jacket and blue jeans with my camera in clear view slung over my shoulder. The cathedral was a living place, even now performing its function as a church, a place of worship and of solace. A bagpiper sounded the end of the service. I tiptoed away and never asked, of course, who the boy was or how he had died.

In the cathedral's equally famous octagonal chapter house lay another surprise: an exhibit in a glass case of what is believed to be one of the four original extant copies of the Magna Carta. In fine gothic script with characters no more than a few millimeters high and on lined white parchment, this famous document had as its purpose the limitation of the powers of the king. Its presence in Salisbury is due, I learned from a pamphlet with a brief history, a translation and a facsimile, is due to the fact that one of its authors and enforcers was a powerful lord from this same district of Wiltshire.

I found of particular interest a short paragraph in the document describing limited obligation to repay debts to Jews:

"If one who has borrowed from the Jews any sum, great or small, die before that loan be repaid, the debt shall not bear interest while the heir is under age... And if anyone die indebted to the Jews, his wife shall have her dower and pay nothing of that debt; and if any children of the deceased are left under age, necessaries shall be provided for them in keeping with the holding of the deceased; and of the residue the debt shall be paid."

Here, in an original document, was true history revealed in a manner that touched me personally as a Jew.

I had found reference to Jews in another medieval English cathedral I had visited the year before, at Lincoln. At the tomb of "Little Saint Hugh," the Christian boy who was said to have been murdered by the Jews of that city in the eleventh century, I found an apology by twentieth century church elders in a typewritten sheet behind glass. The document read:

"Trumped up stories of 'Ritual Murders' of Christian boys by Jewish communities were common throughout Europe during the Middle Ages and even much later. These fictions cost many innocent Jews their lives. Lincoln had its own legend, and the alleged victim was buried in the Cathedral in the year 1255.

"Such stories do not redound to the credit of Christendom, and so we pray: Remember not, Lord, our offences, nor the offences of our forefathers..."

When I left the cathedral at Salisbury I was satisfied that my dream of seeing in reality what I'd seen in the sketch and in the painting by John Constable had been fulfilled. The morning had been a rich experience, but it was still only noon on one of the longest days of the year. There was still time to see the Stonehenge only fifteen miles away. I walked to the central square of Salisbury town, only a modest space surrounded by modern, two-story buildings, the glory of the town, its cathedral, only half a mile away. I found the bus station and asked about the possibility of getting to the Stonehenge and back in time for the train back to London. I studied the timetable that was handed to me and found that there was a bus that left the Stonehenge at 4:20 and that would return to Salisbury in plenty of time.

The bus was full of tourists all dressed casually like myself, most with back-packs and cameras. We were all in high spirits anticipating a visit to the world's most impressive and mysterious pre-historic site. I was not disappointed. I walked round and round the circle of upright stones, many topped with their massive stone lintels.

I listened to the message in the recorded tour guide that explained Stonehenge's plan as I marched from point to point around the circle. I learned which were the "blue stones" and which were the "sarcen stones," and where the stones were quarried and hauled from. I learned that the entire plain on which Stonehenge was built was a holy place and that nearby conical earth mounds were the tombs of chieftains and kings. I was able to see some of these mounds from a distance with afternoon light falling softly on them. A pair of tourists like myself, whose picture I took of them with their camera, photographed me with my own camera, so I was pleased to be able to come away with documentation that I had been there.

I was pleased that so far all of the plans (and more) that I had made for the day were being fulfilled. At four o'clock I set out early to meet my bus. At the corner where the entrance to Stonehenge Park met the main road, many cars filled with families were leaving. I waited there for my bus, but 4:20 came and the bus did not appear. I allowed it a little leeway for being late. More and more family cars were leaving. It was now nearly 5:00 o'clock. The bus couldn't be *that* late. I looked about for the possibility that a less-filled family vehicle might recognize my predicament and pick me up. Now I was becoming increasingly alarmed. Finally I took out my bus schedule and I noticed for the first time that an asterisk marked the notation of the 4:20 bus. A footnote explained the asterisk: the 4:20 bus would be operating from July 2nd to August 30th. There would be no bus. The date was June 26th.

There at the junction of the road to the Stonehenge Park I wasn't truly lost. Just stranded. I stationed myself to try to hitch a ride. I watched as car after car turned out of the park, turned left, and headed in the direction of Salisbury. I had hopes some of the English in those family-filled cars would see me but I realized nearly every vehicle could hold no more. But even if one of those cars was not filled, how good, in England, were my chances of catching a ride? Weren't the English more conservative, less likely to take a chance on a stranger?

The sun was still high on this day near the summer solstice, but still it was getting late. I would miss my train for the return trip to London; I would miss my chance to see *Cats* as the final event of my dream-crowded day.

In the end no English driver picked me. A small car drove up and stopped. There were two people in it, two young Germans spending the summer in England working at a nearby sea-side resort. Their purpose, the driver said, was to improve their English. Indeed, his English was better than my German, so I didn't attempt to speak to him in his language. He wasn't sure where the railroad station was, but after he dropped me off at the center of the town and after a few inquiries I had no difficulty finding it. I crossed a small river, the Avon, that flows southward in the direction of the channel. I wondered if this was the same Avon as Shakespear's of Stratford-on-Avon.

I was on time for the train I'd originally planned on for my return to the city. The theater was packed for the performance of the celebrated *Cats,* a wonder to me since the play had by that time been in continuous performance for thirteen years. The music and the songs were familiar to me but I was too tired to catch the allegory and the symbolism. And tired I was after such a full day when I made my way by the underground once more to our hotel room. Ida and Shoshana had gone to sleep but they had ordered a supper that I found waiting for me.